BARBARIAN
LOVER

BARBARIAN LOVER

RUBY DIXON

JOVE
New York

A JOVE BOOK
Published by Berkley
An imprint of Penguin Random House LLC
penguinrandomhouse.com

Library of Congress Cataloging-in-Publication Data

Names: Dixon, Ruby, 1976– author.
Title: Barbarian lover / Ruby Dixon.
Description: First Jove Edition. | New York: Jove, 2022. |
Series: Ice Planet Barbarians
Identifiers: LCCN 2022008057 | ISBN 9780593548967 (trade paperback)
Classification: LCC PS3604.I965 B375 2022 | DDC 813/.6—dc23
LC record available at https://lccn.loc.gov/2022008057

Barbarian Lover was originally self-published, in different form, in 2015.

"Ice Planet Honeymoon: Aehako & Kira" was originally
self-published in 2020.

First Jove Edition: July 2022

Printed in the United States of America
3   5   7   9   10   8   6   4

Book design by Kristin del Rosario

*For Kim, JoAnn, and Dawn, who selflessly wrangle
the Blue Barbarian Babes group on Facebook.
Thank you for all that you do!
You three might be the only people on the Internet more
pumped to talk about barbarians than I am.* ☺

BARBARIAN
LOVER

PART ONE

PART ONE

Kira

Two caves over, I hear the wet sound of sex, and a woman's whimper. "Oh God yes, like that," moans Nora. "Spank me like that."

A soft thwack echoes in my translator, and I groan and cover the hated thing with both my hands. I try to roll over on my side and push it into the pillow I've made out of scraps, but all that does is shove the translator harder into my ear canal, and it sends a shooting pain through my skull. So, I flip onto my back and stare up at the rocky ceiling of the bachelorette cave.

"Just like that, my big, strong, sexy beast," Nora cries again.

"Nnnngggghhhh," says her big, strong, sexy beast (also known as Dagesh). To make matters worse, I hear another woman giggle, and then Stacy and Pashov—who, because of crowding, share a cave with Nora and her mate—go at it, too.

Gaah.

I hate this translator. Hate it, hate it, hate it. I push the pillow over my face, ignoring the fuzzy fur that sticks to my mouth. It wouldn't be too bad if it just made every conversation happen in stereo as it translates it. Oh no. It also amplifies everything. So I hear every ass slap, every moan, every grunt, every kiss . . . everything.

And the tribal caves are chock-full of people mating lately. With us humans that crashed here, we ended up having to take on what the aliens call a *khui*. It's a symbiont that allows us to live on the planet without the atmosphere killing us. Of course, one of the side effects of the khui is that it decides who and when you mate, and there's no going around it.

Considering that the tribe of alien men—known as sa-khui—outnumber the alien women four to one, I'm not surprised that mating after mating has happened. Out of the twelve human survivors dumped here, six have mated.

I'm . . . not one of them.

It's hard not to feel like a reject at times because my khui is silent. When it finds you the perfect mate, it starts to vibrate. It's a bit like purring, but more songlike. The aliens call it "resonating," and a male will only resonate to his female and vice versa. And despite the insta-mating, everyone that has hooked up is blissfully happy. Georgie adores her alien, Vektal, who's the leader of the tribe. My friend Liz is fiercely protective of her mate, Raahosh. Stacy and Marlene and even weepy, terrified Ariana love their men. And it's clear that Nora is into her mate, if the sounds of sexy spanking are any indication.

All the "leftover" girls—aka the unmated ones—are piled into a cave together. I was lucky enough to get the nook in the corner with a curtain for privacy. Not that it does much to muffle the sounds. I can still hear everything . . . and I can also hear when someone sneaks out to visit a guy, like Claire is currently doing.

Claire's one of the tube girls, so I don't know her as well as some of the others. When we were captured by aliens, several were held in stasis in pods stuck into the wall, oblivious of their surroundings. The rest of us—Liz, Georgie, me, and a few others—were crammed into the dirty, crowded hold like animals and lived there for weeks. You bond when you're in a situation like that, and I miss them.

I don't know Claire as well as I know them. I haven't bonded with her over weeks of hugging to share warmth and melting snow just to have something to drink. In a way, I almost resent the tube girls because they had it easy while the rest of us were scraping by to survive. It's not their fault, and they're just as shocked and traumatized by the alien abduction as we are. We just had it worse for longer.

I call a mental image of Claire to mind. She's pretty, with a soft, downy cap of white-blonde hair cut in a pixie style that frames her small face perfectly. She's extremely quiet and isn't prone to excessive weeping like Ariana is. And she didn't resonate.

So why she sneaks out to fuck one of the aliens, I have no idea. I don't know which one it is, either, but it concerns me. Has she been pressured? Led to believe that she has to give up her body in order to have safety? Are the single men here in the cave too direct and the girls afraid to turn them away?

I make a mental note to talk to her in the morning. I feel responsible for all the girls here. I was the first one to be let out of the stasis pods, so I feel like I'm the most senior. I've turned into the den mother of our human girls, even though Georgie's our unofficial leader. And I worry about them being taken advantage of. The fact is, even though Vektal's people have taken us in with open arms, we are still strangers to their customs and their world. It doesn't hurt to be cautious.

As the sound of more sex starts up again, I clamp the pillow against my translator to muffle sound and wait for everyone to fall asleep.

I don't actually fall asleep until late, and so when I wake up, I'm bleary-eyed and yawning. The translator surgically attached to my ear aches from pressing on it all night, and I'm exhausted. I shuffle out of bed and go to sit near the firepit in the center of the bachelorette cave. Megan's poking at the fire with a stick, while Claire is toasting nuggets of raw meat. There's not a lot of vegetables on this ice planet, so our meals consist of meat, fish, and more meat. The only berries we know of are used for washing. There's a pounded gruel in storage that's saved for travel rations, and herbs for teas. Other than that, it's meat, meat, meat. Sometimes raw, sometimes cooked, depending on your taste buds. Liz eats hers raw like the hunters do, but I can't bring myself to try it. I'm a wuss.

I sit next to Claire and draw my legs up. "Morning."

"Actually I'm pretty sure it's early afternoon," Megan says. She examines the burning tip of her twig, and then sticks it in the fire again. Megan is normally a pretty positive one, with encouraging words no matter how bleak the situation. But since we came to the alien caves, she's been . . . withdrawn. Quiet.

I worry about her, too.

Claire wordlessly offers me a stick and then a large, stone plate covered in gobs of raw meat. I gingerly spear a few pieces for my breakfast and then hold them over the fire. "You hungry, Meg?" I ask.

"Megan ate hers raw," Claire whispers.

Megan just gives me a thin smile.

"You've got a stronger stomach than me," I say. I'm no good at being the cheerleader.

"Tastes like nothing when it's cooked," Megan says, and jabs at the fire again.

She's not wrong. With the khui in our bodies, certain things about our physiology are changing. Smells are less strong—not a bad thing, given that the cave is built around a hot spring that reeks of sulfur. Taste is also less strong. All the sa-khui eat their meat raw and their travel rations heavily spiced. Some humans have adapted. Some of us haven't.

I push my kebob over the flames.

"Aehako came by this morning," Megan comments, poking at a coal with her stick.

"I'm not interested in Aehako," I say pointedly, and then nibble on a chunk of my breakfast.

"He's interested in you." She looks up at me. "If you mated him, you'd get your own cave at least."

I can feel my forehead setting in a frown. "I didn't resonate to him."

"Doesn't mean you can't hook up." Megan is serious.

I'm shocked. "I'm not going to sleep with a guy just because it'd get me a cave. Besides, where would we go? There are no more caves!" I gesture around us. "People are sleeping in the storage rooms as it is."

Megan shrugs. "Might not be a bad thing to have a guy looking out for you here, like Vektal does for Georgie. And Aehako's nice."

I feel my face flushing with embarrassment. Aehako is nice. And handsome, for an alien. And flirty. And . . . I didn't resonate to him, so none of it matters. She thinks Vektal protects Georgie, but Georgie's pretty dang capable on her own.

And it doesn't matter because they resonated to each other. Now they're mates and stuck like glue, and Georgie's pregnant.

Claire's silent at this exchange, but talking about men gives me the approach I need. I choke down another cooked chunk of tasteless meat and give Megan a meaningful look, asking her to leave for a few. She gets up and heads back to her bunk, bundling in the furs and turning to the wall. I'll have to deal with that, too, I think. Soon.

Instead, I touch Claire's arm. "Can we talk?"

A wary look crosses her pixie face. She nods.

I gesture at the translator jutting out of my ear. It's a bit like a conch shell made of metal that sticks out of the side of my head. "I told you what this does, right?"

Again, Claire nods.

"Did I mention that it also allows me to hear a lot of stuff? More than your average person would?"

"Like . . . ?" Her voice is a mere whisper.

I lean in. "Like girls that aren't mated going to visit men at night."

Her face flushes an angry red and she jumps to her feet. "You think you're my mother?"

"What? I—no! I just—"

"I'm an adult," she says, her fists clenched, and for a moment, I think she's going to hit me. I'm so surprised by her anger I can only stare at her. "I can have sex for sex's sake, you know. I can do what I want. And excuse me if I'm trying to find a little fucking comfort in a bad situation!"

"Claire, please. I just wanted to make sure you were all right. That no one's coercing you—"

"Not all of us are stuck-up prudes like you," she huffs. She flings her cooked meat into the fire, uneaten, and then storms away out of the cave.

I'm left behind, my mouth hanging open slightly from that outburst. Wow. My feelings are a little hurt, but I'm mostly just shocked to hear such a violent outburst from such a small, timid person.

Not all of us are stuck-up prudes like you.

Ouch.

"That went well," Megan comments, rolling over in her bed to look at me.

"What's wrong with her?"

"The same thing that's wrong with all of us rejects," Megan says. "She's just trying to find a place for herself."

I bristle a little at her words. "We're not rejects."

Her shoulders shrug. "We didn't resonate. You can't help but feel a little rejected over that."

I did . . . but I also knew why I hadn't. "Don't be discouraged," I tell her. "If you want a family, I am sure at some point you'll resonate for someone. The healer said that sometimes these things take time." Which also explained why I hadn't resonated, but I keep that thought to myself.

She makes a soft snorting noise. "I know why I didn't resonate, Kira. You don't have to try and make me feel better."

"What do you mean?"

She sits up in her nest of furs, and for a moment, the expression on her face is incredibly sad. "I was pregnant, remember?" Her hand touches her stomach. "They sucked it out like it was nothing. And mind you, it was unplanned. Just a stupid night at the club that led to drunken sex. I don't even know the guy's last name."

I say nothing. How can I judge? The life we left behind seems so very long ago.

"But I still think about it," she says in a soft voice. "I still wonder about it." She looks away for a moment, then blinks rapidly. "But I think maybe my khui knows my body isn't ready for another child yet. So maybe it's giving me time before it puts me back on the horse."

"Oh." I don't know what else to say.

"And Josie has an IUD," Megan says. "I think that's why she hasn't resonated. Maybe the other girls are on some sort of birth control. I'm starting to think that all of us that didn't resonate just aren't fertile." She looks at me. "You on the shot?"

I shake my head.

"Huh." She shrugs. "So, yeah. Josie hasn't said, but she's scared that someone's going to figure out that she has an IUD and can't get pregnant, and she doesn't know how they'll react. I can't really blame her for trying to integrate herself."

I say nothing. Josie has been working herself to the bone, learning how to tan, and weave, and everything else she can think of. I thought she just had a lot of nervous energy to channel. God. I truly am clueless. Of course she's scared. We all are.

These alien men are interested in us because of what we represent. We're wombs. We're a chance for family. If we can't give them that . . . at what point do they stop feeding us? Stop housing us?

Suddenly, the walls of the cave feel very narrow and enclosing. I breathe hard. "I . . . think I need to take a walk," I tell Megan. I have to get out of here. I'm starting to feel trapped again. The walls feel as if they're closing in on me. Have we traded one captivity for another?

What are they going to do when they find out that I'm sterile? That when my appendix burst as a child, it infected my ovaries and I won't ever have children?

What will happen to me then?

Aehako

I see Kira's small form hurry out of the caves, and I automatically follow her, a predator stalking its prey.

She's fascinated me since the beginning, this Kira. Ever since we rescued them from the black cave they were hiding in, I have been drawn to the human with the melancholy eyes and the strange device protruding from her ear. I thought perhaps that I would resonate to her, but my khui remains silent.

My cock, however, pays attention when she is around. It comes to life when she brushes a lock of brown hair behind her small, perfect, unadorned ear. It twitches in response when she gives one of her rare smiles to the other human women. And when she flushes and hurries away from me? It ignites the predator inside me.

I want to find her and grip her against me. Push her into the snow and fuck her until my name is on her lips.

But she resists me. It's the human way, perhaps. I've made it quite clear I'm interested in this particular human, but she ignores my attempts to get her attention. She's rarely alone, always surrounding herself with the other humans. This might be my one chance to give her the human courting gift that her friend Leezh suggested.

I race back to my bunk to retrieve the item I've been whittling. I will give it to her, and she will know of my interest. I want to see the look on her face when she realizes it. I want to see her soft, small human mouth part in surprise. I want to touch her smooth brow and find out the other places she is smooth.

I want to touch that third nipple between her legs that Vektal mentioned his mate had. He said it made her squeal. I want to make Kira squeal and lose that careful, calm expression she always wears. I'm good in the furs. I know I can please her.

Thinking about solemn Kira coming undone in my arms has made my cock stiffen in my breeches, and I rub a hand against it through my leathers, assuaging the ache. I haven't had a woman in some time, and my cock responds eagerly to the thought of sinking into the tight, ridged warmth of a woman's cunt again.

"There you are," purrs a voice.

I stifle a groan of irritation as Asha saunters into my family's cave. My bunk is closest to the entrance, and it offers little privacy. Certainly not enough for what Asha intends. "I'm busy at the moment, Asha." My voice is blunt in the hopes she'll get the idea. I hide the gift for Kira in the waist of my leggings, because the last thing I want is someone like Asha seeing what I have before my intended recipient does.

"Hemalo's out showing one of the ugly human girls how to dye leather," she says, and then moves forward to put a hand on my chest. "Want to come back to my cave with me?"

I remove her hand from my tunic. Once, I had welcomed

Asha's forward attentions. She'd been unmated and flirty, and I'd eagerly participated in bedsport with her.

Until she resonated with unassuming Hemalo, one of the tribe's tanners. Asha hadn't been pleased—at the time she'd been moving between the beds of several unattached hunters, eager to frolic and enjoy herself. Resonating meant she had a mate and a family . . . and someone she didn't want. Their joining hadn't been the most joyous of occasions, but I had genuinely wished well for her.

I am also relieved, because Asha can be annoying when she wants her way. I am glad she is not my mate.

But her kit died mere days out of the womb, and she and her mate fight, and now she seeks to recapture her old ways . . . only I am not interested in another male's mate. And Asha is not the only young female in the tribe anymore.

She clings to my arm. "Aehako, wait."

"I am busy, Asha. Go seek your mate if you want sex."

She huffs in irritation and smacks my arm with one hand. "I am not interested in him. We have no children together. Why should I be tied to him?" She follows me as I head out of the privacy of my parents' cave and into the main tribal area. "You enjoyed sharing furs with me before."

"I'm interested in another," I tell her.

Asha gasps and clings to my arm, tugging me backward to face her. "Not one of those humans?"

"Who else would it be?" I chuckle.

"But they're so . . . ugly."

I roll my eyes. "Does it matter?" I do not find them ugly. Different, yes. Intriguing? Definitely. They could be as beautiful as a kas-fish with its opalescent scales, and she would find them ugly because they are competition. Poor Asha is threatened—

before, she had all the young hunters in the tribe at her beck and call. Now she watches them pair off with their own mates and feels unhappiness at her situation.

She pouts. "I miss you," she says, trying another tactic. "Aehako, please."

I give her a quelling look. She's wasting my time, and all the while, Kira is outside alone. This is a rare moment I can spend with her and not have others peering over my shoulder.

"I must go," I tell her firmly, and adjust the gift I am hiding under my clothing. Asha gives me a curious look but steps aside. I jog to the cave entrance, looking for Kira's small body. The humans barely come to my breast, and I am not even the tallest of males in our tribe. They are delicate things, and I worry that Kira will not be safe out here.

There are tracks in the snow, and I follow them out of the caves and onto the nearby ridge, where Maylak's healing plants grow in abundance. They are wedged into a small valley, buffered from the worst of the winds. Kira is here, grabbing leaves off of a plant angrily, a scowl on her face.

She turns and glares at me as I approach. Am I the recipient of some of her anger? I grin to myself. Her cheeks are flushed with that unusual pink color that some find ugly in humans. I find it charmingly adorable. She's so many interesting colors— pink and brown, and her eyes are the vivid khui blue courtesy of the symbiont. "Hello, my small friend," I call out in greeting.

"Not your friend," she mutters. "And I'm not small."

I chuckle at that. "You should pull a few of the intisar plant there," I tell her. "It's good for eyesight."

She shoots me another glare.

I don't mind. I prefer her angry expressions to the sadness in her eyes that is so often there.

"I don't need herbs for my eyesight," she tells me.

"No?" I tease and move to her side, then point at another bush. "That one is for potency."

She gives me a shocked look, and the pink returns to her cheeks.

"I do not need it, of course," I tell her. "My cock can stay erect for many hours without flagging. It is mostly for the elders or men that have been ill for a long time and wish to couple with their mates."

The noise she makes is strangled. "I don't want to hear about your . . . penis." She shoots me another vicious look. "Maybe you should go and talk to your friend about it more. She seems interested."

"Are you jealous?" I ask, pleased. I've tried to make it clear to Kira that I am interested in courting her, but she's rebuffed me at every turn. Has she changed her mind? I admire her fine brown hair as it blows in the wind and imagine it spilling over my chest.

And then I have to adjust my breeches again.

"Jealous? Ha! Why should I be jealous? I'm ugly, remember?" She taps the shiny metal shell attached to her ear. "I heard every word of your conversation!"

I cannot keep the delighted grin from my face. She did hear me speaking to Asha. And she *is* jealous. This pleases me greatly.

Perhaps Kira is not so aloof after all. It's time to present her with my courting gift.

Kira

But they're so ugly.

Does it matter?

The words ring in my ears as I rip leaves from one of the wintry plants. Jerk. Jerk. Jerk. I like how he doesn't care what I look like as long as he gets laid. "Why don't you just go inside and leave me alone?"

"How can I leave you alone?" Aehako still has that teasing note in his voice that makes my stomach flutter . . . and makes me want to punch him at the same time. He puts a hand over mine. "You're plucking all the leaves from this plant. If I leave you, I'll find the entire hill bare." He tsks. "Maylak will be most displeased."

I glare over at him, but I stop denuding the bush I'm attacking. He's right—I've taken way more leaves than I should have, but the man gets me so darn frustrated. "I'll stop with the plant. You're free to go now."

He doesn't leave, though. Instead, he reaches out and touches the translator sticking out of my ear. His fingers brush against the shell of my ear where it's attached, and I have to fight back a shiver. "Does this thing hurt you?"

"It doesn't feel good." His touch does, though. His finger feels insanely warm against my skin, and a prickle of awareness runs up my arms. "It's heavy and I can't sleep comfortably. It gets cold, too." That, and I can hear every conversation for a mile around.

"Can you take it out? Do you want me to try?"

I pull away from him. A rush of horrible memories burst through my mind and I hug my furs tighter around my body. "They surgically implanted it. I tried pulling it out myself but it's in deep. I'll just have to live with it."

It could be worse. They could have raped me like they did Josie. They could have removed my baby like they did Megan.

"I want to help you," Aehako says softly, and all the teasing is gone from his voice.

I give him a faint smile. "That's sweet and all, but I'm fine. Really." I drop the crushed leaves into a leather pouch. He's right that I'm squeezing them to death. I don't even know if I can give these to Maylak. They look pretty mangled.

"You're angry at me, aren't you, Sad Eyes? Is it something I said or did?" He leans in close and I catch a whiff of his scent. He smells like the berries they use for soap, and a hint of sweat that somehow smells wonderful on him. "My goal is to make you smile, not bring more sadness to your face."

"I'm fine," I say, even though his earlier conversation with the female sa-khui still stings. To me, it matters if he finds me attractive or not. I'm only human—ha.

"You're not fine."

"Yes, so you like to point out," I respond automatically, then mentally wince. Ugh. Why did I go there?

"What is this word? I am not understanding." He tilts his head. "Is 'fine' the wrong word? Raahosh says he doesn't understand half of what Liz says, so I worry our language barrier is worse than we thought."

"Don't worry about it," I say quickly. I step away since he's awful close and it's making me fluttery. "I think Maylak needed more tea leaves." I hurry over to the next plant.

"'Fine' means . . . Ahhhh." He chuckles and follows me. "You heard my conversation."

I shrug my shoulders as a nonanswer.

"You did, and your feelings are hurt because you think I do not find you attractive."

"That's not it at all," I lie, averting my face. I feel like my emotions are painted across my forehead and he's going to be able to see right through me.

"Mmm. Is that so? Then look me in the face, Sad Eyes, and tell me this."

I don't. I pluck a few leaves off of the newest bush, because it's a nice distraction.

"Look at me, Kira," he commands again.

I peek over at him. It's weird that I'm so attracted to an alien. Back on Earth, my relationships were nonexistent. I'm the type of girl invisible to guys. I don't dress in sexy clothing, I don't flirt, and I rarely wear makeup. My hair's an uninteresting brown and sits flat against my head, and my face is a little too long to be pretty. I'm not even a great conversationalist. I'm a virgin but not because I'm holding out for marriage.

I'm a virgin because I'm boring and unsexy. Normally I don't care. But Aehako? He's masculine and utterly breathtaking. He's one of the few sa-khui who keep their hair cropped super short. His is a short buzz against his scalp, which just draws attention to his big, handsome smile and the enormous horns that jut from his brow line. The plated, bumpy ridges down his face are also more prominent, and it makes his face—especially his nose—seem blunter than most. But he's got such an endearing smile that you can't help but find him handsome. He's tall and muscular, thickly built instead of lean like Liz's Raahosh, and his entire body is a pale slate blue that I find intriguing.

To say he rings my bell is an understatement. And I hate that I don't do the same for him. I look away again. "I don't care if you think I'm ugly."

"I don't think that at all," he murmurs, and I feel the heat of his big body as he moves closer to me again. "I simply did not correct Asha because I wanted to get rid of her, not continue a conversation."

So he thinks I'm pretty? A happy shiver races through me.

I squelch that line of thinking. It doesn't matter if he finds me attractive. Leading him on is just a mistake, and I can't afford to get my heart caught up in matters.

I'm sterile. There's no way he's ever going to resonate to me. He can flirt all he wants, but a relationship with me is a dead end. "We're just friends," I say, when he leans in even closer.

"If we are just friends, why do you care so much?"

"I don't," I protest again. I look over and his face is inches from mine. It makes that weird flutter start in my stomach once more. "Why . . . why are you standing so close?"

That lopsided, too-sexy grin curves his mouth. "Because you keep backing away." He leans in. "And I like the scent of you."

"Aehako," I say, my voice soft. I can't lead him on. He needs to know that flirting with me will get him nowhere. He should save his attentions for a woman that might someday be able to be his permanent mate. "Listen . . ." I stop, because he's pulling something out from under his tunic. "What are you doing?"

"I am giving you a courting gift." He pulls something long and thick and wrapped in leather out of his tunic and holds it out to me.

"A gift?" I take it from him, touched. We humans have so little and I already feel like a big mooch with all the things that the kind sa-khui people have given us. Now he's giving me a gift?

"A courting gift," he emphasizes. "I worked very hard on it."

A . . . courting gift? Is this a sa-khui thing? "I see." I shouldn't take it, but I have to admit that I'm curious as to what it is. It fills my hands and is about a foot long, and thick like a baseball bat. I unwrap it slowly . . . And then stare. Surely that's not . . . "Is this your, um, penis?"

He nods proudly. "It's a very good likeness. I worked hard to get it just right. Of course, the others think I'm mad for staring at my own cock for hours while I whittle." He shrugs. "Do you not like it?"

It's a dildo. I stare at it in a mixture of horror and disbelief. It's made of bone, and I'm a little terrified of what sort of crea-ture comes with bones this . . . thick. Oh God, I'm blushing. It's really thick, though. And long. Surely these cannot be the actual dimensions of his penis. But there's no mistaking the heavy crown on the end, and the veins tracing the length of his, ahem, equipment. It's definitely a penis. There are even ridges along the top like the ridges on his brows and big muscular arms. And there are even balls attached, and something that looks suspi-ciously like a pinky finger above the cock.

Dear lord, that has to be the "spur" Liz mentioned. I thought she was making fun of us.

Turns out, not so much.

I push the . . . thing . . . back toward him. "I can't take this!"

For a moment, he looks crushed. His laughing smile disappears and his expression turns fierce. "Is it another? Has your heart already been claimed?"

I give my head a small shake. "What are you talking about?" I'm baffled. I push the dildo back toward him.

His brows draw together and his hands go to his hips. "Is this not an appropriate courting gift?"

"Humans don't do courting gifts!"

"But Liz . . ." He breaks off as realization crosses his face.

"I am going to kill her," I say grimly.

Instead of being angry, Aehako throws back his big, horned head and roars with laughter. He clutches his sides, incredibly amused. I'm glad one of us is having fun at this little joke. I have no idea what I'm supposed to do here. "Take this back," I say, pushing it toward him.

He raises a hand and shakes his head, still chucking. "Ah no, it was meant for courting, and I do intend to court you, my sad-eyed human. Keep it." His eyebrows wiggle. "Unless you would like to see the real thing?"

"I—what? No!" I sputter. "I don't want to see your penis!"

"Are you sure? It's quite a nice one. Look at how fine my gift is!" He gestures at the bone dildo. "I would give you much pleasure with it. I'm quite good in the furs."

"I don't want to hear about your sexual prowess," I hiss. I wrap the thing in the leathers again because I'll be damned if I'm going to wave a big dildo through the entire cavern, and he doesn't seem to be taking it back.

"No?" He looks momentarily frustrated. "How do human men court the women they like, then?"

"Not with dildos. They give them flowers and chocolates and kisses and things."

His arms cross over his chest. "I thought you said they did not give gifts."

"Kisses are not gifts!"

"What are they?"

I blink at him, stumped. He doesn't know what a kiss is? Is he joking?

"This is a trick, right?" I say, gazing at him suspiciously. "I'm supposed to tell you what a kiss is and then you insist on demonstrating and then the next thing I know, we're playing tonsil hockey together."

His brows furrow as I speak, and it's clear he has no idea what I'm going on about. "Tonsil . . . hah-kee?"

"Stop it already." I'm exasperated by both him and Liz, since they seem to be conspiring against me. "I can't believe Liz would tell you about dildos and not kissing."

"So they're similar?" A speculative gleam enters his eyes.

"I'm done with this conversation." I move away, edging closer to the bushes. "You should go."

"Why is it so hard to believe that I wish to be with you, Kira?" He moves closer to me, ever determined, and his big hand touches my shoulder. It takes everything I have not to lean into that small touch. I'm so starved for love and affection that I don't trust myself not to just fling my panties off simply because he represents some stability in this weird new life.

"Because we didn't resonate to each other," I say, tired. And we won't, because my body won't produce children, no matter how much I might want them. Or the guy standing next to me.

"Can we not take what pleasure that our bodies offer us?" He leans in closer, and I feel the heat of his body against mine even though I won't look at him. "Can we not know the joy of touching another?"

"And then what?" I ask. "What happens when you resonate to someone else, or I do?"

He shrugs, his big body utterly casual. "Then life goes on and we celebrate the new union."

And no one has any hard feelings? I find that hard to believe, but I keep my thoughts to myself. No jealousy? No burning resentment? No envy that someone else gets your lover?

He might be able to turn his feelings off with a switch, but I know I'm not built like that. I know that when I commit, I'm going to want to actually commit. To have a relationship, not just a fuck-buddy. To be loved and love in return.

Unfortunately for me, all Aehako can offer is a fuck-buddy.

"Not interested," I lie, and give him my best Serious-Kira-Is-Serious face. "So you might as well give up now."

He sighs and gives his big head a small shake. "We will talk again, Sad Eyes. I am not giving up on you even if you have given up on yourself." He reaches out and brushes a finger over my cheek, then walks away.

I'm left tingling from that small touch, and full of aching need. Why me? Why must I be the unluckiest girl alive?

Because I know the moment I give in to my wants and have a relationship with Aehako, that's the moment he's going to resonate to another woman.

And I'll be left alone. Again.

It's not until he's halfway down the ridge that I realize I still have the leather-wrapped dildo in my hands. "Wait," I call. "Take this back!"

He ignores me.

I remain outside until I can't stand the cold any longer. Then, my fingers nippy with frost, my face chapped from the wind, and my bag full of herbs, I finally return to the caves. The dildo is shoved into my herb bag since I don't know what else to do with it, but it sticks out an obscene amount. Fact of the matter is, it's huge. There's no way any guy's dick is this big. Not that I'm an expert on dicks, of course. I thought briefly about burying it in the snow, but after all the time and effort Aehako put into it, it seems wrong.

Plus, I might want to study it a bit more when I'm alone.

I head inside and blow on my fingers to warm them. Gloves are a priority, as are snowshoes. Actually, we need a little bit of everything, if I'm being honest. Bras, panties—and I shudder to think what it's going to be like when I get my period again. I missed it last month, but I've never been regular. Thank goodness, because these people wear leather, and it doesn't make a great pair of underpants. Our options are pretty limited, though, and beggars certainly can't be choosers. We're lucky to be warm and fed.

The main cave is fairly quiet, though I wave at a few people that are hanging out in the central pool. During the day, a lot of the men go out and hunt for small game nearby, and the crafters work. Josie mentioned to me that Maylak's husband, Kashrem, has a cave a short distance away that he uses for tanning, since it smells so bad that even our blunted senses get offended.

I head for the healer's cave and tap the wall outside since the leather curtain is drawn over the entrance. "Maylak?"

"*Kay-sah,*" she calls out. *Come in,* the translator intones in my ear.

I enter, and she's not alone. Megan's lying on the mat in front of the healer, and Maylak's three-fingered hands are spread wide over her belly. Her eyes are glowing fiercely, which I have learned happens when she's deep into her healing. In the corner, Maylak's little girl, Esha, plays with a few bone toys.

"Oh. Is this a bad time?" I say it in English because we still don't know the alien language.

"It's okay," Megan says with a soft smile. "I was just having Maylak check me out and stuff. To see if, you know . . . all my parts are working correctly or if the Little Green Men damaged something."

When they gave her the abortion? Oh. I hadn't even considered it. I sit down at the end of the mat while Maylak gives me a shy smile and then continues her work, pressing her hands gently on Megan's stomach. The baby—she has to be two, max—sees me and toddles over with a happy gurgle.

No translation, the translator says. It's baby talk. I grin and hold my hands out for Esha, and she hops into my lap, fearless. Her small blue hand immediately goes to my brow and she rubs it, feeling the difference between her ridged brow and my own.

"I was picking herbs and thought I'd drop them off," I say by way of explanation. "Has she been able to find anything wrong?"

Megan shrugs but doesn't get up. "There's a bit of a language barrier, but so far she hasn't freaked out."

"That's good," I say, then stifle a laugh when Esha peels back my lip and examines my square teeth. Her own are sharp little fangs.

"Esha," Maylak calls out and gives a small shake of her head.

"It's okay," I say, and bounce the baby a little. "I don't mind." I like children. I know Liz complained that she wasn't ready to be a mom, and Georgie said she never thought about children, but I do. I think about them all the time. Maybe because I can't have any.

Maylak pats Megan's stomach and the hard glow in her eyes softens a bit. *"Finished,"* Maylak says in her language, and the translator automatically pings in with the words.

"She's done," I offer to Megan, who is looking at me, waiting.

"Am I okay?" Megan asks Maylak, sitting up. She puts a hand to her stomach and then moves her hands in a cradling motion, indicating a baby. "Is everything working properly?"

The healer nods and spouts a stream of the fluid alien language, gesturing at Megan's stomach and then looking at me. They all know I can translate. *Your womb has been wounded recently,* Maylak says. *There was a baby there once, but no longer. Your khui is repairing the damage. It is almost done, and when it is, there should be no reason why you should not be able to carry a child like any other woman. Give it a turn of the Little Moon and see.*

I translate for Megan and wince when Esha's small, grabbing hands discover my translator and pull on it. I gently tug her little fingers free, feeling envious of the growing smile of relief on Megan's face.

"I'm so glad to hear that." She gestures at the healer, who is looking at me. "You want to get her to look at you? See if there's a reason why you're not resonating?"

I bite my lip and then shake my head. "I know why I'm not."

"What is it?" Her eyes are wide.

I hesitate. I'm so frightened to tell someone but I also feel the need to share my burden. I want someone to understand why I'm so uneasy. "My appendix burst when I was thirteen. I nearly died, and I was in the hospital for a long time. It caused several of my organs to become infected, and when I was better, the doctors told me I'd be unable to have children." I shrug. "I know I won't resonate because I'm not fertile."

The look of sympathy in her eyes hurts. She glances at Maylak, who is unable to understand our conversation. "Maybe she can look. Maybe . . ."

I shake my head and snuggle Esha, watching out for the little horns jutting from her baby head. They're tucked flat against her skull for now, but they'll grow larger and more protruding later. "It is what it is. I just worry they'll boot me out once they find out the truth."

"I won't say anything," Megan says fiercely. "You have my word."

"Thank you." I give her a soft smile.

She returns my smile and then her expression changes and grows weird. A giggle escapes her throat. "Um, you got something you want to tell us?"

I'm confused about what she's referring to, and then Maylak chuckles as well. "Esha!"

I look down and the baby's found my . . . courting gift and is examining it with great intensity.

"Oh my lord," I murmur and take it from her, wrapping it with leather again. "Aehako gave this to me."

"Uh-huh," Megan says, voice teasing.

"Blame Liz. She told him it was what human men do to court women."

"Ooo, a romance blossoming?" She clasps her hands. "That's so awesome."

I shake my head. "It's not going anywhere. I'm never going to resonate. How do I know he won't resonate to you tomorrow? Or to Josie? Or Claire?"

Then I'll be abandoned again. It's the story of my life. Every time I meet a guy—a rare enough occasion as it is—and we start to connect, I feel obligated to point out that I can't have children. And since I don't put out, their interest dies. I'm not a long-term girlfriend. I'm a short, not-very-fun sort of fling until they meet the one they want to spend the rest of their lives with.

And it's never, ever me.

This time, Megan's sympathetic look of pity bothers me.

"It is what it is. Here," I say, opening my pouch to turn the conversation. "I brought you herbs, Maylak."

Things are quiet for several days. The humans keep themselves busy enough. Josie's decided that she wants to learn how to cook, and Tiffany's still working on trying to make dvisti wool into yarn of some kind. Megan is with Maylak tending to the herb plants around the caves, and Harlow is scraping skins. Claire hides with her alien boyfriend and watches the small children when the parents are busy.

Everyone's staying busy, including me. There's granulated salt from the "great salt lake" a few days' travel away, and it's precious to everyone, so I'm trying to figure out how to salt or smoke meat to make it last longer. Food's precious, though, so I take the unpleasant bits that people don't like the taste of and experiment on those. Even that feels wasteful, though. One of the caches of frozen meat was buried under an avalanche, and the tribe is worried that there won't be enough food to feed everyone when it gets "really cold," so we're all in work mode. There are extra mouths, pregnant women, and lots of clothing needed, so there's no time to be idle.

Aehako hasn't been around lately. He's been out hunting as well, and it's weird, but I miss his flirting and his laughter. I tell myself that I shouldn't, but everyone else seems to be blending in just fine with the group . . . except me.

I feel weirdly lonely. Maybe it's because my closest friends all seem to have found love. I hate that I feel envy when I see Vektal feeding Georgie choice bits of meat, or the fact that Liz and Raahosh prefer to stay out in the field because it means a lot of alone time for them. I'm even envious of Ariana, because her mate, Zolaya, bends over backward to make her smile.

The only person I have is Aehako, and I chased him away.

The hunters have been afield all week long, and it makes the caves quiet. Nevertheless, when Aehako returns from a hunting trip with extra furs and a wink for me, it's hard not to feel flushed with excitement. Especially when he insists on saving the furs for me to make a cloak for myself. He's so thoughtful.

Of course, then I remember the dildo, complete right down to the veins, and get all embarrassed again.

That day, Liz and Raahosh stop by with a sled full of meat for the tribe and will stay overnight. They've come in at the same time as Cashol, one of the many single hunters in the sa-khui clan. I hug Liz, happy to see her. She's utterly radiant, glowing with good health and love for her mate.

"How's the hunting?" I ask, beaming at her. "That mate of yours keeping you fed?"

She laughs and steps to the side as Cashol slings a dead dvisti over his shoulder, bringing it into the caves for the tribe to eat. Someone directs him toward the bachelorette cave, probably because Tiffany's trying her darndest to make something with all the dvisti wool. Liz giggles and catches my attention again. "God, yes. When we're not fucking like bunnies, we're eating. So much food." She pats her belly. "Raahosh is determined to make me expand early."

The scarred-up alien leans in and gives his mate a kiss on top of her head. "I must go say a greeting to my chief." He heads off in Vektal's direction.

Liz watches him go with a possessive smile, and then she turns to me. "How are you? How's life in the crowded caves?"

"Crowded," I agree. "We're all stepping over each other. They're talking about starting a second cave again in a few years, once all the babies are here."

"They are?"

I nod. "Apparently there was a second smaller one nearby back in the day, but after the sickness everyone moved in to just the one."

"So why not open it up again?" Liz slings her arm around my waist as we head toward the bachelorette caves to sit for a bit.

"Because they're not sure if we have enough supplies to feed two caves," I tell her. It's been a topic of much conversation lately. "The caves are a half a day's walk during good weather, and impossible to get to during bad weather. They're afraid someone might starve in the winter. For now we're going to stick around here and see what happens."

I'm torn over the thought of another cave. It might be nice to have a bit of privacy . . . but I also worry that it will turn into a "send all the rejects over to this other place" situation, and I don't want that to happen, either.

"I don't mind the crowding," I add after a moment. "I—"

A high-pitched squeal echoes in the cavern. Liz and I share a look and then we both race for the bachelorette cave, which is where the squeal came from.

When we get there, Megan's got her arms wrapped around Cashol's neck. He holds her against him, his face tucked against her, and her feet aren't touching the ground. She giggles and squeals again, and then we hear it—the faint sound of purring in symphony.

"Oh shit," Liz says, and gives a happy clap. "Did you two just resonate?"

"We did," Megan says, and presses a kiss on a stunned Cashol's face. "Are you okay?"

"My mate," he says reverently, and then swings Megan around again. "My mate!"

She kisses his face over and over, and then gives him a smacking one on the mouth that confuses him.

By now, there's a crowd forming at the entrance of the cave, but Megan and Cashol are oblivious. She's staring happily into his eyes and he can't stop touching her. We might as well not exist. The purring in the cave is loud enough to make my own silent chest feel over-quiet.

"This is a good day," Vektal says behind us. "Our tribe continues to grow and thrive."

"Yo," Liz says as Cashol starts to undo the laces in his pants. Megan's equally oblivious, now tonguing his mouth with an enthusiasm that's a little obscene to watch. "I think we should give them some privacy."

Georgie strides forward, pushing past all the onlookers, and she pulls the curtains over the entrance to the bachelorette cave shut. "Let's leave them alone," she says brightly. "Most of the hunters are back, and we've got good news. I'd say this calls for a celebration."

A few happy cheers echo in the air, and chatter begins, drowning out the happy couple's purring. I step away, feeling a little lost and lonely. I should be happy for Megan. I should. For some reason, I glance over at the edge of the cavern and see Aehako.

He's watching me.

And my heart aches a little more because I can't have him.

Aehako

There's a fermented tea called *sah-sah* that Maylak's husband, Kashrem, is an expert at making. It smells like the backside of a scythe-beak, but the taste is pleasantly warm on the tongue and it loosens inhibitions. The tribe is breaking out skin after skin of the sah-sah in celebration, and everyone is feasting, laughing, and happy. Old Kemli and her mate pull out their drums and flutes, and happy music fills the cavern, covering any noises that the now-resonating couple might make as they give in to their khui's demands.

Kemli's daughter, Farli—still young enough to be nothing but a sapling—has out her paints and draws decorative symbols on the skin of anyone who will sit long enough to let her. I have a soft spot in my heart for Farli, so I'm one of the first to fall prey to her pretty begging, and when I'm done, she's painted spirals on my horns and sweeping symbols across my face and chest. The elders smile at this—it was common for people to decorate their bodies in celebration of a mating back in their time, and they like to see the custom revived.

The humans are enthusiastic about the painting as well, and I watch as Joh-see gets blue shapes painted on her pale skin. Kira of the sad eyes sits nearby, watching. There's a smile on her face but it doesn't reach her eyes. It rarely does. Occasionally she glances over at me, and then just as quickly turns away.

Even amongst a celebration, she seems alone.

"Can I have this?" I ask Farli, reaching over for a pot of the reddish paints. She and Joh-see are giggling at the stripes she's painting, and the red is unused.

"Of course," Farli says in sa-khui. "Are you going to paint someone?"

I nod and gesture at Kira. "She looks as if she could use more celebrating."

Joh-see grins. She doesn't understand our words, but she knows who I'm talking about. "Try to make her smile, please? She is bringing me down."

"Bringing you down where?"

Joh-see just giggles again. "Never mind."

Strange humans. I take the paint and a skin of sah-sah, and before I head over to Kira's side, I lean toward Joh-see once more. "Do you know what a kiss is?"

She gives me a flirty wink. "You hitting on me, big guy?"

I chuckle. "You are too much of a handful for me."

She giggles, and it's clear she's been hitting the sah-sah for some time. She hands another color to Farli, and then rolls up one of her fur sleeves. "Do my arms!"

I wait as Farli gestures and then begins to paint colorful circles on Joh-see's skin.

"A kiss," Joh-see says, musing. "I think Georgie and Vektal referred to them as mouth matings."

Ah. I have seen this for myself. Vektal plants his mouth on

his mate when he thinks others are not looking, and they lock together. It even seems like he sticks his tongue in her mouth, which is interesting. I have tongued a cunt before but never a mouth, and I'm eager to try it.

I look over to Kira. She's moved away from the boisterous tribe, hiding in a corner to stay out of the way of the dancers that are beginning to move to the beat of the drums. Another kit on the way and another happy resonance is always a cause for celebration. It doesn't matter that there's no place for the new couple to make their home. There is always room for one more, even if we have to sleep piled atop one another.

I would not mind sleeping atop Kira.

Asha saunters in front of me as I walk through the busy cavern. "Is that for me?" she asks when she sees the sah-sah skin in my hand.

"No." I stalk past her and ignore the irritated sound she makes. I head straight for Kira, who has hidden herself in a corner. She sits on a stuffed pillow, and there is an empty one next to her. Good.

The human gives me a frustrated look when I drop onto the pillow next to her. "I don't want company."

"You never do, Sad Eyes." I offer her the skin of tea. "Lucky for you, I am not easily dissuaded."

Kira sniffs the drink and wrinkles her funny, tiny human nose. "What is this?"

"It is . . ." I cast about for the right word. "Burns in the belly and makes you feel good? Yes?"

"Alcoholic," she corrects. She sniffs it again and offers it to me. "You first."

I take a healthy swig from the skin and grimace at the sharp taste, but the warmth floods through me a moment later. "Strong."

She takes the skin back from me and sips it. I watch her small lips curve where mine were just a moment ago and lust shoots through me. Kira is a difficult one to chase, but I am determined.

She grimaces at the taste but takes a second swig. "It's awful."

"Drink more. It will start to taste better."

She takes another healthy mouthful and then coughs, wiping at her mouth. "I think you're lying."

"Perhaps a slight exaggeration," I say, and when she tries to offer it back to me, I decline. "Keep it. You need a bit of alcoholing."

"Inebriating," she corrects.

"Your language is confusing," I tell her, and dab my finger into the small red paint pot. "Your words are nonsense much of the time."

"You're not wrong. We should probably learn your language. Go back to the mother ship and get the brain dump Georgie mentioned."

By "mother ship," I assume she means the elders' cave, which the humans swear is another ship that our ancestors landed from. They might not be wrong, but it's still odd for me to think of it as a ship. As she drinks again, her gaze strays to the group of dancers in the center of the cave. A few of the newly mated human women are with their men, dancing around the heated pool and having a wonderful time. Nearby, others lounge. My friend Zolaya is being fed tidbits by his doting mate.

"They all look so happy," Kira says in a soft voice. "I should be glad for them, shouldn't I?"

The fermented tea must be working quickly on her; she's actually speaking to me of her own accord. I look over at the others. "Should they not be happy?"

"No, they should." She looks over at me with those sad, sad eyes again. "It's me that's the problem."

I drag my paint-tipped finger down her small nose, creating a stripe. "Because you are not happy that they are happy?"

Her eyes cross and she peers at the stripe. "Why are you painting me?"

"It's custom when we celebrate. We show our joy with color."

The sad look enters her eyes again. "Then maybe you should save your paint for someone else."

"Nonsense." I dab a bit on her chin, and then make two colorful streaks on her delicate cheekbones. She's silent as I do, watching me. I want to say flirty things to her, to bring a smile to her small face, but she just looks so forlorn that any jokes I make will seem foolish. I finish with her face, study my art, and then dab my finger into the paint pot again and begin to draw lines on the delicate cords of her neck. Her skin feels so soft under my touch that it makes my cock ache instantly. "You bring me joy. Does that not count?"

Instead of the eye-roll I expect, she just looks even sadder. "You should give up on me, Aehako. Spend your attentions on a girl where you might go somewhere with her."

"Go . . . somewhere?" This is another baffling human phrase. We have the words, but the way these humans use them does not make sense.

Kira just sighs and tries to look away.

I catch her chin before she can. "I found out what a kiss is," I tell her, pleased with myself. This will distract Kira and bring the sadness from her eyes. I expect her to flinch away, to pull back and chide me for flirting with her again.

Instead, her gaze goes to my mouth. Her lips part slightly and she leans in. "Oh?"

I know an invitation when I see one. I lean in and brush my mouth against hers. I'm uncertain about the details of kissing but I'm sure I can figure it out. If it's anything like licking a cunt, I'll just watch for her cues.

Kira's lips are soft and pliant, and my mind automatically imagines them on my skin. My cock feels like rock inside my breeches. She presses her small lips to mine, and I pause, uncertain where to take this. Vektal always looks as if he's devouring his woman.

But then Kira's tongue brushes against the seam of my mouth, and I part to let her in. She's taking the lead on the kiss and I'm fascinated—and aroused. Her hands curl in the front of my tunic and I pull her against me, feeling how fragile the human is compared to my stocky, muscular body. She has no horns, no plated ridges to protect her soft parts, and her vulnerability frightens me.

Then her tongue touches mine and I forget all about her fragility. Lust roars through me, and I tentatively flick my tongue against hers. She tastes like the fermented tea, a sweeter, more delicious version. And her tongue is smooth and slick, unlike mine, which has the textured ridges that all sa-khui's do. She realizes this and a soft sound of surprise passes from her mouth.

But she doesn't pull away. Her hand goes to my cheek and she caresses my jaw, and we continue to kiss. My mouth slants over hers, and I tongue her back, mimicking the motions she began with. When she doesn't stop, I continue, my flicks stronger and bolder, questing. Over and over, I fuck her with my tongue. This, I realize, is what the appeal is to humans. This is a tease with mouths, a promise of what a mating will be like. It feels incredibly deviant.

It also feels amazing.

I can't stop kissing her. I see why humans are so addicted to this.

She pulls away after a moment and looks up at me. There's dazed lust in her eyes, too, and her hands are clinging to me.

"Come," I murmur, leaning in and flicking my tongue over her lips again. "The others are busy celebrating. My cave will be empty. We'll have time to be alone." And I'm eager to explore her human body and find out what she likes.

She blinks rapidly, and then shakes her head. "No, not yet. I . . ." Her voice trails off and her eyes become glazed. Her hand moves to the silvery shell that juts from one ear.

Then, a look of horror crosses her face.

PART TWO

PART TWO

Kira

They're coming back.

A small part of me had always hoped that we'd never see their spaceship again. That they'd forget all about the cargo they dumped and let us live out the rest of our lives here in peace with Vektal's people. We'd settle in, make the best of a strange situation, and eventually forget all about our initial kidnappers.

Wishful thinking, I guess.

But when the birdlike tones of the Little Green Men filter in through my translator earpiece, my entire body tenses with a wash of memories. Of being pulled from my apartment in the dead of night and waking up on an examining table. Of the horrific first encounter with the aliens, and their frustration with me when I couldn't understand them. Of being held down while they forced—painfully—the translator into my ear. Of weeks spent terrified in the hold, reeking of filth. Of being afraid to make the slightest sound.

Weather conditions on the planet are not ideal. Equipment retrieval will be delayed.

That's the only thing that comes through, but that's all I need to hear. They're coming back to pick things up.

And I still have a translator in my ear.

My breath rasps in terrified pants, and I cling to Aehako's arms.

"What is it?" He touches my chin. "Kira?"

They're going to find me. They're going to find me, and because the translator won't come out of my ear, they're going to take me back with them. Oh God. I swallow back a sob.

"Surely the thought of visiting my cave is not so terrible as that?" His voice is teasing and sweet, and anchors me back to this place. I cling to his arms, gripping him tight.

I can't tell anyone about this. The others will panic. My mind is whirling. If they're coming after the translator earpiece, maybe I shouldn't be at the caves.

My thoughts are so far away that when he leans in to kiss me again, I automatically draw away from him.

His expression darkens. "Is it me, then? Do you not want my attentions?"

"I . . . It's just . . . complicated." I shake my head at him. "I think I'm going to go sit by the fire, all right?"

Maybe if I'm surrounded by all the others, their happy voices will drown out the fear surging through me.

Aehako

Something's wrong. I watch as Kira gets up and woodenly approaches the central firepit. She has a wan smile on her face for the others. And even though she sits with them, I sense her thoughts are not in the cave, or with anyone in particular. She is distant, staring into the fire, and the troubled crease has returned to her brow.

Perhaps it is me after all. Perhaps my attempts to court her unsettle her. Frustrated, I get to my feet and return the paint to Farli. The celebration no longer holds any joy for me. I watch Kira for a few moments more, and even though she smiles and talks to the others, it is clear to me that she is distracted and unhappy.

Never before have I been turned down by a woman I have approached. I've shared furs with two women my age, and both were eager for my attentions until they found their own mates. My own mother refers to me as a charmer. Yet this one small human with the sad eyes cannot wait to get away from me.

Troubled, I hand Farli my skin of sah-sah and head off to my furs. I've moved back in with my mother and father and my brothers since there is so little room in the caves. I don't mind—

it's not as if I have a mate, though I'd gladly find a quiet spot and share pleasure with Kira.

When I get to my furs, though, they're already occupied. Asha is there, and curls a finger at me, urging me forward. This is not what I need tonight. Weary, I scrub my face with my hand, smearing the paint Farli worked so hard on. "Why are you here, Asha?"

"Everyone is at the celebration," she says, breathless. Her hand strokes over my bed. "Come and join me. I've missed you."

I shake my head. "Go find your mate, Asha. I want no company tonight." It's a lie, of course—if Kira showed up in the next moment, I'd gladly take her into my furs. But Asha has a mate, and I'm repulsed by her careless attitude toward him.

"I don't want him," she says, pouting. "I want you."

"I don't want you," I say as gently as possible. Asha is an old friend, for all that she is determined to make me miserable now. "Our khui will never unite, Asha. Stop seeking the past."

She stands up and straightens her leather dress, glaring at me. "That human won't have you, either, Aehako. Best take your pleasure where you can."

I ignore her as she leaves. I hate that she's right.

The next morning, I watch Kira as I sit down in the central cavern and work on my carving. I am making a toy for Esha, who is getting to an age where she is into all her mother's herbs and needs something to distract her. When Farli was little, I made her bone rings, linked through careful carving, and she enjoyed the rattling sound. I will do the same for Esha. I take one of the long dvisti thighbones and start working on it. Making a rattling chain for a kit involves a lot of hollowing, and it allows me to sit quietly and watch the humans in the cavern.

One in particular always has my attention. Kira is seated near the banked fire this morning. That she is not in her cave tells me she is looking for someone. That she does not approach me stings, but I'm curious to see who she is waiting for. She looks tired, circles under her eyes, and the colorful, playful streaks I painted on her face last night are gone. Two other humans sit with her, chatting, but she is distant.

When Vektal and Georgie enter the cavern, though, she grows alert. Ah. So she is waiting for the chief. I strain my ears, curious to see what she will say.

She greets Vektal and Georgie easily enough, and then she launches into her plan. "I would like to take a trip to the elders' cave."

"The ship?" Georgie asks, curious. "Really? Why?"

Kira looks uncomfortable as she responds. Her body shifts and she touches the silvery shell in her ear. "I'd like to see if I can get this removed. If I can, I'll need to get the language from the computer there. And I've been thinking." She gestures at the cave. "Look around us. This cave isn't a natural formation. The doors are too smooth, the ceilings too perfect. I think that when Vektal's people landed here, they must have found a way to do stone cutting of some kind. I'd like to see if we can do so again. Maybe we can cannibalize parts from the ship and make new cutters. We'll need more room for everyone."

Vektal rubs his chin. "It is a good idea."

"I'll just need one person as a guide," she continues on quickly. "Just send me out with one of the hunters and I'm sure I can find my way back once someone shows me the way—"

I'm standing before she can even finish her sentence, my protective instincts getting the better of me. I stride over to where she's speaking with the chief. Her plan is a mad one. The humans do not know anything about this place. They are not familiar with the snows, the creatures, the dangers. Kira would never make it back if left on her own. I won't let that happen. "I will take Kira to the elders' cave."

She looks over at me in surprise, but I notice she doesn't protest. She simply firms her little human mouth and then looks at Vektal.

This worries me. She wants to leave so badly she is willing to endure my flirtations? She is indeed troubled by something.

"You should take more," Vektal instructs. "Other humans need the language as well."

Kira's expression grows even more troubled. "Oh, but if it's a fruitless mission, I don't wish to waste the time of others. Really, it's all right."

"We can keep the group small," I compromise. "Perhaps three hunters and three humans?"

Vektal nods. "When will you set out?"

I look to Kira.

She looks frustrated. "I would like to go as soon as possible."

"Tomorrow, then. First light. I'll ask around and see which hunters wish to go."

"We have to take two humans?" Kira looks unhappy.

"What's the matter?" Georgie asks.

Kira gives a quick shake of her head and puts a false smile on her face. "I just hate to waste everyone's time."

That's not it. She's hiding something, but what it is, I am not sure.

I intend to pry it out of her, though.

After being pressured, Kira agrees to bring the two humans called Harlow and Claire with us. Harlow is the one with the orange mane and the speckles covering her skin. I remember her because of her unusual coloring. Claire I remember nothing of save that she is extremely quiet. That, and she is apparently sharing furs with Bek whenever she gets a chance.

Bek, of course, immediately volunteers to join us with our traveling party. No doubt he will see this as time to spend with his human lover away from the overcrowding of the cave.

I don't blame him; it's why I shadow Kira. In addition to protecting her, I secretly hold out hope that one of my flirty barbs will hit the mark and she will melt in my arms.

I'm less pleased that three other hunters are volunteering to go with us. They do not care that our party is supposed to be small, only that they might get the opportunity to spend some exclusive time with the unattached human women.

"After all," Harrec says. "Is that not how Raahosh resonated to his woman? He kept her away until she gave in." He nods at the women preparing their packs nearby. "I would not mind having time alone with one of the women. Perhaps I can convince their khui that I am ready for a mate."

I frown at his words. "This is not about mating the females."

"No? Tell Bek that. He thinks the tiny one with the small voice is his property, for all that they are not properly mated. I'll stay away from her, though." He shrugs. "Either one of the others will do for me. The one with the shell in her ear has nice eyes."

A hot surge of possessiveness blasts through me. "You can go next time," I lie. "Haeden is coming." When Harrec starts to protest, I add, "He has to check his traps." And I storm away, furious that he thinks to approach my Kira.

He just wants a mate—he doesn't care that Kira's eyes are sad or that she feels alone. He's not right for her.

When the other two hunters ask when we are leaving, I give them the same excuse—our party is full. And then I approach Haeden and tell him that I wish for him to join us. My surly friend is not amused.

"You volunteered me?" he asks, sharpening the head of his favorite spear with a stone. "Why?"

"Because you are the only one I trust not to think with your cock when it comes to the human females." I cross my arms and watch him, trying to keep my voice casual.

He grunts and glances up at me. "You wish to keep them away from the one you picked out, you mean."

I laugh, because Haeden has always been able to see through me. "Perhaps. But can you blame me?"

The look he gives me is sour. "Which females are going? Is Joh-see?"

"No, she is not."

"Good." He stands and blows the bone-dust off of his spear tip. "Then I will go."

"Did you want her to go? I can speak to Kira . . ." My voice trails off into a chuckle at the scowl he gives me. "No? Joh-see is harmless."

"She talks incessantly," he says in a curt voice, placing a small, leather protective case over the tip of his spear. "Regardless of whether or not I am interested in hearing her words."

Amusing. "Perhaps if you spoke to her instead of ignoring her, she would realize what an unpleasant fellow you are."

"And perhaps I should tell Harrec you changed your mind."

I raise my hands in surrender. "No need to get testy, my friend. Will you join us? We leave in the morning."

He gives me a quick nod. "But if Joh-see shows up, you are going without me."

Kira

As I pack my bag, the translator in my ear makes it impossible not to hear Aehako's conversation with Haeden. A hot flush covers my cheeks. He's chasing the other hunters away because he wants to be the one to spend time with me. I'm flattered, even though I tell myself I shouldn't be. Aehako has no claim on me.

I just . . . wish he did.

But now the aliens are coming back, and I guess it's a good thing that I'm alone.

At my side, Harlow makes a face as she tests out one of her snowshoes she's made. "This one's splitting, I think. The wood isn't green enough. Or, um, pink?" She pulls the shoe off and examines it. It's made from leather straps and the wood from the pink, whippy eyelash trees clustered outside of the caves. "I need a new branch." She gets to her feet and dusts off her soft leather pants. "You guys want to come with me? We need to make a pair for Claire anyhow."

I stand, abandoning my pack. The guilty part of me wants to continue to listen in on Aehako's conversation, but I shouldn't.

"I'll go with you." I already have shoes but Claire rarely leaves the cave, so she does not.

"I'll stay inside," Claire says in her small voice, and she busily works on repacking her bag. A quick glance around shows Bek hovering nearby. Ah. I shrug on my fur cloak and a pair of mittens, and then get bone-handled knives for myself and Harlow.

We head out of the cave into the snow and walk a bit farther down the path, toward the thick copse of the pink, flippy trees. I hear footsteps crunching behind us and know that one of the hunters is shadowing us. They're always very careful to keep the humans watched—not out of anything negative, but simply because we're clueless about this world. They don't want us to get hurt.

Harlow studies the trees. "I wish they had a lot of branches like the trees at home. That would make this so much easier."

I nod, moving into the "forest" of trees. Some of them have a split branch at the top where it forks outward, but for the most part, the trees are straight up into the air, with just feathery fronds for leaves that jut out of the bark. They do look like one big eyelash covered by a lot of smaller ones. "Let's just use saplings, then? It'll be less cutting."

Our snowshoes are simple creations—they're one long piece of wood twisted into a teardrop shape and lashed together at the heel. Leather has been crisscrossed to make a mesh for the center, and they're strapped on to the foot. The good news is that they don't require a lot of construction, so we should be able to take care of them easily.

Harlow and I pick out a likely tree. It's a little shorter than we'd like, but if we cut directly at the root, it should be long enough for Claire's light weight. Harlow picks out a nearby sapling and we both get to work cutting at the stem. The weather's colder than usual today, with big fat snowflakes falling out of the gray skies. I worry that they're going to think the weather's not good enough for us to travel and delay our trip.

I need to go. Soon. The sooner the better.

I dig at the snow with my mittens, searching for the root. The ground here, once I dig down far enough to find it, has a curious bluish tinge to it, and I swipe at it in surprise. Just another example of how this place is different from home, I suppose. I clear a bit more of the dirt away, noting idly that I've dug almost two feet down in snow, and we're on the hillside, which means it's less deep here than other places. A moment later, I uncover something whitish, and I begin to dig at it.

This plant doesn't have a taproot, like I expected. It has a . . . bulb. Like a turnip? Excited, I dig with my knife and my mittens, ignoring my original task in favor of this new one. By the time I've uncovered the plant in its entirety, I've found a root-like bulb about the size of a beach ball. It smells woodsy and is whitish in color, and when I heft it onto the snow, Harlow comes over to my side to take a look at it.

"Is that a potato?" she asks excitedly.

"I don't know. Do you think it's edible?" They only seem to eat meat around here.

"I'm willing to try it," she says with a laugh. "I was a vegetarian before. This has been hard for me to adjust to."

I'll bet.

We saw off the woodsy stem for the snowshoes, and I carry the tuber itself inside, pleased. Maybe we can bring a few aspects of our human diet to these people and increase everyone's food. I like the thought of contributing instead of just constantly taking.

That night, we eat slices of roasted root along with our raw meat. The root itself is declared edible by Kemli, an elder woman who is the tribe's expert on plants. She's confused about why we would want to eat it, but everyone tries out the cooked slices and I see hands reaching for seconds. I'm pleased and happy.

I'm less pleased when Aehako pulls me aside. "Do you want to delay the trip? It's growing colder by the hour."

"What? No! Don't be ridiculous. It's fine."

His brows draw together and he nods at the cave entrance. "Come. I'll show you."

I finish my bite of not-potato and head after him. A bitter breeze is coming in from the front of the cave, but I suppose it would just reinforce his decision to stay if I go get my cloak. So I suck it up, cross my arms over my chest, and follow him as he leads me outside into the night air.

Another foot of snow has fallen since early this afternoon, and the air is definitely colder. Aehako takes a few steps out, and then turns to look at me. "The wind has changed patterns," he says, gesturing at the sky. "It's now blowing from the east." Well, the word he says isn't "east," but that's what the translator turns it into. "It will hit the mountains and then turn back here, which means even more snow."

"So?" I say, trying to sound nonchalant. "It always snows. What does it matter?"

He steps back toward me. We're out of the warm light coming from inside the cave, and it's darker out here than I expected. I instinctively move closer to the cave wall to block the breeze, and I can't say I'm sad when Aehako moves in front of me, blocking even more of the chill wind. "Humans are fragile," he says. "I would not want you to hurt yourself on this journey." He reaches out and brushes a lock of hair from my face. "You may be fierce in spirit, but your body is puny."

"Puny?" I sputter, and then give his arm a light smack when I realize there's a playful grin on his face. He's teasing me.

"Your hands are already like ice," he says, taking my fingers in his. "Even your khui cannot keep up with this kind of cold." His grip radiates warmth and he pulls my hand to his mouth and blows warm air on it.

For some reason, this makes my nipples prick. His touch is tender and caring, and the teasing look he gives me is flirty and totally Aehako.

"We have to go very soon," I tell him in a soft voice. "It's imperative."

"Something troubles you," he says, cupping my hand between his and rubbing my fingers to keep them warm. "Will you share with me what it is?"

Oh God, I really want to. I move closer to him and offer him my other hand so he can give it the same treatment, and he takes it, gently cupping it and then rubbing his fingers on my cold ones to warm them. But if I tell him, will he try to mobilize the others to save me? Their spears and slings won't do much against aliens with the technology I've seen.

So I come up with a lie. Or a half-lie, anyhow. "I just . . . worry that the aliens are going to come back. I worry that each day here is going to be our last. That I'm going to wake up tomorrow and find myself back in the alien ship, a captive again."

I expect him to give me comforting words. To tell me that it isn't the case. That I'm safe with him. Instead, he gently blows on my hands again and says, "No one can predict what will happen tomorrow, Kira. I might fall off of a cliff and break my neck. I might catch a khui-sickness. Or . . . I might live to be old and grizzled like Kemli and her mate, Borran." He shrugs his big shoulders. "But I do know that living in fear of what might happen prevents us from enjoying what we have today."

Oddly enough, his words make me feel better. I slide a little closer to him, sharing his warmth. "I'm afraid I can't turn my mind off enough to live in the moment. I wish that I could."

"I can show you how," he murmurs.

I stare at his mouth, fascinated by the flashes of sharp teeth behind those soft smiling lips. I shouldn't kiss him. I shouldn't want to kiss him. My time here is limited. The bad aliens are coming back, and they're going to come straight for me, because I'm still wearing this stupid earpiece. But I'm so ridiculously attracted to Aehako that it's insane. I want him to touch me. I want his kisses and his attention. I want to flirt back with him, even though every ounce of my being says that it's a bad idea.

Damn it, I want flirting to be a good idea.

"Life can be sweet, even if you take it one day at a time," he murmurs, and his fingers go to my tangled hair, brushing it away from my face.

I lean into his touch. I can't help myself. I've felt so isolated and alone since we were taken. I want to be able to relax in safety. I want someone to hold me close and tell me that everything's going to be all right. "I'm afraid I might not have many days left," I confess to him. My hand covers his, and I hold it to my cheek. He's careful not to touch the hated translator piece jutting from my ear, but I'm all too conscious of it there. Even now it hums and chirps conversations from inside the cave into my head. I hate that it won't be quiet. I want silence. I want an end to all the worry and anxiety.

Aehako leans in and tilts my face up to his. Intention is written over every line of his face. He's going to kiss me. He's also moving in slow enough that I can stop him at any time if I don't want it.

But I do. So I grab one of his big horns and pull him down closer to me, closing the distance between us. His mouth meets mine, and then we're hungrily kissing. His mouth slicks over mine, his tongue questing deep into my own mouth, and for a time, I forget all about aliens or the chatter inside. I forget about the translator surgically attached to my ear. I forget about everything but the soft lips of the man kissing me, and his wonderful taste. Of the gentle clash of our teeth when our kiss gets too enthusiastic. Of the way his tongue coaxes against my own, encouraging me to be just as aggressive as him.

His hand slides up to my breast and he pushes me back—and to my surprise, I realize I'm pressed up against the cliffside, the smooth rock hard against my spine. His hand goes to my breast, his mouth never lifting from mine. I give a small squeak in surprise against his lips when his thumb grazes my nipple. That small touch sends skitters of pleasure all through my body, jolting nerve endings that I didn't realize I had. My pulse hammers through me, and I want him to do it again. I break our kiss and stare up at him, panting. "I . . ."

"Is it too much?" he asks, voice low and husky and so sexy it makes me want to melt right into the snow. "Are you too cold?" His knuckles lightly trace a trail between my breasts. "Shall we go inside?"

Once again, he's letting me lead. I'm more skittish than a fawn, unsure and trembling all at once. I know what I want, but it wars with common sense.

What if I let myself get attached to Aehako and he resonates to someone else tomorrow? What if the aliens take me away just when I give in to the longing that's rippling through me?

His thumb brushes across my swollen lower lip. "One day at a time, Kira," he murmurs.

It's as if he can read my mind. Even if tomorrow goes to hell, we have today. Maybe I need to claim today for myself. Maybe I need to make a few memories to carry me through the bad things that are certain to be ahead.

So I take his hand in mine and stare down at it. We're so different, he and I. My skin is the pinkish-white of untanned human flesh; his is the blue of his people, and suede-like in feeling. Three big knuckles lead to three thick, strong fingers tipped with shiny bluish fingernails in blunt squares. My hand looks positively tiny against his, but I don't feel threatened with him.

I feel safe. And so I jump.

"Your hand is cold," I tell him in a low voice.

For a moment, disappointment flickers across his normally laughing features. He starts to pull away, seeing my response as a decline of his attentions.

But I grip his hand, not willing to let it go. Instead, I guide it under my soft leather shirt and place it against my warm stomach, my gaze meeting his.

I'm letting him know that I want to go on. That I want more of this. More of him. That I'm living for today.

A low groan rumbles through my translator, and he leans forward, pressing his ridged forehead against my smooth one. "You will undo all my good intentions, Kira."

"I didn't know you had good ones," I tell him, feeling breathless and a little flirty. This isn't me, to be a tease. But I like pushing my boundaries with him.

And I love his response.

His fingers stroke against my stomach under my shirt, and it feels ticklish. I squirm a bit, and when his nose nudges mine and then his mouth brushes against my lips, I open up for him, accepting his kiss. I want to point out to him that he hasn't mentioned his good intentions, but they suddenly seem unimportant. I just want more caresses. More touching.

Aehako's hand strokes over my ribs and then moves up my shirt, to caress the globe of my breast. I suck in a breath, realizing just how big his hand is. My boob must be positively tiny to him. I think of the big, strong women of his tribe. I'm still a little frail from weeks of starving and captivity. My boobs certainly aren't what they used to be, and they weren't super impressive then, either.

But his fingers trace the curve of one breast and he kisses my lower lip, sucking gently on it. Jesus. For a man that didn't know how to kiss until yesterday, he's pretty darn good at it. "You are beautiful, Kira. As delicate as a scythe-beak."

The compliment strikes me as a strange one, and a nervous giggle escapes my throat as I picture a killer toucan. Not a sexy mental image. "What's a scythe-beak?"

"Shhh," he says. "It isn't important." His thumb brushes over my nipple again, and then circles it.

I suck in a breath. His touch feels like utter perfection. I close my eyes, my legs weak against the onslaught of sensation. I feel his big arm go around my waist, supporting me even as I sag against the wall. He won't let me fall. All the while, he presses soft, attentive kisses to my face.

"Tell me if my touch is too much," he murmurs and then slicks his mouth over mine.

It's never too much. It's so good that I can hardly think straight. For once, the endless chatter in my earpiece doesn't seem to matter. All that exists is Aehako's big body pressing against mine, his arm gripping my waist, and that thumb that drags over my pebble-hard nipple.

"You are so soft, Kira," Aehako says, nuzzling at my unmodified ear. He gently bites my earlobe and it sends shivers all through my body. I cling to him, lost in sensation. "Are you this soft everywhere?" he muses. "If I explored you between your legs, would I find you this soft?"

Oh God. A soft protest rises to my lips and then remains unspoken. I don't want to stop him. I want him to discover all of me and to keep touching me. I've touched myself before, but it's never felt half as good as his caresses.

My breath is gasping and ragged as he gently brushes his mouth over mine, and then his hand goes to the waistband of my leggings. It's a drawstring, since buttons and zippers haven't been invented here, and I seem to come apart the moment the knot does. My pants slide down my hips a few inches, loose, and my entire body is tense with anticipation.

His fingers stroke against my belly. "You are allowed to touch me, as well, Sad Eyes," he says in a low, amused voice.

Oh. I blink my eyes open and realize my hands are fists curled up against his chest, unmoving. Of course he'd like to be touched, too. I'm such an idiot. I flatten my palms and grasp at his tunic. There are laces at the collar and I fumble with them, ever conscious of his gaze on my face and his hand stroking the soft skin of my lower stomach.

I don't know how I'm expected to concentrate with all this going on. So I focus, trying to drown out everything but the task at hand. Operation: Touch Aehako. I pull at the laces of his collar, loosening them until they gape open and reveal an expanse of blue, muscled chest. My hand slides under the fabric and I touch him, surprised to feel the rough texture of more ridges over his heart. I always forget that these aliens have tougher, ridged skin over sensitive parts of the body. "You're rough here," I murmur to him, gliding my fingers over the strange patch of skin.

"And you are so smooth everywhere, are you not? I find it fascinating." His fingers dip lower and brush against the curls of my pubic hair. "Ah . . . and this. I forgot about this."

My legs automatically squeeze together, and I reach to pull his hand away in humiliation. That's right. The aliens don't have body hair like humans do. We must be gross to them. "I-I-I . . ."

I can't think of a thing to say. *Sorry about the bush? There's no razor here?*

He ignores my pressure on his wrist and drags a finger through my curls, exploring them. "It's different than the hair on your head, is it not?" He rubs his mouth over my long bangs, testing them with his lips. "So interesting."

"Aehako, please," I whisper, my face burning. "I just . . ."

"Do not be ashamed. I am learning your differences. I like them." He leans down and kisses my mouth again, then gently tugs on my lower lip and sucks on it. That distracts me and turns me into mush again, and when he releases it, he whispers, "I will add it to my list of sensations to think about when I rub my cock."

My eyes widen. He's going to think about my pubic hair when he jerks off? Why is that so . . . filthily arousing? I inhale deeply and stare at his big, broad chest again. I could stop him, but . . . I don't want to. Despite my embarrassment, I want his exploring hand to go farther down, for him to get even more fodder for his spank bank.

Which is terrible and naughty of me, but I can't seem to care at the moment.

I slide my hand sideways into his collar, feeling along one

thick pectoral. God, it's like a slab of rock. I brush against something hard and realize it's his nipple. Curious, I drag my fingers over it, exploring. I never thought of my own nipples as soft until I feel his. It's as rough as the platy skin over his heart. So odd.

"And now you are adding to your sensations, are you not, Kira?" He breathes, his eyes glowing hot. "So you can think of me when you touch yourself in your bunk late at night."

I can feel my face growing hot at the thought of doing such a thing. I want to protest that I wouldn't, but . . . I'm afraid that'd be a lie. And he's arrogant enough to assume that I'd be thinking of him.

Which is also not a lie.

I bite my lip and pull my hands from his collar, then move to his waistline. I want to keep touching him, but the moment my hands leave the warmth of his clothing, the chill of the outdoors creeps in again. I move under the skirt of his short tunic and brush my fingers over his strong thighs. He wears knee-high boots but there's bare skin under there that shocks me. It's like a Scotsman with a kilt, and I wonder if he's wearing anything under that kilt.

And I wonder if I'm brave enough to find out.

His breath hisses out when my fingers drag up one corded thigh muscle. "Keep exploring me, Kira. I don't intend on stopping with you." And his mouth captures mine again just as his fingers move lower and touch my folds.

He groans into my mouth and swallows my gasp of surprise at the touch. With his fingers there, I can feel so many things. I can feel how big his hand is, how thick and blunt his fingers are. How warm his skin is.

How very, very wet I am between my legs.

I have no panties on. There's no leather that makes a good

alien panty, and so I've learned to go without even though it feels shockingly bare. Right now, though, I'm glad for the lack of panties, because his fingers stroke through my wetness and he groans again. "I bet this tastes like the sweetest nectar."

I moan again, my fingers digging into his thigh at the thought of him tasting my juices.

Aehako's tongue flicks against mine even as his fingers explore my folds. They drag over my labia, find the entrance to my core that makes me gasp and stiffen, and then glide back up to my clitoris.

When he touches that, my breath explodes.

"Ahh," he says, and he sounds so pleased with himself. "I have found your third nipple."

My—what?

I should correct him. Really should. But his fingers are gliding over it like he did with my breast and it feels so incredible that I cry out and cling to him, unable to do anything but lose myself to the sensation.

His mouth captures mine once more even as my leg hooks around his, and then I'm practically straddling his hand as he begins to play with my clit, his thumb rubbing it back and forth as I whimper and grind against him, full of desperate need. My tongue flicks into his mouth and I'm mindless with lust. I'm so close to coming, and I should tell him to pull his hand away—

But then he changes the kiss, flicking his tongue against my mouth, and then presses more kisses to my jaw, my cheek, and moves to my ear. He nibbles on my earlobe again and then sucks on it, even as the pads of his fingers drag over my clit.

And I'm lost. With a low moan, I come. I come so damn hard my entire body quakes with the force of my orgasm. The world tilts, and there's nothing but the rasp of my breath and the feel of the hot, hard body pressed up against me, and the insistent rub of his fingers against my clit. A burst rockets through me and I come, and instead of Aehako pulling away, he continues to stroke my clit, driving me into an even higher fever pitch. I—I don't know what to think. Every time I've touched myself, the moment I come, I stop. Job done. But he's still touching me, and I can't handle it. A loud cry escapes my throat as I come again, harder, sharper, and his mouth covers mine to muffle the sound. And I just keep coming.

By the time the aftershocks finish rolling through my body, I'm twitching and sensitive, and I give a small little mew of protest when his fingers slide away from my clit. I look up at him, dazed, as Aehako kisses me on the nose one last time and then brings his wet fingers to his mouth. It's so cold outside they're already icing up, but he licks the frosty dew off of them and his throat rumbles with pleasure.

And I just stare.

What have we just done?

Aehako

Kira's hands are clenching my ass, so close to my tail that it's making me twitchy. I don't know if she realizes what she's holding—judging from the glazed look in her eyes, I don't know if she's aware of much.

And I'm smug at the thought. I like that I've made her utterly senseless.

She's mine. Resonance or not, Kira is my female, my mate, and I'll challenge any male that thinks otherwise. I hold her possessively, watching the expressions moving over her small human face.

The moment she comes to herself, though, the sad look returns to her eyes. I can't let that happen. So I nudge her with one more kiss and then whisper, "Are your hands warm enough?"

She blinks at me, hazy, and then jumps away as if burned when she realizes she's holding my ass. Her face is cherry red, her nose from the cold and her cheeks from embarrassment.

"We shouldn't have done that."

The possessive male side of me instantly becomes growly at the thought. Why shouldn't we? I watch as she hitches her pants back around her hips and ties her laces. "Why should we not? Did you not enjoy yourself? Did I not make you shudder with pleasure?"

Her fingers press to my mouth to silence me, and she glances around to see if anyone else is watching. I find this amusing, considering that a moment ago she was keening her pleasure as she came. When she is satisfied that no one else is around, she looks up at me again, reproach in her eyes.

"Why shouldn't we do that?" I question again. "It felt good."

"Yes, but we're not attached! With my luck, you could mate someone tomorrow."

"Ah," I say. "But this is tonight." And I lean in for another kiss and am frustrated when she turns her mouth aside.

"I'm a virgin," she says.

"I am not familiar with this word."

"I've never had sex with anyone." Her face is adorably red again. I wonder if it will stay like that if she grows embarrassed enough?

"And?"

"And I should save myself for a mate! Provided I ever get one." Her expression grows sad again.

I'm confused by this logic. "Why should you save yourself?"

"Won't he want to be the only one to touch me?"

I snort. "I should think he would rather you know what you are doing. What kind of male would hold your pleasure-seeking against you?"

Her eyebrow goes up, but a hint of a smile curves her mouth. She's softening toward me. "That's not a very human way of thinking."

I open my arms wide and gesture. "Look at this male before you. Does he look very human to you?"

Kira gives me another half-smile and then shakes her head. She looks up at the sky, where a heavier snow starts to fall, coating us in the pale flakes. "Do you think that will let up before tomorrow?"

"I do not."

She looks disappointed.

"We can delay the trip. A day or two will not matter."

Again, the panic crosses her face. She shakes her head. "We can't."

"Kira," I say, putting my hand to her cheek. This isn't about pleasure, or mating. This is about something else that is wrong, and she's going to tell me what it is. "What is it that you are not sharing?"

She blinks up at me, and I can see the thoughts churning in her head. Something is bothering her and she is terrified to share it. Her big eyes are so sad that it makes my chest ache. I would take this sadness from her if I could.

If she will let me.

She bites her lip. "It's nothing."

"It is not nothing, and if you do not tell me, I shall go into that cavern and tell everyone what we just did together." Not that they would care, but I know shy Kira will be bothered at the thought.

Her lips fall open, and for a moment, I think she wants another kiss. But then her mouth snaps shut and she scowls at me. "You're not being fair, Aehako."

"I am not," I say agreeably. I will not be fair when it comes to her. She's mine. I touch her cheek. "But you will tell me what bothers you anyhow."

She bites her lip again and her fingers touch the strange metal thing that projects from her ear. "If . . . If I tell you, you cannot tell anyone. Not Bek, not Vektal, not *anyone*."

As if I would tell Bek anything. The male has nothing but snowdrifts between his ears. But I nod.

Her hands tense into fists and then she crosses her arms over her chest. Not in anger, I realize, but . . . hugging herself. Protecting herself. "The others are coming back," she whispers. "The aliens. And I think they're going to be able to find me."

PART THREE

Aehako

"Tell me everything."

She wrings her small human hands and then does just as I command. Her worries spill out—the things she hears from the strange shell in her ear and her concern that the aliens are coming back to get her. As she speaks, I see the stark terror on her face, and I ache with knowing that she has been hiding this inside her, that Kira feels it is a burden she must shoulder alone.

She's not alone, though. She's mine.

When she's done speaking, she wipes at the corners of her eyes, pushing away her tears before they can freeze to her cheeks. "Say something?" she asks me.

"Can we remove the shell from your ear?"

She shakes her head and touches it. "I've tried. It's attached to my ear and sometimes I think I should just cut the whole darn ear off, but I worry there's a part that goes deeper into my head." She bites her lip. "I don't want to lobotomize myself."

I don't know this word, but I understand what she is saying—she is wise not to fool with things she does not understand. "Then we must get it out of you." I stroke a hand over her hair. "I will still go with you, Kira, but we must tell the others. It is not right to bring them with us if it will put their lives in danger to be around you."

Her face crumples a little. "Do you think I'm putting them in danger? That's the last thing I want. I want to get away from the cave so no one's in danger but me."

"If you think they are coming after you," I say, considering the alien device stuck to her head, "then it is best we are not near the others. Do you not agree?"

"You're right. I should have said something earlier." Kira looks defeated.

"There is no shame in fear," I tell her, and tip her chin up so she will look at me. "I have not abandoned you. Fear not."

Worry creases her brow. "But it's not safe."

"What in this world *is* safe?" I tease. "I could die tomorrow from a fall or bad food."

"Don't say things like that." Kira's eyes shimmer with more tears. "You'd be safe if it wasn't for me."

"I'd be lonely and sad if it weren't for you," I tell her. "Do you think you are not worth a little risk?" At her silence, I continue. "I do."

The brave smile she gives me wobbles a little. "I'm scared."

"Shall I come to your furs tonight and distract you until you are no longer scared?"

She buries her face against my chest. Only her small chuckle tells me that her mood has lightened a little with sharing her burden.

It's enough that she trusts me with this. Soon, she'll trust me with all her secrets. Then she will no longer fight the thought of being my mate. But first I must help her rid our skies of those that would seek to take her from me.

I mentally add more weapons to my travel supplies.

Kira

THE NEXT MORNING

It's not easy to confess to Vektal and the others the truth about why I want to visit the elders' spaceship. I feel ashamed, as if it's my fault. I see the worry on Georgie's face, and the others', and I feel responsible. I've burst their happy bubble and brought fear back.

Only Aehako's strong hand on my back keeps me from running away like a coward. I don't understand why he supports me through all this, but I'm grateful for it. So, so grateful.

"Have you heard them again?" Georgie asks. Her voice is calm but there's a furrow of worry on her brow. As I watch, Vektal tangles his hand in her curly hair, as if to anchor her to him.

I shake my head. "It's better to be safe than sorry, though. I want this thing out of my ear, and all traces of them gone. If the elders' ship can do that, it's worth a try."

"And if it doesn't work?" Georgie's voice is gentle, even though her question pierces me to my soul.

I don't know what I'll do if I can't remove it. I can't come back and be a danger to others. "I'll cross that bridge when I get there, I suppose."

"Bridge?" Vektal asks.

"Figure of speech, love." Georgie pats his shoulder. "It's nothing to worry about."

"Whatever happens, I won't bring them back here, I promise," I tell her. Even upon pain of death—or worse, my own re-captivity—I won't sell out the others. I just hope the aliens will leave well enough alone.

She bites her lip and looks at her mate, the chief. Then, Georgie looks back to me. "I don't want to tell the others if we don't have to. I don't want to worry them over nothing. Ariana's no longer crying at the drop of a hat and Claire isn't cringing when I talk to her. And Megan . . ."

I nod. Megan just mated with Cashol. She's radiating happiness. I can't take that from her. "I'll tell the others that plans have changed and we no longer need them to go."

"I'm still going," Aehako says, stubborn. "I will not let Kira leave my side. I shall keep her safe." He looks down at me, and I have to fight hard to keep the blush off my face, remembering what happened last night. "I suspect Haeden will accompany me, if I ask. He has no family to endanger."

"I can go by myself," I protest. I don't like the thought of putting others in jeopardy. "Just point me at the ship—"

Aehako frowns fiercely at me, stunning me into silence. "I will not allow it," he says. "I will keep you safe."

"So protective," Vektal comments. "Are you sure there is no resonance between the two of you?"

"If hope was enough to waken my khui, my chest would be thundering, my friend," Aehako says easily.

I say nothing. I just sit there and blush. "I'll, um, let Claire and Harlow know that plans have changed." At Georgie's worried look, I amend, "Don't worry. I won't say the truth. I'll sugar-coat."

I wouldn't wish the knot of fear in my stomach on anyone else.

We separate a few minutes later, and I head off to the human "bachelorette" cave to talk with Claire and Harlow. Claire is fine with not going, especially once I tell her Bek's no longer heading off with us.

Harlow, however, is stubborn. She shakes her head and shoulders her bag, her manner unchanged. "I'm going with you."

I take her by the elbow and steer her to a corner of the room, where I'm sure Claire won't overhear us. "Harlow, it's not that I don't want you to come along, it's that . . . things might be a bit more dangerous than we originally anticipated. It's best to keep the party small."

She stares at me with her bright-blue glowing gaze, evidence of the khui strong inside her. It looks odd against her red hair and pale, freckled skin. "The elders' cave. You said it's a spaceship, right?"

"Well, y-yes, but it's several hundred years old and it doesn't fly anymore," I stammer. "The computer inside it is still working, but I don't know that much else is—"

"Then I'm going," Harlow says. "You can't really stop me."

I frown at her, frustrated by her pigheadedness. "It might not be safe," I stress again.

"Because of the weather?"

"Because of other things," I hedge.

She considers for a moment and then shakes her head. "I'm still going. I'll take my chances. I need to see that ship."

For a moment, I stare blankly at Harlow. Does she have a

listening device somewhere, too? Or is something else going on? "Anything you want to talk about?"

"Nope." She hoists her pack and adjusts the strap against her shoulder. "When do we leave?"

I sigh, defeated. "Very soon. Come on."

I get my pack and Harlow and I meet Aehako and Haeden at the front of the cave.

Aehako immediately takes a bedroll from my pack and ties it to his. "You are carrying too much. Let me help."

"I'm fine," I say, feeling a little embarrassed. Haeden's not hovering over Harlow like Aehako is with me. Then again, Harlow and Haeden probably didn't do what Aehako and I did last night. I blush hard just thinking about it.

I know twenty-two is old to be a virgin, but I've never given it much thought until now. There's just never been much opportunity to have sex with someone. Now, it seems like opportunity is knocking with a sexy alien . . . and the timing couldn't be worse. How can I even think about getting involved with someone?

Of course, to him it might just be playful, fun sex. Meaningless except for a night between the covers. But that's not how I'm built. I can't just tumble into bed with a guy for fun and not think about it again. I need to make Aehako aware of this. Oh no. A terrible thought occurs to me. What if he's focusing so much attention on me simply because I'm available for "fun"? Maybe it's a cultural thing and women that aren't tied down by a resonance-mating should be wild and free with their bodies? There's nothing wrong with that . . . but that's not who I am.

I feel guilty that I've led him on for this long. I need to talk to him. I touch his arm. "Can we talk?"

"We should hurry. We need to make good time before the weather gets worse. It's going to slow us as it is."

I look at the others, waiting on me, and tap on Aehako's big shoulder. When he arches an eyebrow at me, I sigh in frustration and indicate he should bend down so I can whisper in his ear. It's not an easy task considering he's seven feet tall. When he finally does bend down, I lick my lips, suddenly nervous. "I think I should go alone."

"Why? I thought we settled this—"

"I don't want you to think, well, that things are different between us."

He rears back and gives me a guarded look. Then, he leans in again and pulls me close to him. "How should I think things are between us, then?"

I wring my hands in a maidenly gesture, but damn it, I'm feeling a bit maidenly at the moment. "It's just . . . I just . . ." I blow out a nervous breath. "So last night? What happened between us? I realize you're all fun and games and party time and not thinking about tomorrow, but that's not how I'm built. I can't form a casual relationship. I'm not set up that way. So I don't want you to think that I'm into just having sex for sex's sake and nothing else out of it. I don't think I can do the things we, you know, did—"

"We did not do very much," he interrupts, a dry note of amusement in his voice.

I ignore him and continue.

"—without thinking there's going to be something between us in the long run. And I don't want you to think that you have to sign up for a relationship with me." Gosh, I'm getting all flustered now because he's just staring at me. "I'm just telling you that I'm the wrong kind of girl for fooling around with. And I don't want to lead you astray."

The big alien gazes down at me in silence.

"Well?" I ask.

"Are you finished vomiting excuses at me?"

My arms cross over my chest. "Those aren't excuses."

"Then you are not done?"

"No, I'm done—"

He puts a big hand behind my head and tugs me in, bending down to my height. We're eye to eye and nose to nose, and he's so close I can smell his faint scent and breathe in his same warm breath, which feels oddly intimate. "Listen to me, Kira. My interest in you is not just for sex. Though, I would gladly take it if you were to offer it."

I look around, horrified, because he's not speaking in a whisper. He's loud enough for everyone in the cave to hear.

Fingers tip my chin, forcing me to look back at Aehako. His gaze is intense and I can't look away.

"I am interested in you. All of you. Your sad eyes, your soft smiles, your tears, your courage, and your worries. I am at your side now, and I will be at your side until you tell me to leave. I do not need a khui to tell me who is the mate for me. You are mine and I will take every moment with you as a gift."

"But what about—"

"If my khui resonates for someone else? I will not let it." He grins, utterly confident. "My heart is for you and you alone."

"That's not how it works, Aehako."

"That is how it will work for me," he says, ever stubborn. "And if your khui should resonate for another, I will send you to his arms with gladness for your happiness."

Hot tears prick my eyes. The knot in my throat prevents me from speaking, but if I could, I'd probably just gurgle a few insensible words about what a good man he is. Because he's the best.

"You were mine the moment you landed on this planet,

Kira," Aehako says. "It does not take a khui to tell me that. Nor will I let anyone take you from me. So, come, we shall remove this shell from your ear and free you from worry, and then you will fall into my arms and lick every inch of my skin to show me your appreciation."

A choked giggle escapes me.

"There, that is better, Sad Eyes," Aehako says. He tenderly touches my cheek. "Now, we should go. We have a lot of ground to cover before it grows dark."

If I thought Haden and Aehako would set an easy pace for us because we're humans and a bit frailer than they're used to, I'm dead wrong. They make sure we're bundled well against the cold winds, check our snowshoes, and then set a breakneck pace through the ridges and valleys of the snow-covered land. I huff, my breath freezing against the furry scarf that covers the lower half of my face, and I'm walking so fast it feels like I'm jogging. In snowshoes.

It's ridiculous, but even Harlow is walking faster than me, so I can't complain. I just do my best to keep up with the others.

The height of the aliens—along with the different makeup of their broad, spread feet—means they don't have to use the snowshoes like we puny humans do. They slow me down and make every step feel like effort. Before the cave has even disappeared from sight, Aehako jogs back to me, plucks my pack off my back, and then gives me words of encouragement so I will keep up.

If all it took were determination, I'd be at the front of the pack. Instead, I'm at the back, and it just gets more difficult as the storms pick up and snow pours from the gray skies. I put my head down and march on, grimly determined to keep up with the others. Georgie said the ship was only a day or so away from the tribal caves, so it can't be that long of a journey. I just need to suck it up and keep moving.

We pause after a few hours to eat. Haeden has killed a critter of some kind with his sling, and the two men cut raw bits off of it and offer them to us. I'm not used to eating my meat au naturel, but Liz has assured me before that it's fine. And again, Harlow is eating quietly, so I feel like I can't be the one to demand a fire. So I gag the warm, bloody bites of food down. It's fuel, I remind myself. Fuel that is desperately needed, because I suspect my "tank" is going to be on empty before the day is over.

Once food is eaten, we get to walking again. Aehako drops down beside me, and his steps seem impossibly slow. "Are you well?"

"I'm hanging in there," I assure him. I feel like a putz for being so slow, what with him carrying my bag and his, but I'm having a hard enough time as it is.

He nods and gives me a quick squeeze over my fur-covered shoulders, and then paces ahead at his regular, fast gait.

Hours pass and my world becomes nothing more than placing my feet in the path that Harlow's snowshoes have trod ahead of mine. I'm no longer aware of the cold, or the travel. I thought coming to the tribal caves the first time was exhausting, but now I'm remembering how much of the time we were carried, too weak to walk. I kinda wish someone was here to carry me now. The snow continues to pour forth from the skies, making it nearly impossible to see farther than a few feet ahead. I don't know how the guys can tell where we're going, but we seem to be heading in a straight line. That's encouraging. I think.

A hand touches my arm. "Kira?"

I look up and realize that the scarf over my mouth has frosted to my face, and my teeth are chattering. "Wh-wh-what?"

It's Aehako, his big face concerned. He pulls his hood back from his horns, and he looks no more bothered by the weather than if it's a rainstorm and not the Snowpocalypse. "Come," he says, pulling me against him and wrapping a supporting arm around my waist. "We're near a cave. Come."

I sag against him and more or less let him drag me the rest of the way to the cave. I didn't realize how tired I was until he broke me from my trance, and now it feels as if every ounce of strength has left my body. The translator feels like a block of ice against my ear, and I can't feel my toes. Or my fingers. My teeth are clacking like they're tap-dancing, and all the while, the snow just keeps pouring down.

Maybe we should have waited after all.

I don't even have the energy to protest when Aehako slings me into his arms and carries me the rest of the way to the cave. At least there will be warmth there, and fire. Gosh, I love fire.

But when we get to the cave, it's dark inside. There's no fire.

"Predators in this area," Haeden explains. "It's a dangerous place to have a fire. We'll have to share body heat."

I look over at Harlow, who is just as bundled in furs as I am. It's gonna be a cold night.

Harlow, however, takes one look at me as Aehako gently sets me down, and then drops her pack next to Haeden. She unrolls her bedroll and strips off her wet, snowy clothing and then inches against him like a big furry worm in a blanket.

Which means I'm with Aehako.

I should have seen that coming, I guess. I stand there like a big snow cone as Aehako tugs my gloves off my frozen hands and then blows on my chilled fingers to warm them. "H-how c-come H-H-Harlow's not as c-c-cold as me?" I chatter. "How c-come I sssssuck at traveling so bad?"

"She was not sick for two weeks like you were," Aehako says easily. "You will get stronger with time."

Harlow yawns and scoots farther into her furs. "If it makes you feel any better, I'm cold and exhausted, too."

It doesn't, because she doesn't look as if she's about to fall to pieces like I do. Sure, she's cuddling up to Haeden, who really isn't the most cuddly of people. But I'd feel better if I wasn't the only one struggling.

"Get some sleep," Haeden says. "We'll eat in the morning and then set off again."

Aehako strips me down to my last layer of clothing, spreading the others out to dry. The cave is small but there's no bitter wind, at least. I watch as Aehako lays out my furs and then his, pushing them both together. Then he guides me down into the bed and pulls the covers to my chin.

It doesn't feel warm at all. I'm about to whine about this when Aehako's enormous body gets into the furs next to me and he pulls me against him, my face pressing against his bare chest.

And . . . oh. Okay. This is where the warmth comes in. Because sleeping with Aehako is like sleeping with a space heater. A soft, velvety one with lots of muscles. I'm pretty sure he's naked, too, or at least down to a loincloth.

Man. Now I wish I'd been paying more attention.

My teeth stop their chattering and I press my cold hands and feet against his skin. He doesn't protest, just hugs me closer. Delicious warmth seeps through my body, stolen from him, and I start to feel good for the first time since leaving the tribal caves hours and hours ago.

"Are we almost there?" I whisper to Aehako. "To the elders' cave?"

"About halfway," he says in a low voice. His finger traces my

ear and then my jaw, sending shivers up my spine. "We're moving slower than we'd like. The storm is hindering things."

The storm, and the slow-ass human, I think, but I don't say
it aloud. He knows I'm doing the best I can. I snuggle closer to
him and rub my fingers on his stomach. Gosh, he feels good. My
fingers glide up and down the flat plane of muscle that is his
belly, and I explore him with my touch even as he caresses my
face.

I should be really embarrassed that Harlow immediately as-
sumed I was sleeping with Aehako. But . . . I find I can't really
care. I'm glad. I don't want to cuddle up to her because she's not
warm and delicious—and I sure don't want to snuggle with
Haeden. I'm glad Aehako and I are under the blankets together,
even if it's just for warmth.

And I think about what he said earlier. About wanting to be
with me no matter what. Heat pools through my body, and even
though I'm utterly exhausted, I find my hands sliding lower to
check if he's wearing a loincloth after all.

My questing fingers encounter nothing but muscular, lean
hip. Oh. So . . . there's that. There's no waistband. No leather.
No nothing. Just me and big naked alien that I have to burrow
against for warmth.

Gosh, it is so hard to be me sometimes.

Aehako leans in and brushes his lips against my forehead.
"Your fingers are feeling playful. Are you not tired?" His voice
is whisper-soft so the others can't hear.

"I'm exhausted," I tell him. I'm still curious, though. Can't
blame a girl. He's big and warm and velvety and I can't stop petting him.

"You should sleep."

"I will." Soon enough. I just want to explore him for a bit

and keep touching. I'm addicted to the feel of his soft skin over all those hard muscles. I keep petting his stomach, because I'm not quite brave enough to go lower. Something brushes my arm and I gasp and pull back, scandalized. Was that his . . .

"Don't be shy. You wanted to explore, then explore." There's a challenge in his voice, along with amusement.

That sounds an awful lot like a dare. I'm both outraged and fascinated. I shore up my courage and reach down. My hand encounters hard, hot flesh. A lot of it. I'm . . . not entirely sure that this is a normal size, but maybe it's normal for aliens. I grip his cock in my hand, wrapping my fingers around him.

His hand immediately cups my face and his groan of delight is so soft. It's just for me.

And I'm a little addicted to this. To his responses. I release him and slide my fingers up and down his length, exploring him with touches. I can feel veins, and there's a thick set of ridges running along the top that reminds me of his brow. The head feels bigger than the rest and my fingers encounter slickness there. "Are you supposed to be wet?" I ask, a little scandalized.

"My seed cannot seem to stay inside when you touch me," he murmurs, and his mouth traces my brows. "Your touch is too exciting."

My touch? Me? I don't think anyone has ever used the word "exciting" to describe me, ever. I bite my lip and slide my hand lower, grazing new anatomy. Balls. The word seems like a silly one. Sac might be better. He's hairless down here, the skin even softer than I imagined. I circle the thick base of his cock and my fingers brush up against . . . oh. That has to be his spur. It's a hard, horn-type thing above his cock, about the size of my pinky finger. Such a weird, strange piece of anatomy. I wonder how it's going to match up with my anatomy. I assume it can, since neither Georgie nor Liz has had any complaints. I stroke it with my fingers, and I can feel him tense against me. Ooh. An excited throb starts between my legs, and I press my thighs tight together. "What should I do?" I ask him.

He leans down and kisses my mouth gently. "You should stop."

That . . . wasn't what I wanted to hear. I pull away as if burned. "Did I do it wrong?"

"Not at all." Aehako nips my mouth with his teeth, sending another pleasurable jolt through me. "I just have no idea how I'm going to explain to the others how my seed was sprayed all over the cave if you continue."

A horrified giggle erupts from me, and Aehako's hand covers my mouth.

"Quiet," snarls Haeden from a few feet away.

Oh lordy. Aehako's right. We should be quiet. Still, it's hard to take my hands away from him and place them back on his nice, safe chest.

He must be feeling the same way, because he kisses me hard, and then releases me. "Sleep," he murmurs. "You can explore more when we are alone."

As I drift off to sleep, I think the idea's one that has a lot of merit to it. I hope I dream of warm blue skin and spurs and fun things like that.

Aehako

Rousing myself from my furs the next morning is an ordeal. Not because I'm tired, but because Kira's sweet form is curled against me, her small body pliant and pressed against mine. I don't think I've ever wanted to remain in one place so badly.

The other human is still asleep, though Haeden's furs are empty. There is no connection between them, then. Not surprising—I think Haeden is even more remote than Raahosh. At least, he has been since he lost his mate before he could claim her. Who can say what that will do to a man's heart?

I ease myself from the furs without waking Kira, and dress quietly before heading out to the mouth of the cave. Haeden is nearby, staring at something on a snowy crest. I join him, and he points at the snow.

"We're not alone," he says.

My hackles rise at the sight of the footprints in the unspoiled, thick snow. They're not deep enough to be mine or Haeden's, and the shape and size are wrong for human feet. But it's clear that during the night we were visited by someone.

Or some*thing.*

I squat down next to him and touch the track. The snow is crusted, meaning that the track is several hours old. "I don't recognize this creature," I say to him, keeping my voice low so the humans will not hear it. "What has three toes like this?" The track itself is twice the size of my own foot, shaped into three long prongs for toes. I have three toes but . . . not like this. It's curious.

It also makes me angry and fiercely protective, thinking of the fragile humans sleeping in the cave. To think something came this close makes me feel helpless.

"Do you think it's the aliens that Kira mentioned?" Haeden glances up at me. "The tracks circle around our cave and disappear a short distance away, crossing a stream."

I lick my thumb and test the wind. It's against us. If there's a scent trail to follow, it's long gone. Curse it. "If it was the aliens, why did they not attack while we slept? Under the cover of the storm? Kira thinks they want their shell back from her. If that is what they truly want, why not take it?" I rub my forehead at the base of my horns. I'm angry at myself—angry that someone came so close to our cave and threatened my woman. Angry that I didn't set a watch and instead crawled into bed with her to share a few fleeting minutes of pleasure.

Haeden shrugs and gets to his feet. He's not bothered. To him, this is just another hunt, another day. Sometimes I wish there was something that would take that deadness from his eyes. To wake him up and make him realize what is at stake here for me. He puts his hands on his hips and glances at the fresh snow, then at the sky. "Whatever the reason we are followed, we should hurry and take the women to the elders' cave before our new friend returns."

He's not wrong. I nod and go to wake the women up. I debate telling them of the situation, not sure how they will react. Kira's frightened enough as it is.

When I enter the cave, though, Kira is sitting up, a troubled look on her face. "We're being followed?" Her voice is soft.

I look over at the other human's still-sleeping form. She hasn't heard a thing. How did Kira catch my conversation with Haeden?

As if guessing my thoughts, Kira touches the shell in her ear. "This lets me hear . . . pretty far. I heard you speaking with Haeden. Are we in danger?"

I'd forgotten. I consider downplaying the danger, but Kira deserves to know. I spread my hands. "I don't know. Something came close to the cave and left, and we don't know what it was. But we had best hurry on to the elders' cave."

She nods and jumps to her feet.

Kira

Yesterday's snowstorms have disappeared and left behind the weak, thready sunlight from the two tiny suns and an extra foot of fresh, powdery snow on the ground to trudge through. My heart sinks at the sight of it, but there's no time to sit around and hope it'll melt. We need to get to the elders' cave, and soon.

We break camp and set off at a fast pace. It seems even faster than yesterday's brisk hike, but maybe it's because I'm tired. Whatever it is, I struggle to keep up even more than usual, to the point that Aehako has to come and retrieve me a few times. It's embarrassing, but no one calls me out because it's obvious I'm doing the best I can.

The next time Aehako jogs back to where I'm lagging, he unslings the packs he's carrying. "Come," he says. "I'll carry you on my back the rest of the way."

His words make me sputter. Carried? Really? My pride is insulted, but this mission isn't really about pride, is it? I'd gladly strip down naked and lick the feet of every single alien on this planet if it meant that the Little Green Men wouldn't be a threat. So, with a small sigh, I nod. "All right. Let's do it."

"Be careful of my tail," he teases.

No sooner does he say that than it bats me across the legs, like a big, playful cat. I arch an eyebrow at him and just shake my head. Even in all this stress, it's hard to keep the grin off of Aehako's face. I wish I could be as easygoing as him. Even without the worries from all the alien abductions, I've always been a serious sort.

I still have no idea what he sees in me.

He crouches low in the snow and pats his thigh. "Take your snowshoe off and put that puny human foot here."

"I'll put it in your balls," I mutter as I pull off my snowshoe. "Puny human, indeed."

Aehako's laugh of delight makes me feel better, and I climb onto his back and lace my arms around his neck. He hikes my thighs around his ribs and then grabs our bags, one in each hand, and tosses one to Haeden as he sprints to catch up.

Oh sure, make it seem effortless.

Haeden turns and gives Harlow a sour look. "Do you need carrying, too, human?"

"I'm fine," she says, shouldering her pack to adjust it. "I can keep going."

I'm envious of the redhead's seemingly endless reserves of strength. I hate that I'm the one that has to be babied.

As if sensing my thoughts, Aehako squeezes my thigh and says, so low that only I can hear it, "Most likely she just doesn't want to be around Haeden's pleasant personality for any longer than necessary."

I stifle my giggle.

A weird chirp sounds nearby, and I glance around, looking for birds.

Weather update? my translator intones.

I stiffen. That wasn't a chirp. That was one of the Little Green Men.

More chirping echoes in my translator. *The storms have stabilized. We should be able to find a sufficient landing area very soon.*

Look for the cargo hold. If the ones in stasis are still there, we can recover them.

We'll set down near it.

"What is it?" Aehako looks at me from over his shoulder.

It takes me a moment to realize that I'm clutching his neck so tightly I'm practically choking the man. I relax my grip, though my anxiety remains. "They're coming. The storm's gone and they want to land."

"Then we have to hurry," Aehako says. He looks to Haeden, and the man nods. Before Harlow can protest, she's slung over his shoulder like a pack, and then both aliens are off, running through the snow at a speed faster than our human legs can move.

As more alien chatter feeds down, I can only hope we get there before they realize the translator is nowhere near the old cargo hold and come looking for me.

I want this thing out of my head *now*.

Even though the sa-khui—our blue alien friends—call it the elders' cave, it's actually a spaceship. Some three-hundred-and-change years ago they crash-landed here much like we did, and over time lost the use of their technology. The ship is still there, and the computer works. And if they have the advanced technology to have had a working spaceship once upon a time, I'm hoping that they also have some sort of working medical equipment that can get this thing out of me.

At this point? I'm willing to chop off my own ear to get rid of it. The implant feels like an anchor, weighing me down with worry.

I'm relieved when the snowy expanse of the ship appears on the horizon. It's enormous, like a gigantic, overly flat hill. Off to one side I see the "cave" opening. It represents safety, even as I hear another sequence of alien chirps come through the translator.

"Hurry, please!" I squeeze Aehako's neck as something bright zips past in the skies overhead. It's not headed in this direction . . . yet. Doesn't mean it won't, though.

Aehako picks up the pace, and with me clinging to his back, he heads for the entrance to the ship in a full-on sprint. Haeden follows close behind.

As we approach, I see the rounded door entrance. It's iced over and dark, but the interior is deep. The snow around the door itself is high, masking any steps. We race inside, and I see that off to the sides there are doors tightly hugging the rounded walls.

"Can we shut the doors?" I ask frantically. The chirping is filling my ear to the point that it's making my anxiety go wild.

"*Mja se fah-ree*," calls out a computerized voice. *Door sequence initiated*, the translator tells me.

"What's it saying?" Harlow asks, sliding off of Haeden's back.

Aehako releases me gently, pulling out one of his bone knives from his belt and eyeing the skies. "It says it is quenching doors. I do not know what this means."

"Sequencing," I correct. "That means it's about to shut them." I pull Aehako back a step or two, watching. I'm a little unnerved that the computer's listening to us. We'll have to be careful what we say.

There's a heavy groan of metal, and then the snapping of ice. Harlow shields her face and Aehako protectively steps in front of me as ice flies everywhere, and then the doors to the hatch roll shut. The sunlight disappears, and we're in utter darkness.

Somewhere in the dark of the interior, a red light blinks.

"Hello?" I call out. "Can you turn on the lights?"

A big hand clasps my shoulder, nearly making me crawl out of my skin. "Stay close, Kira. We do not know if it's safe—"

"North American English, Planet Earth. Is this the default language you wish to use?"

"Um, yes please."

"Accepted."

I glance around. Maybe the computer is like an overgrown version of Siri from my iPhone. "Computer, turn on the interior lights, please."

Something sizzles and I jump closer to Aehako. A flicker, and then a dim light comes on overhead.

"There is a malfunction in regards to the lighting in the main bay. Please contact a service technician."

"Computer, please turn off malfunctioning lighting and turn on all other lighting," I correct. I don't want anything catching on fire. I rub my arms, mindful of the chill in here. Temperature control might be a bit too much to hope for. "Are we safe with the doors shut?"

"The doors can be opened upon request. Do you wish to initiate a lockdown sequence?"

Oh, I absolutely do. "Yes, please."

"Would you prefer biometric passkeys or verbal authorization?"

Aehako looks at me in confusion in the dim lighting. "I do not understand any of this."

Harlow leans in. "We want verbal authorization. A password."

She's right. I nod. "Something that'll be easy to remember. Any ideas?"

Her smile is thin. "Earth?"

I glance over at Haeden and Aehako. They look uneasy, both of them gripping weapons. "I'm not sure that if things get ugly, they'll remember where we came from. Maybe we'll just go with Georgie? Since she's Vektal's mate and all."

Harlow shrugs. "Works for me."

"Computer," I call out. "Please lock down all doors to the exterior. No one can enter or exit without the password of 'Georgie.'"

"Password 'Georgie' accepted."

I move to Aehako and squeeze his hand. "If you guys need to leave for whatever reason, just say her name."

He nods, still looking around with something akin to awe. Underneath the ice that coats the interior of the ship, there are lights and panels and instruments. This must seem very foreign to him.

Heck, it's foreign to me, but I'm starting to get used to weird things at this point.

Harlow takes a few steps forward and shrugs off her thick, furry overcoat. "You think it's okay for us to explore?"

I gesture at the air. "Ask the computer?"

"Right." She gives me a sheepish look. "Computer, are there any living things inside the ship other than us?"

"Performing bio scan. Please wait." A low hum fills the room and a red beam flashes from one side of the cavelike hold to the next, scanning us. "Four life forms detected, two modified sakh and two modified human."

Modified human? I touch my chest, where my khui is wrapped around my heart. "You mean us, correct?"

"That is correct."

"Cool," Harlow says. "I want to go have a look around, if that's okay with you guys."

I shrug. I certainly can't stop her. She's her own person, and this isn't my ship. I have my own agenda here, and if Harlow doesn't want to talk about hers, that doesn't bother me. It must be personal.

Aehako's big hands tug on my icy cloak, helping me take it off. "Is it safe to build a fire?" he asks.

"I don't know if we should. There might not be a vent for the smoke, and we might set off smoke detectors in the interior. I don't know how the ship will respond to that."

"Smoke . . . detectors?" Haeden asks, a frown on his face.

"Long story," I say. Another chirping sequence of flight commands comes through my translator, reminding me why I'm here. I clutch it and approach one of the frozen panels. "Computer, do you have a medical bay somewhere on this ship?"

"Medical bay is located on floor two, section D."

I look over at Aehako. "That's where I'm going."

He steps forward. "Not alone."

For some reason, I appreciate that. I smile at him, feeling shy. "All right."

Haeden moves toward the snowy portal that we entered through, now shut. Muddy, slushy footprints mar the flooring. "I'll stay here and guard the door."

I want to tell him that we're probably safe, but . . . I don't know that we are. For all I know, the computer can think we're safe and the aliens can show up with some new technology that will bust the doors open. So I nod and start forward. There's a dark hall off to one side, and Harlow disappears down it, her hand tracing along the wall as she explores. She's fearless. I envy that.

"Computer," I say. "Can you show me the quickest way to get to the medical bay?"

The track lighting on the edge of the floor flickers off to one side. There's a door there, and after a quick command to open it, it rolls back and exposes a different, dimly lit hall than the one Harlow went down. Exposed wires hang from a missing tile in the ceiling, and it leads on into darkness.

This feels . . . creepy.

I touch the translator in my ear. It doesn't matter if it's creepy or not, I need to take action.

Aehako's hand touches the small of my back, and that small gesture bolsters my courage.

I plunge into the ship.

PART FOUR

PART FOUR

Kira

The ship is a lot bigger than I originally anticipated. It looked big on the outside, but moving through the empty halls makes me realize just how vast the interior is. The long hallways wind and twist, and I pass door after door, some of them rusted shut, others with flashing red lights on their panels. It's obvious that this ship has been in a crash, and it's also obvious that it's been cannibalized for parts at some point. There are panels removed and loose wiring here and there, and stacks of things set into corners. Old footprints cover the floor gratings from long-dried mud. There's a faint musty smell in the air.

Aehako's big body is a few steps behind mine, and each movement makes the floor shake and rattle, as if a hundred metal plates are upended with every step. I cringe at each movement, worried the floor won't hold us both.

The track lighting in the floor stops in front of a yawning archway with a seam down the middle. It looks as if it might be double doors. It looks like part of the wall, but there's writing of some kind on one side, and a control panel on the other. A broken light flickers overhead and then goes dark.

The moment it does, the chirping sounds in my earpiece again. *Report back on what you see. Are the stasis pods intact?*

"Please, open up," I say, pressing my hand to the door. "I need this thing out of me!"

The metal is warm under my hand, which surprises me. It gives a small shiver and creaks open, and I step inside.

"Kira?" Aehako asks as I enter. "Be careful."

The time for being careful is past. I just want this thing gone. I put a hand to the translator and walk into the room, gazing at my surroundings.

I'm not going to lie, it looks a bit like a laboratory. That's scary. There are tables, and a few benches, and a row of futuristic-looking cots jutting from a wall in the distance. Another wall is nothing but screens and monitors. As I step inside, they fire up one by one, scrolling unintelligible words across the screens.

I swallow hard. I don't like the looks of this, but I've never been a fan of the doctor's office. "Do you have something that can remove foreign objects, computer?"

"There is a self-assisted surgery compartment," the computer intones. "I shall activate it."

Self-assisted surgery? Not high on the list of things I want to have done. I'm even more alarmed when one of the walls opens up and spits out a long bed. Monitors flicker and dance with messages.

"Please enter the surgical compartment."

I swallow hard and walk slowly toward the bed. I can do this. It's just like getting a CAT scan back home, right? No big deal. I'm sure these people have—or rather, had—some sort of anesthesia or pain numbing sort of thing. Even if they don't, my earpiece still has to come out.

I still have nightmares of when the aliens implanted the thing in my head. Of being held down and strapped to a table, their voices chirping around me. Of the cool metal object placed against my ear . . . and then things burrowing into my brain, sending blinding pain through my body. I'd had a migraine for a week after it was implanted.

I can't imagine what the extraction is going to be like.

Mouth dry, I sit gingerly on the edge of the bed.

"Please lie flat upon the indicated pallet." The computer's voice is changing, turning into a gentle, soothing counterpart. Bedside manner, perhaps. Whatever it is, I relax a little and start to lie down.

Aehako immediately appears at my side and grips my hand in his. "Kira."

"What is it?"

He looks at the walls, full of monitors and flashing lights and computerized technology that I can't comprehend. He looks . . . more than a little alarmed. This must be terrifying for him. His hand squeezes mine. "You do not have to have this thing removed. I will protect you from the aliens with my life."

I give him a wan smile. "Aehako, they have laser guns and technology that both you and I can't even comprehend. Spears and slings won't do much against them. If they want to take me, there's nothing I can do to stop them. I'm trying to get rid of this thing because I want to hide, not because I think you can't protect me."

His broad face studies me, and I can see the worry etched in his ridged brow and the set of his jaw. He doesn't like this, not one bit. It's startling to see in one as easygoing as Aehako.

"You can let go of my hand now," I tease, trying to keep my voice light.

"Kira," he says, and his voice is low and husky. Instead of moving away, he leans in. He clasps my hand tighter in his and presses it against his breast. "Be my mate."

I stare up at his big body in shock. Was that . . . the alien version of a marriage proposal? "Your mate? But I thought we had to resonate—"

He shakes his head, big horns cutting through the air. My hand is pressed against his thudding heart, the tough, platy ridges covering it. "We will not be resonance mates. Just mates."

"What's the difference?"

He stares at me, so intent and serious. His other hand reaches out and brushes lightly along my jaw in a tender caress. "We choose to be mated to each other until we are separated."

"Separated?"

"By death or by khui."

I can't decide if this is romantic or heartbreaking. "But if you resonate for someone—"

"I will not."

"But how do you know?"

"I don't. All I know is that you are my mate, and I will not listen to anyone or anything—even my khui—that says otherwise."

Yeah, and I'm sure his newly resonated mate would just *love* that.

He's looking at me, waiting for an answer, though. And I'm . . . torn. Not because I don't want to be his mate. The thought sends happiness shooting through me. Aehako and I have flirted for weeks now, and he's shown himself to be caring and funny and kind and just all-around wonderful. If I could pick a guy for my mate here on this frozen ice ball of a planet? It'd absolutely be him.

But I'm barren. I can't have kids.

We'd just be mates until his khui decides that it's time for him to add to the gene pool. Then he'll mate with Harlow, or Claire, or one of the other unmated humans, and I'll be left all alone. Again.

And I don't know if I can take the abandonment. I'm not strong like Liz or Georgie. I'm weak and wimpy and the thought of being put aside for a new mate hurts fiercely. And I've seen Aehako around the others. He comes from a good-sized family. He loves his mom and dad, and his younger siblings. I'd be robbing him of everything but my company if I agreed to be his mate. I can't have children. I'll never resonate for him. If he pins his hopes on me someday resonating for him? He's in for a rude awakening.

It's something he deserves to know before I make up my mind.

I should tell him. I look up at his big, broad face.

The words that come out are, "Do you want children?"

Aehako blinks in surprise. I can tell the question wasn't one he expected. But it's worth asking. If he doesn't want children, I'll feel better as his "mate." Maybe because at that point, I'll know that I'll still have a place in his heart even if his khui kicks in and decides he should be a daddy. But his words shatter that hope. "Of course I want children." A slow smile curves his mouth. "What man doesn't dream of a family of his own?"

I feel about as big as an ant. A tiny smushed ant ground into the carpet. I let go of his hand. "Okay, that's what I wanted to know. Thank you."

He laughs and cups my face in his big hands. "Kira, do not

worry so. I have seen the khui resonate amongst those mated for many years. It is as if it can sense the love between two people and decides to unite them in every way."

Yeah, right. More like the khui gives up and gives one last shake just to get a little something out of its host. I don't think it's as romantic as he thinks. And it wouldn't happen anyhow. I give him a thin smile. "We'll talk about it when I get out, okay?"

Worry clouds his expressive gaze and he leans in and gives me a quick, soft kiss. "I will wait here."

I slip from his grasp and lie flat on the pallet. "I'm ready," I tell the computer. The bed immediately begins to recede into the wall with me on it, and I watch Aehako's worried face disappear from sight.

Lights flicker and then go dark.

I suck in a breath, because this isn't like a CAT scan after all—more like a slab in a morgue. What if the machine breaks down and won't let me back out? I start to breathe rapidly, full of anxiety. My hand touches the panel over my head. It's less than a full arm's length away, ditto the sides. Lights begin to hum, and I watch the walls come to life with more writing and dancing charts—probably my vital signs.

"How can we assist you today?" the computer's smooth voice asks.

"I need a foreign object removed." I point at the translator in my ear.

"Please remain still. Our systems will scan you to make a health determination."

I put my arm down and lie flat on the bed, careful not to move. I look around, wondering at the technology. I'm a lot smaller than the bed itself—I think even Aehako's brawny form could fit in here—which tells me that the sa-khui haven't changed much since the crash. There's a headrest—maybe in case the patient has extremely large horns—but it's too big for my neck and I ignore it, tilting my head off to the side.

"Our sensors have noted two foreign bodies," the computer informs me pleasantly. "Would you like for us to proceed with extraction of both?"

"T-two?" I stammer, shocked. "What do you mean?"

"Our sensors indicate a nonorganic compound attached to your human sensory organ. Further scans indicate that you have also acquired a parasite native to this planet—"

Oh. The khui. I keep forgetting that Aehako's people crash-landed here and had to take the khui, same as we did. No wonder their computer views it as a foreign object. "I want to keep the parasite and get rid of this thing." I tap the translator. "The nonorganic compound attached to my, um, ear."

"Please turn on your side so we may examine the object in greater detail."

I roll over, and immediately, computerized arms sprout from the wall and begin to touch the translator. Things whir and chirp, and I have to bite down on my lip to keep from jerking every time something taps on the metal, as it sends feedback screeching through my skull.

"Object identified," the computer informs me. "Sensors indicate it is a *strbde qreiduvp scipqrei.*" The computer rattles off a sequence of unintelligible sounds. "Would you like to proceed with extraction?"

I notice no one's offering anesthesia or novocaine or any sort of medication to numb the pain. I lick my dry lips. "Is it going to hurt?"

I mean, I still need to get it removed either way, but I want to know what I'm in for.

"Sensors indicate that the equipment is attached to sensitive neural tissue. It will take some time and effort to remove without damage, but the probability for successful extraction without requiring additional surgery is 97%."

That sounds encouraging. "Let's do it, then."

The table underneath me whirs and shivers, and a sleek metal cuff slides around my neck.

"What?" I yelp, jerking as another cuff locks around one of my wrists, and another on my ankles.

"Kira," Aehako bellows, and his voice sounds far away, muffled through the machinery.

"Please remain still," the computer admonishes me. "You are being restrained for your own safety. The slightest movement can affect the operation. Do you still wish for us to proceed?"

"Kira!" Aehako shouts again, and I hear a clatter of equipment, and an angry chirp from the computers.

"It's okay," I call out in a small, thready voice. "I'm all right! Tell him I'm all right, computer."

It's silent for a moment, but I don't hear Aehako shouting anymore, so I suppose that's a good sign. I force myself to relax, trying not to think of the cuff around my neck as choking me. It's just like a blood pressure cuff. That's all. No problem.

"Please remain calm during the procedure."

"Okay." I close my eyes so I don't see the robot arms moving around. Something pings and I feel a tug against the translator, and my body tenses.

"Your blood pressure is abnormally high. Shall we provide soothing music?"

The question strikes me as utterly absurd, and I swallow my hysterical giggle. "I'll calm down," I promise.

"Do you have any other questions you wish to have answered?"

My stomach chooses that moment to rumble, and I decide to make a joke. "Is there a snack bar around here?"

"Query: what is snack bar?"

Oh. Now I have to explain. I feel a bit childish. "A place where you go to eat."

"This ship has three dining locations. However, current food and water supplies are exhausted."

Of course. The people that crashed here probably cleaned out the pantry. "How many people were on this ship?"

"At the time of landing, this vessel had one pilot and sixty-two passengers."

Interesting. I hear the computer arms humming and the thing in my ear tugs. I squeeze my eyes even tighter shut, trying to relax. "So what kind of trip was it? The one that crashed?"

"The charter for *Se Kilahi* reads: A voyage for those to commune with nature."

Se Kilahi must be the ship. It sounds pretty. "Commune with nature? Was this a . . . camping trip?" If so, they got a heck of a camping trip. Maybe they were a back to basics kind of group and that would explain why Aehako's people went from advanced technology to leathers and hunting/gathering in the course of three hundred years.

"Query: what is camping trip?"

"Never mind." Something tugs on my ear again and I cast about for another question. "So what's the weather going to be like for the next week, Siri?"

"Query: what is Siri?"

"Never mind." I smile inwardly at my own joke.

"The atmosphere indicates that more snow will return at this planet's sunset."

Yaaay. I never thought I'd be so happy for snow. Maybe it'll prevent the other aliens from landing. "Can you tell if there is another ship in the atmosphere here?" Worth a shot.

"Affirmative. Sensors have located an alien ship three drumah away."

I have no idea how far a drumah is, but I hope it's far. "How many aliens on board?"

"Sixteen."

Ulp. "You can tell there's sixteen? Seriously?"

"Affirmative. This unit is connected to a satellite orbiting the planet that allows the ship's computers to track and record information."

"Like how many sa-khui are here?"

"Affirmative. There are thirty-four modified sakh and twelve modified humans currently on the planet."

Huh. I wonder what the point of recording all the information is for. Before I can ask, there is a sharp tug on my ear and I yelp.

"Please remain still as the extraction begins," the computer's sweet voice tells me.

Then, there's a blinding, red-hot shot of pain that seems to jolt directly to my brain and the world goes black.

Aehako

My heart stops beating when the wall spits Kira out. She's crumpled on the strange bed, small and still, and there are bloody bandages pressed over her ear. Her strange metal shell is gone but her face is so pale, and she's unconscious.

Mouth dry, I touch her cheek to rouse her. When she doesn't stir, I collect her in my arms and take her away from this room. I don't trust it. I don't trust the elders' cave, with its strange magic and glowing walls and disembodied voices. I want to take Kira back to my own cave and lay her down in my furs—

Well, it's not really my cave but my family's cave, and it would be awkward to lay her down in my furs and mate with her with my younger brothers and my parents looking on. But I'd find someplace quiet to take her and comfort her. To hold her and make her mine.

None of that matters, though. Kira's unconscious and not well. I scent Haeden somewhere nearby and follow my nose until I locate him, still at the front entrance, staring at the strange stone doors with a grim expression. He gets to his feet at the sight of me with Kira in my arms, his scowl deepening.

"What is wrong with her?"

"They removed her shell," I say. "But she won't wake."

He grunts. "She might be tired. Perhaps the walls chatted her ear off."

I cradle her closer to my chest. "Are they talking to you?"

He nods. "It keeps asking me if I wish for anything. I wish for silence and for stone walls not to speak to me."

"Ask the stone walls where a bed is. If Kira is going to sleep, I will stay with her until she awakens." I look around. "Where is the other human?"

Haeden shrugs. "Does it matter? She has to come out through here to leave." He gestures at the closed cave-mouth.

My friend has no love for the humans. He might be the only one in our tribe who was not beside himself with joy at the discovery of so many women. I turn and look at the strange stone walls with their flashing lights and moving wiggles. I decide to address it. "Where is a cave? I wish to set my mate down to sleep."

Haeden arches a brow at me but I ignore his silent question. Kira is my mate, even if neither my body nor hers realizes it yet. They just need time.

The computer speaks in the human language. "Living quarters are in the south wing."

"Lead me there," I demand.

The floor lights up as it did for Kira, and I hold her close, pushing my way into the bowels of the cave. I don't like this strange place, but it seems to be safe from predators. The strange lights lead me down another winding path, and stop at a cave with a half-open door that shivers as if trying to shut itself.

There is a broken piece of the wall hanging down from the ceiling that prevents it from closing, and I slide under and into the cave itself.

It's a small, too-square compartment with more of the flashing panels, but I'm pleased to see that there's a square pallet covered with a soft, squishy, strange-feeling animal skin. I toss my cloak down over the pallet and gently lay Kira down onto the bed so I can examine her again. Worry makes my heart pound and I smooth a hand down her arms and legs and chest, looking for hidden wounds I might not have seen before. She seems healthy in body. I peel back the bandages over her ear. There are reddened holes along her lobe, and dried blood crusted inside her ear canal, but otherwise I see no issues.

There's nothing to do but wait for her to awaken.

I slide onto the bed next to her and wrap my arms around her. She fits against me so perfectly. I sweep my hand over her hair and press my mouth to her strange, smooth forehead. "You are safe with me, Kira," I murmur in a low, soothing voice. "No one will harm you while you are with me. I will fight to the death to keep you at my side. Enemies will look upon my spear and recoil in fear." I run my hand down her small back. "Then, you and I will get a cave of our own. I am not sure how, but we will manage. And we will set up a nest of warm, thick furs to keep your fragile human body warm, and I will press my mouth to every inch of your soft skin and show you how much you mean to me." My fingers graze over her face, tracing her small nose, her tiny brows. She is strange looking compared to the women of my tribe, but I have a great appreciation for her flat brow, pale face, and sad eyes, and her small mouth, which so rarely curves into a smile. I decide right then and there that I will act a fool around her if it will only bring a happy look to her face.

I will do anything for her.

I settle into the bed, describing in great detail how we shall set up our cave. How my mother will fuss over the thought of having a daughter, as she has only sons and none of them mated. Of how my father will shake his head at my ways, but it won't matter because it is all for Kira.

"The biggest, warmest bed in all the caves," I decide. "Dvisti fur is the warmest and I will line our nest with that, and then ask Kashrem—that's Maylak's mate—to create soft coverlets that are softer than a kit's bottom, but warm enough to please you. It will cost me much, but Kashrem's always been jealous of my carving, so I shall create him some new tools, I think. Perhaps a few baubles for his kits." I consider thoughtfully. I've always given away my carvings with ease, not concerned with getting anything in return. Now that I have a mate, I shall have to consider things more carefully, so I may provide all the things she wants. "And we shall need furs for the entrance of our cave," I tell her. "To muffle your shouts of pleasure when I take you every night."

Perhaps that is my own male pride talking there. I do not think Kira is a shouter. Not like Asha was. She will be the quiet type, the kind that comes with a widening of her eyes and a parting of the lips, and no more than that.

I picture it, and my cock grows uncomfortably hard. Time to think of other things. I stroke my hand down Kira's arm. "I imagine that the first brutal season with my people will be hard on the humans. You struggle right now, but I will do my best to ensure that you are always warm and well fed. And when the snows are too high for even the hunters to go out, we shall stay in our furs all day long."

Strange, how badly I want the life I am envisioning. My heart thuds hard, thinking of Kira, warm and smiling up at me from a long night of vigorous mating. Kira, with her belly rounded with my child. Kira, nursing a tiny human-sa-khui halfling, with a pink tail and stunted horns. What would our child look like?

Lost in pleasant thoughts, I continue to talk to my unconscious mate.

Kira

My head feels like a cracked-open melon. Pain pounds in my brain, and I remain completely still, hoping that the lack of movement makes the agony dissipate. As I do, I hear a soft, low voice.

"I might have to stack the back of our cave with extra dung so I can keep a fire going for you at all times. I'll just have to figure out something to disguise the smell. Maybe some of Maylak's herbs. And I know you like your meat cooked, so there's that to consider. And when it gets too cold at night, we can heat some snow in a quilled-beast bladder. You can preserve them a certain way and place them at your feet to keep your furs warm at night. Either way, I'll make sure you're happy and comfortable." Aehako's big fingers trace my jaw. "But I'll take care of you."

My headache fades a little at his soothing touch. I'm cradled against him with my face pressed to his chest and my hand nearby. His arms are wrapped around me, hugging me against him, and it feels . . . like home. I keep my eyes closed, relaxing in the low thrum of his voice as he tells me all about his plans for "our" cave and how we'll weather the brutal season—the winter—together and all the plans he has for us. I have to admit that hearing him talk about his plans for the two of us together fills me with an incredible amount of yearning and muted joy. Joy because setting up a cozy cave with him sounds incredibly wonderful and I still can't believe someone as fun and sexy as him is interested in someone as quiet as me.

Yearning because he starts talking of kits and when I have his children.

Which will never happen, because I'm still barren. A small sigh escapes me. He wants me and a family, but he can only have one of those things.

"Kira?" I feel his big body move under my cheek and my hand. "Are you awake?"

I nod and lick my dry lips. "Head hurts."

"The shell is gone," he says, keeping his voice low.

I reach up and touch my ear. It sends a new round of blistering pain through my head, but I also feel . . . lighter? I trace along my earlobe and feel the new holes there. It's really gone. "Did you destroy it?"

He tenses against me. "Should I?"

"Please," I whisper. "They might be able to track me with it."

"I'll take care of it," he says, getting up from the bed. "But first you must drink."

I nod and manage to pull myself into a sitting position. He pulls out his waterskin and holds it to my mouth carefully so I can drink, and when I'm done, he helps me lie back down in bed and then gently tucks the blankets around me. My heart is brimming with affection for this giant, laughing man that can be so tender with me.

I hate that I can't keep him. That I'm flawed and I'll never be what he wants in a woman. In a mate.

I sigh softly and close my eyes again to relieve my pounding head.

"Rest, Sad Eyes," he tells me, and caresses me once more before heading toward the door. "I shall handle everything."

I close my eyes and hope he's right.

When I wake up later, my headache is all but gone and my stomach is growling. I sit up in the bed, conscious of a big warmth curled around my backside. It's Aehako again, and he's returned while I've slept, and we're spooning.

Gosh it's hard to be me.

Aehako's big hand goes around my waist, curling me against him. "Kira?" His sleepy murmur of my voice sounds like honey, and I can feel the rather . . . prominent erection he's sporting pushing against my backside. "How is your head?"

"I think I'm okay," I tell him. "I need to find something to eat, though. And a bathroom."

"Bath . . . room?"

I nod sleepily, peering at the room we're in. It looks like a small private bunk of some kind, maybe someone's quarters. There's a faded poster on the opposite wall, and I can't make out what was on it. A few more wires hang from the ceiling and there's a fine layer of dust over everything. The room has been stripped, right down to the bed, which is nothing but a mattress with our furs placed atop it.

I swing my legs over the side of the bed and get to my feet, testing my strength. I seem to be fine, my surgery-induced migraine gone. If this is a private cabin, I'm sure there's a potty around here somewhere. By running my hands along a few interesting-looking seams in the walls, I manage to find what I'm searching for. It's a cubby with a strange basin that's a *leetle* too high off the ground for human legs. Off to one side is what looks like a shower.

God, I would love a shower. I manage to wiggle my way onto the alien toilet a moment before wondering if it's even functioning. "Um, computer? Are the facilities working?"

"Query: what is facilities?"

"The toilets and the showers?"

"I can reactivate them with stored snow. It will take twenty-seven seconds to melt and heat. Would you like to proceed?"

"Oh, yes!"

By the time I finish my business on the toilet, there's water pouring from the spout in the shower ceiling. At first it drizzles a muddy color, but then runs clear, and I run my fingers under the water to test the heat.

It's perfect.

With a small sigh of pleasure, I strip off my leathers and toss them to the dusty floor, then move into the shower itself. Some things are eternal, I suppose, because it's almost exactly the same as a human shower, and I wipe my wet hair off my face with pure bliss. This is exactly what I need.

"Kira?" Aehako knocks at the door. "Are you well?"

"I'm fine," I call.

The door opens a moment later. "Then you will not mind if I come and spend time with you?"

I squeal, covering my girl parts with my hands as he steps inside. "What are you doing?"

He spreads his arms. "Is it not obvious? You hide in here so I will join you."

"I'm trying to shower!"

"Shower?"

"Bathe!" I hate that the language that the sa-khui learned is three hundred years old. A lot of our language has changed since then. "Washing!"

His eyes gleam and he looks me up and down. Aehako's gaze is scorching. "I have soap-berries in my bag. I shall be more than happy to help you wash."

The blush on my cheeks feels like an inferno. "I'm naked."

"I noticed." The look he gives me is appreciative. "And your parts are as fine as I imagined."

I know I should tell him no, to go away. But then it hits me . . . why should I? What is the point in being modest? Who is there to judge or shame me? I want him to come shower with me. I want his big, blue body rubbing up against mine. I like it when he takes care of me. It makes me feel loved and cherished, and those are two emotions I am utterly hungry for. But . . . I don't know how to invite a man into a sexy situation. It's not in me to flirt back. So I just give him a mute, helpless look.

As if he senses my agony, he hesitates. "Do you wish me to leave, Kira?"

I stare at him for a long moment. At the big, seven-foot-tall alien male wearing only a loincloth that doesn't do much for modesty. He's got horns and ridges and should be frightening. And instead, I'm terribly attracted to him. So I steel my courage and shake my head. I don't want him to leave. "G-get the soap."

He flashes me one of those quick, pleased Aehako grins and heads out of the alien bathroom, leaving me only moments to try and make myself, well, pretty. I smooth a hand over my wet hair and glance down at my legs and arms and my pale body. I'm not at my hottest. I . . . guess it doesn't matter. He doesn't have other humans to compare me to except the ones I came here with. When he comes back with his small pouch of berries, I'm nervous but . . . so excited. My nipples are already pointing and hard, and I flash him a quick, shy smile, hoping that he finds me pretty. Which is weird to think about, considering he's blue and horned, but I still want him to be attracted to me because of me, not just because I have a vagina.

Aehako sets the bag down on a nearby counter and scoops a few of the berries out. I push back the glass door of the shower at the exact same moment that he whips off his loincloth.

And . . . okay. So that looks a lot bigger than I'd initially "felt." It's one thing to see pictures of naked men and statues and the like, and it's another to have a fully aroused guy standing right in front of you. With a spur. Can't forget the spur. And here I'd thought his big carved "present" of his cock was . . . well, an exaggeration.

Doesn't seem like it.

His cock looks as long as my arm, though surely it can't be. It's also flushed a darker blue than the rest of his skin. I can't help but stare at it as he enters the shower with me.

And then I have to squeeze against the back wall, because Aehako's big body is enormous and the shower clearly wasn't built for two. A nervous giggle escapes me. "Should I get out?"

"I can fit," he says, stooping a bit lower to get his big horns into the shower. "It just means we'll have to stand a little closer together." And he gives me another flirty look that makes me giggle.

"You're hogging all the hot water." It cascades off of his body and his horns but doesn't seem to hit me at all. He'd make a great umbrella, not such a great shower partner.

"Hogging?"

"Taking," I correct, then think about it. "I should probably get the language dump while we're here. I want to know your speech."

"It can wait another day," he tells me, and smashes the berries in his fist. "Shall I rub this on you?"

A shiver moves through me, and my skin prickles with awareness of him. Even hunched over, Aehako's size is intimidating . . . but I know he can be oh so gentle. And if I move in any closer, his penis is going to be rubbing up against me.

It's a bit like sensory overload. I want to explore him, and I want him to explore me . . . but I mostly just want to kiss him.

"Aehako," I breathe, and reach up to wrap my arms around his neck. Water immediately dumps in my face. I sputter, and then wipe my face clean. "Will you kiss me?"

"You need never ask, Sad Eyes. All you need is to turn your face toward me." His big arm goes around me and pulls me against him, and I'm startled at the contact of our wet skin. It feels decadent and strange and I want to run my hands all over him and explore him.

But then his mouth covers mine in a hot, hard press, and I moan in surprise and delight. His tongue flicks against mine in invitation, and then we're kissing wildly, the water streaming down on both of us. Lips locked, we kiss over and over again until I'm pressing up against him as much as he's holding me to him. My nipples rub against his chest and it sends shivery bolts through my body . . . so I make it a point to rub against him repeatedly.

"Kira," he groans, and then pulls away, which leaves me dazed. I nearly stumble without his big body to lean against. The look on his face is sober as he indicates I should turn around. "Let me wash you before we continue."

I stiffen even as I turn, my back going ramrod straight. "Is it because I smell?"

"No, it is because I don't have many berries left and I need to wash, too."

Oh. I stand obedient as he rubs the berry juice over my back and shoulders and then into my hair. He rubs at my hair for a bit and then smooths his hand down my arm, washing my skin. It feels good, like being stroked. Almost like a massage.

Then, his hand comes forward and cups my breast and I forget all about massaging. The breath explodes from me and I gasp in shock and startled pleasure.

"You are so delicate." His hand moves over my breast, then glides to the other. "Soft and delicate all over."

I tilt my head back and I'm surprised when Aehako's other arm goes around my waist, pulling me against him again. The feel of his cock against my back is like a stabbing spear, but he holds me against him and smooths his soapy hands all over my body and I'm helpless to do anything but stand there and let him. It feels way too good.

His mouth nuzzles at my neck and he licks and then playfully nips at my skin, even as both of his hands move to cup my breasts. I moan with pleasure. I've touched my own breasts, but when he does it, the pleasure goes from simply "good" to "off the charts." I press back against him and my hands go to his arms. I'm desperate to show him that I want more of this lovely, exciting touching, but I don't know how to show him. "Aehako, what do I do?" I scratch my nails over the plated ridges on his forearms.

His low growl of pleasure surprises me. "Anywhere you touch me is a pleasure. Just like it is for me when I touch you. And right now, I intend on taking my pleasure from my mate."

Aehako's passionate words are like a slap of cold water in the face.

His mate.

Oh no. I need to tell him. "Aehako," I say softly, and turn around to face him.

"No, Kira." He leans in and nips at my mouth to silence me. "I will hear no protests. You will be my mate. We need no khui to bind us. You are mine and I am yours. Our khui will simply catch up later. It has happened in many a mating. You choose, and then eventually the khui chooses."

I shake my head. "It won't ever choose me, Aehako."

"You do not know that—"

"I do," I say, and before I can even think about keeping the words in, I spit them out. "I'm barren."

PART FIVE

Aehako

It takes me a moment to digest the word "barren." The mental visual the translation gives me is that of scorched, fallow earth with no animals and no plants, no water, no anything.

Then I realize what she is telling me. "You cannot have kits?"

Tears pool in her sad eyes and she nods. "When I was very young, I got sick and nearly died. I was in the hospital for a long time, and when I finally healed, they told me that my reproductive system had been compromised by the illness and I'd never have children." The tears spill down her cheeks and she swipes at them with quick, angry motions. "That's why we can't be together. Because you want to have a family. And I have to tell you that if you choose me, you'll never have one. I won't ever resonate, because I can't have children."

I feel a sharp pang of regret, but it's quickly banished. Is this why she's so sad? Is this why she holds me at arm's length when it's clear she is desperate to be loved? That she craves affection the way I crave her smiles?

I touch her chin and force her to look up at me. There's such misery and heartbreak in her eyes. She truly thinks I shall cast her aside now that I find she cannot create life in her belly? "Is there anything else?"

A half-sob turns into a laugh and she swipes at her tears again. "I think that's plenty, don't you?"

"What if I told you it did not matter to me if you could have kits or not?"

Her small brows furrow. "But you said you wanted a family. I wouldn't deprive you of that."

"Do not worry on my behalf, Sad Eyes. There are no children without resonance, and now I do not have to worry about another male snatching you out of my grasp." I stroke her cheek gently. "A few moons ago, I had resigned myself to a lonely life of hunting and the only companionship that of my hand." My crude words make a small, horrified laugh erupt from her, and I continue. "Now, I have met you and I see a life ahead of me of laughter, and caresses, and loving. Does it matter to me that we will never resonate? It does not. Just to have you in my life is enough for me. You are my heart, Kira, and you should be my mate."

She starts to cry again. "I don't want you to feel trapped with me."

"Trapped?" I laugh. "Trapped with a beautiful, strong, smart mate in my furs every night? I welcome such traps."

"But children—"

"If we have no kits, then we shall always have our cave to ourselves," I tell her, pulling her against me. Her wet skin sticks to mine and creates a delicious friction between us. I can feel the small nubs of her nipples rub against my stomach and it makes my cock jerk, desperate to be inside her. "And we shall scandalize all of the others by being the loudest mated pair in the caves."

A horrified little giggle escapes her, and I'm so relieved that I've made her smile that I squeeze her tight against me.

"If you're sure . . ." she says softly.

"I was sure the moment I saw your face."

She pulls back, surprised. "You were?"

I nod. "I saw you and thought, if ever there was a female that needed a male to make her smile, it was you. And that we would be perfect together."

Kira bats at my chest in mock annoyance, but I can tell she's pleased by my words. She's softening against me, and the tears are drying. "I just . . . I never said anything. Your people were so excited about the fact that we could resonate and have children. I never wanted to admit that I was flawed. I didn't know what would happen if I was. Would I be welcome any longer?"

"Of course you would be welcome. We would not cast you out simply because you cannot bear kits. Do we cast out Farli?"

She snorts. "Farli is too young to have children. That's not even a fair comparison."

"Then Asha? Whose kit died too young? Or my mother, Sevvah, who is now too old to have more kits?" I touch her cheek. "You bring more to the tribe than just your body."

"I'm not so sure," she says softly. "The only thing I was good at was translating, and I just had that removed."

"Then you will bring new skills and joy to the tribe. We just have not seen them yet."

Kira gives me an exasperated look. "Do you have an optimistic answer for everything?"

"Yes." I grin at her. "That is what I bring to the tribe. Well, that and my carving skills."

Another small giggle escapes her, muffled under the falling of the bathing waters. "Yes, I still have the present you made for me."

"Ah. Because it is such an impressive likeness?"

Her giggle turns into a snort and she buries her face against my wet chest, her arms going around me. "Because I wanted to compare the sizes. I figured it was exaggerated."

"Shall I show you just how accurate my carvings are?" I slide my fingers down her wet back, and then take her hand and place it on my aching cock. I hear her suck in a breath, but she doesn't pull away. Instead, she caresses me and explores. "Be my mate, Kira."

She looks up at me, hope in her eyes. "But the aliens—"

More excuses? "Let them do their best to separate us. They will fail." I touch her cheek again. "And let us not predict doom for our future. Let us live for today, yes?"

I have always been a practical male. I have seen too much sorrow to let it guide my life, like Haeden does. If it means I must smile one day and weep the next, then I shall enjoy the day of smiles all that much more. I want Kira to realize this—that life is sweetest when we take what it offers with no worries.

She squeezes her fingers around the base of my cock and then gently glides her hand up, stroking me. "Today," she says in a low voice, "is a really, really nice day to be with my mate."

My heart swells with affection. "Yes, it is."

The water changes temperature from a delicious heat to an ice cold, and Kira yelps at the same time I do. She rinses the berries from her hair and then quickly jumps out of the water, and I follow a moment later.

"I guess we ran out of hot water," she says, her arms pressed against her chest as she shivers and gives a little hop.

"Was that not supposed to happen?"

"No!" She laughs. "No one can bathe in that cold of water."

I shrug. I don't understand anything about the elders. But as

I watch Kira delicately pick up her leathers from the floor, quivering with cold, I decide there are other ways I can warm her. Ways that are as old as time. I scoop her up in my arms and ignore her startled squeal. "You are entirely too cold, my lovely mate. Let your male warm you up."

Instead of the shy protests I expect, she wraps her arms around my neck and clings to me. My cock feels like aching stone. I've wanted this since I saw her. I carry her into the other room and gently lay her down on the bed. Kira looks up at me with trusting eyes, and my heart swells again with affection.

This is my mate.

It doesn't matter that our khui haven't chosen or that she cannot bear kits. She is mine to claim. Mine to pleasure.

"You are beautiful," I tell her. She is. Her human limbs are dewy with water, her skin gleaming with smoothness. Her eyes—blue with khui—seem big and bright in her face, and her hair is slicked back against her skull, making her seem even more fragile than usual. Her chest heaves with nervousness, and each short breath makes her breasts jiggle enticingly. Her legs are curled together, but soon I shall lick her between them and taste her honey.

Kira smiles up at me and reaches out for my hand. I lace my fingers with her smaller ones, noting again our differences. She has four small fingers and a thumb, where I have three and a thumb. Her toes are the same—four small toes next to a large one on a slender foot. My own foot is more than twice as large as hers, and my toes—one less than her—are more spread to balance my larger form. There are no plated ridges on her body to protect it, only softness everywhere.

I cannot deny that I find the thought of all this softness incredibly arousing.

I free my hand from her grip and touch her chest, eager to feel that smooth skin. The valley between her breasts feels as soft as the underbelly of a quilled beast. She trembles at my touch, her gaze on me, and I watch her nipples harden in response to my touch, going from soft pink circles to hard, ruched little tips. I don't touch them yet, though. I'm still exploring, still admiring my mate's body. This is our first chance to be truly alone and unclothed with each other, and I would like to enjoy it.

Her belly is flat, with a tiny dip for a navel that makes me want to kiss it. Her hips flare out slightly, rounded and inviting, and between her thighs is a thatch of dark hair that hides her honey-covered folds and her third nipple. It's begging for my mouth, but I suspect my shy Kira would jump right off the furs if I spread her legs and buried my face there, so I must woo her with kisses and caresses.

I want to feel her against me, so I climb into the bed and lie next to her. My body dwarfs her smaller one, and she shifts a little. I lean my weight on the side so I don't crush her, and throw a possessive leg over her thighs so she can't squirm away from me.

Then, I lean in to kiss her, pulling her body close to mine.

She sighs and leans into my kiss, her tongue flicking against mine. I deepen the kiss, make it more explicit, more obvious as to what I want from her. I fuck her sweet mouth with my tongue, and she responds with soft cries and wriggles of delight under me. My cock aches to claim her, but I must go slowly. Kira has never mated before, and she is skittish.

I nip at her mouth, enjoying her responses—noises of pleasure. My mouth grazes her jawline and then I lick at her neck, which sends trembling through her entire body. She likes that. I lick the soft skin there and gently bite down on it, and her fingers dig into my shoulders. "Do you enjoy my mouth on your neck?" I murmur. "Or shall I move it elsewhere?"

"I like your mouth everywhere," she says in the softest, breathiest voice. It makes my cock twitch. I'll give her my mouth everywhere, then.

I lick and suck at her soft human skin, tracing along her collarbones. With each press of my mouth to her flesh, she gives a low moan, and her hands move over my shoulders and arms, fluttering. It's as if she doesn't know where to place them but wants to touch me. She can touch me as much as she wants; I will gladly take it. But for now, I'm concentrating on her. She's had so much worry on her mind lately I want to make her come undone.

Also? I want to make sure she has no doubts about being mine.

I move down over her smooth breastbone and then graze my lips over one breast. The tip is pebbled with arousal, and I lick it enticingly, then wait for her reaction.

"Oh," she breathes, her voice trembling. When I lift my head, she blushes and looks shy.

"Show me what you want, Kira."

Her cheeks are bright pink as she grabs my horns and pulls me back down to her breast again in a silent command. It didn't take much convincing, and I'm pleased that my mate is enjoying my attentions. She's so small and delicate, and I worry one as big and brutish as I am is going to be frightening to her. But the way she directs me makes me suspect I have been overthinking things. That she's as hungry for my touch as I am for hers.

I capture her nipple in my mouth and flick at it with my tongue. She gasps when the ridges on my tongue drag against the tip, so I make sure to do that over and over again. "My Kira," I murmur, cupping her breast so I can better feed it to my mouth. "My sweet mate. You taste as good as I've imagined."

She makes a soft little groan, and her hands skim down my arms again, her hips undulating on the bed under me. The scent of her arousal perfumes the air around us, and I rock my hips against the furs, my cock desperate to sheathe into her warmth. Patience is difficult when your mate is under you for the first time. I want nothing more than to fling myself on top of her and bury deep inside her. I want to watch her lips part with awe as I stroke into her.

Instead, I trail my mouth lower on her belly, my impatience getting the better of me. I drag my teeth against her skin, enjoying it when she shivers in response. My tongue circles her navel, and then I dip lower, to the curls between her legs that shield her folds from me. My mouth waters with anticipation.

They say no taste is sweeter than that of a resonance mate on a male's tongue, but we are not resonating. We never will. I do not think she will taste any less sweet, though.

Her thighs press together and her hands slide over my horns. "Aehako," she murmurs. "I don't know . . ."

"Have you ever had a male lick your honey before?"

Her face flares a bright crimson. "Just you. Before."

Ah, yes. It's a good memory, and one that fuels my lusty fantasies. Of my hand dipping between Kira's legs and teasing her until she comes, then licking her sweetness off my fingers even as it frosts. "Then I shall be your first and last," I tell her, and find a bizarre amount of pleasure in this bold statement. She will never be anyone else's but mine. Ever.

I nip at her thigh, entreating her to open for me. She makes a nervous sound and her legs tremble. "Open for me, my mate. I want to lick all of you." To prove it, I drag my tongue down her hip bone, all the way to the curly little tuft of hair. "Part your legs for me."

I feel Kira tremble again, but she does. Her legs open and I take my hand and push them even farther apart, until she's spread for me. I hook one knee over my shoulder so she can't close her thighs again. Then I get to admire my mate's spread cunt. The folds gleam with wetness, making me salivate once more. Her folds are pretty and a deeply flushed pink, like her cheeks. I drag one finger through her wetness and my cock aches when she squirms and makes soft noises of pleasure.

"I'm going to taste you."

She presses a hand to her forehead and her eyes close. "Oh God."

Interesting. She's not pulling away, though, so I lean in and explore her with my mouth. The first burst of her taste on my tongue is like nothing else—she's like salt and musk and Kira . . . and utterly delicious. I growl low in my throat, feral with need. "Sweet."

Kira's breath shudders in her throat.

I grip her legs and want more. Pulling them farther apart, I lift her off the bed so all of her is open to me, and lick her from her third nipple to the entrance to her cunt. A low moan escapes her, and I lick her fully again. This time I start at the pucker of her bottom and circle it, then drag my tongue all the way up through her folds, to her third nipple.

"Oh my God," she moans again. "You did not just do that."

"I can do it again," I tell her. I will gladly do so. Her taste is sweeter than anything I have ever had. I repeat the action, making sure to swirl my tongue around the entrance of her bottom and then slowly move upward through her folds, coated with delicious honey, and swirl again around the hood of her little nipple.

When I do that, she cries out and her hips jerk.

Aha. I repeat the motion, my tail lashing with my own excitement. I love making her respond to my touch, love that shy, contained Kira moans and cries when I lick her cunt. I could lick her for hours and never get my fill. I tease and nibble at the nipple between her legs, and she presses her hand to her forehead again and cries out.

"More?" I tease, and suck on the tiny bit of flesh.

A cry escapes her throat and I feel her body shudder underneath me, her trembling increasing. Her hips rock against my mouth, and so I continue to suck at the tender spot until she is moaning and boneless with pleasure. "Oh mercy," she pants. "That was . . . something else."

I lick my lips, tasting her on me. "Your cunt tastes sweeter than I ever imagined."

The blush on her face becomes fierce, and she pants, still pressing that hand to her forehead.

"Is your head hurting you?"

"What? Oh, no," she says quickly, and her hand flops down on the bed. A small giggle escapes her. "I guess I was just . . . trying to hold my brains in before they all fell out." And she chuckles.

Strange words, but I chuckle, too. I like making her smile. I press another kiss on the small thatch of hair and then lick her again. Kira shudders, her skin prickling with small bumps at the caress. I press a finger to the entrance of her cunt to see if she is wet enough to take me, and it comes away soaked.

My mate is more than ready. The fierce need to claim her burns through me, and I move over her, my bigger body pressing her into the strange bed. Her arms wrap around me and she welcomes my kiss, and another little gasp of excited pleasure escapes her when I grab a fistful of her hair and arch her neck back so I can lick it again. I bite gently at the cords of her throat and slide my hips between her spread legs, my cock resting against the cradle of her hips.

And I grind it against her so she can feel it.

Kira's small gasp as I rock against her is incredibly pleasing. Her thighs spread a little wider, and I pull one around my hip. Instead of plunging into her, though, I kiss her again, my tongue dancing along her mouth, sipping at the small moans that erupt in a steady stream. The look in her eyes is dazed with need. I rock my cock through her folds again, dragging up and down, wetting my length with her honey. She moans louder, and her fingers dig into my skin.

She's ready.

I grip my cock and hold it at the entrance to her cunt. The thick crown presses against her heat, and her nails dig harder into my skin.

"You feel . . . really big," she says, a note of concern in her voice.

"That is because I am," I tease, and then kiss her worries away. "But you can take me. This I promise. Are you ready to be claimed by your mate?"

She looks up at me with such big, soft eyes. Her hand moves to my cheek and she strokes it, and my heart aches with love for her. "I'm yours," she tells me. "All yours."

"Mine," I agree, and sink deep. I know I will cause her pain—she's never mated before and she's small and tight, but it's best to get it done quickly, like the resetting of bone.

Her sharp cry of pain wounds me, though, and I hold her gently. "Shhh."

"Ow," she tells me, and her fist thumps against my arm. "That hurt!"

"It is a pain that will be soon gone, I promise." To make up for it, I kiss her sweet mouth over and over, until her frown gentles and she starts to respond to my caresses again. My cock feels like a throbbing brand, so tightly sheathed in her wet warmth, but I dare not move until she is ready for me again.

When she gives a small sigh at my latest kiss, I drag my cock slowly out of her, and then stroke in again. She stiffens but doesn't mention the pain. Her gaze is on me, her eyes trusting, and my heart breaks with the beauty of her. She is beyond lovely, my mate. Lovely, and soft, and sweet, and giving. "You have my heart, Kira," I tell her again, and nuzzle her throat.

I stroke in again, careful to gauge her reaction, and when she remains relaxed against me, I shift my weight to one side and caress her breast, teasing the peak until the tip is hard and aching, and she is moaning and wiggling against me.

"Everything feels so different with you inside me," she says, and she sounds breathless and full of wonder.

"Still hurt?"

"I don't think so." She bites her lip and looks up at me. "Do something and I'll let you know."

Do something? I will do everything to her. I knot my hand in her hair again, anchoring her against me, and stroke deep.

She gasps. "That felt . . ." Her startled eyes flick to mine.

"Good?" I can practically feel my chest puffing out with pride.

"Do it again?" Her voice is small and timid, but she arches her back, pressing her body against me.

I do, and she gasps again. Her cunt seems to tighten around me, and when she quivers, I feel it through every span of her body.

"I think I'm going to . . . again." She bites down on her lip, her body tensing under mine.

"Good," I tell her, and stroke deep again. Her next gasp is followed by an intense dig of her nails into my arms, and a definite clench of her cunt around my cock.

"Oh God!"

Yes, she's definitely going to come again. Pleased at how responsive my mate is, I claim her mouth in a brutal kiss and begin to push into her in a steady rhythm, over and over again, slicking deep into her soft body.

"Ridges," she gasps against my mouth. "I feel ridges! And oh God, is that your spur?"

It might be. I surge deep again and she jerks against me, her hand sliding between us to go to her cunt. "It's too much," she says, shielding her folds from me. "I can't handle it all—"

"Then let it take you away," I tell her, grabbing her hand and pushing it back into the furs. I capture her mouth with mine, and pump into her again, and she moans, her hand gripping mine tightly. When she comes again, she cries out sharply, so loud that it rings in the chamber.

Not nearly as loud as my own shout as I come, but almost. We are going to be a noisy pair, I think with pleasure as I collapse onto the furs next to my gasping, panting mate. They will have to move us into one of the back caves so our late-night antics do not wake all the kits.

I pull Kira against me and kiss her sweaty brow, well pleased with my mate.

Kira

My brain is mush. Good mush, but still mush. I slowly drag myself awake. Aehako has his leg over mine and his hand over my breast. I turn over in bed and his tail flicks, then swats me.

"Go back to sleep," he mumbles.

"I need to stretch a bit." I ignore his request and slide out of bed, taking a few ginger steps toward the bathroom. I feel a bit sore between my legs. Okay, a lot sore. But it's a good sort of sensation, and I don't mind it in the slightest. It just reminds me that I belong to Aehako, and I enter the bathroom with a dopey grin on my face.

The first thing I do is check my ear out in the reflective glass of the shower. It feels weird to not have the translator in anymore, and I've got a few new ear piercings in weird spots as a memory of the device. Overall, though, my ear seems to look okay? There's a vague ache deep inside, but I imagine I'm still healing up. And Aehako said he got rid of the device, but . . .

"Computer?" I whisper. "Has the translator that was removed from my ear yesterday been destroyed?"

It beeps for a moment, and then a tinny voice pipes into a speaker over the sink. "The device was destroyed upon request. It was disassembled and then crushed in the trash compactors. Do you wish retrieval?"

"No, that's okay," I tell it, relieved. "I'm good." One problem down, at least.

I clean up with water from the sink, do my business, and then dress in my leathers. Maybe it's because I did a lot of sleeping yesterday post–translator removal, but I'm pretty awake. I enter back into the bedroom, but Aehako is still sacked out. I contemplate getting back into bed with him, but I worry about Harlow. It's no secret that she and Haeden aren't exactly rubbing along, and this is an alien spaceship . . . and I've probably been unconscious for about a day. I should check on her.

I exit the room and head down a hall, until I realize I have no idea which way is back to the front. "Computer, can you lead me to Harlow?"

"Please follow," it indicates, and the lights edging the floor go in the opposite direction as I'm heading. Oh. I turn around and follow its twisting path through debris-strewn halls. Several corridors later, I hear the sound of what seems like a power drill, and when I enter, I see Harlow with a pair of oversized protective goggles on, drilling something together and peering at a computer screen.

"Hi?" I call out.

She looks up at me and the goggles slide down her face. "Oh! Hey!" She pushes at the goggles. "These stupid things do not fit human heads very well."

I stifle my laughter and approach, gazing at the bits and pieces she has strewn on a metal table. "What is all this?"

"Well," she says, setting the drill down and putting her hands on her hips. "This is a bunch of junk at the moment. But I'm having the computer read me a manual about how to create a rock cutter."

"A rock cutter?"

"Yeah, so, did you ever notice that the bachelorette cave has one wall that's rougher than all the others?" Harlow peers at me and pushes back her wild red hair. Her freckles crinkle around her eyes as she swipes a hand over her forehead and leaves a greasy mark there.

"Um, you know, I don't think I ever did." Now I feel a little silly. "It's unfinished?"

"Yeah, and I always wondered about that. But you know most of the cave is supersmooth. So I figured that when they left here, they probably cannibalized a lot of the computer parts to make rock cutters, and the computer told me I was right. I guess they just ran out of juice when they got to our cave." She shrugs. "So I thought I'd see if we could put together some new cutters in order to hollow out a few more home caverns for people, since we're so crowded."

That's so thoughtful of her. And here I was just having sex and thinking about myself. "You're wonderful, Harlow. You know that?"

A surprised smile crosses the redhead's face. "Thanks," she says shyly. "I was just trying to think of ways I could help out, you know? My dad was a mechanic and so I know my way around a few things, but I have to admit that all of this is baffling to me." She spreads her hands out and gestures at the metal junk on the table. "Luckily there's lots of pictures on the computer, so I'm mostly going off of that."

"Smart," I say, examining the table. All of the pieces look like nothing I've ever seen before. Even the drill Harlow is using isn't exactly normal looking.

"How's your ear?" she asks, picking up a piece of metal and holding it up to get a better look at it.

"Better. Translator's all gone." I hesitate, then ask, "You get what you came for?"

Harlow gives me a guarded look. "More or less."

I can take a hint. She's clearly still not talking about whatever it is she tagged along to find out. I understand that sort of thing, what with my infertility and all. Some things just aren't open for sharing with strangers, and I don't know Harlow as well as I know some of the others. There's always just been so many people around that we've never really gotten to bond.

I feel guilty about that.

"You need help?" I volunteer. "I'm not sure how much help I'll be, but maybe another pair of hands can't hurt?"

"You sure?" she asks. "This isn't a fun job and I don't even know if it's going to work at the end of the day."

I shrug. "Aehako's still asleep and will be for a while, I imagine."

"Mm-hmm. Yeah, I heard you guys down the hall. So you and him are a thing?"

My face feels white hot with embarrassment. It never occurred to me that someone might be able to hear us. "He decided I'm his mate," I say, moving closer to the table. "And I decided he was right."

"If you're happy, I'm happy," Harlow says, and runs her hand over a bunch of small pieces of copper-colored metal.

"I am happy," I tell her, and it is true. Other than the nagging worry about the Little Green Men returning, I'm incredibly happy. My translator's gone, and I have . . . Aehako. Big, flirty Aehako who treats me like I'm the best thing that's ever happened to him. Really, it's the other way around. He's the best thing that ever happened to me. I think even if I were offered a ride home back to Earth tomorrow, I'd decline, just so I could stay with my big alien mate.

Maybe that makes me crazy. But what did I have back on Earth? No one that cared about me, an entry-level job in finance, and a mountain of student debt. Here I have an entire tribe of people, and Aehako.

"Let me know if you see a silvery-looking cross-shaped piece," Harlow says, picking through the bits. "About the size of your pinky."

I nod and start at the other end of the table. My fingers brush over the different kinds of metals, and there seem to be hundreds of pieces here. Harlow's set herself up with a daunting task . . . and I notice she hasn't had any help until now. "Have you seen Haeden?"

Harlow snorts. "He's guarding the entrance. I think it's just an excuse to get some alone time. He's not that good with people."

"I noticed." Aehako mentioned to me that Haeden has a sad past. I guess he can't really move past that. I find a cross-shaped piece and offer it to Harlow. "This it?"

"Yup," she says, plucking it out of my hand and taking it to another table. "Let me solder this bad boy on and we can move forward."

The time with Harlow passes surprisingly fast. There's a schematic projected on one of the walls, and if it flickers every now and then, it's still better than consulting a paper version. Harlow's a genius with the metal parts, piecing things together and soldering, drilling, and basically making me feel like a useless hack. To pass the time, we talk about our old lives back on Earth.

Harlow's dad ran a car garage and fix-it shop in Minnesota but passed away last year. No mother in the picture, and she'd recently sold the business and wasn't quite sure what to do with herself. Turns out that isn't an issue anymore, I suppose.

"The ironic thing?" she tells me. "I wanted to travel. I guess now I got my wish, right?"

I manage a wan smile at that.

We talk about foods that we miss, and things that we lack here—like regular shampoo and even porcelain plates. Instead of getting morose, though, Harlow grows thoughtful. "I'm sure we can bring our knowledge to the tribe and maybe improve things. And we can scavenge around here. Tiffany said she was good with makeup and hair stuff back home, so maybe she could make us soap."

I like that Harlow doesn't dwell on the past. Instead, she's looking ahead to the future, to how we can improve our situation here versus mourning about what we've lost. It's a great attitude.

When we take a break, we both decide to get the language dump from the computer. We take turns and Harlow goes first, and I have to admit, it's pretty scary when she slumps and goes unconscious after the laser beam hits her right in the eye. She's awake a few minutes later, and I hand her the waterskin she brought. She sips it, rubs her forehead, and gives me a rueful look. "I guess it could be worse. They could speak several languages, right?"

I laugh at her words, but it makes me think about the Little Green Men. Should I learn that one, too? Just in case? I won't be able to speak it, but it'll be handy to know.

When it's my turn, I call out, "Computer, can I learn more than one language at once?"

"I can insert up to three languages into your memory at once," the computer tells me. "Which languages would you like to download?"

"The sakh language," I tell it, the computer's name for Ae-hako's race. "And . . ." I pause, because I don't know the name of the race for the Little Green Men. "Um . . ."

"What are you thinking?" Harlow asks me, curious. When I explain to her my idea, she nods. "Maybe if we narrow it down to sentient races in or around this planet?"

"Good idea." I'll need to narrow it down a bit more. I think for a moment, and then clear my throat. "Computer? How many language-speakers are there on this planet?"

The computer calculates for a moment, then answers. "Sensors indicate there are thirty-four modified sakh, twelve modified humans, three szzt, and one—" The computer makes a weird chirping sound that sends shivers up my spine. It sounds just like the Little Green Men. The szzt must be their guards. I rub my arms, uncomfortable. Maybe I should learn both languages.

"Huh," Harlow says next to me.

"What?"

"I thought there were thirty-three in the tribe." She wrinkles her freckled nose. "Did someone have a baby?"

"It's too soon," I tell her, but I realize she's right. The numbers are off. I move to the table and mentally count out who lives in each cave, using pieces of the small scrap metal to represent the big blue aliens. When I'm done counting, I'm still one number short of the computer's tally.

How is it that we're missing an alien?

I turn to Harlow, about to ask her that same question, when a searing sound cuts through the skies overhead. It reminds me of a jet plane . . . except there are none on this wintry planet.

The other aliens have arrived.

I turn back to the computer, grim determination on my face. "Computer, please give me the languages for the sakh, the szzt, and the last one you mentioned."

"The ___?" Again, the bird chirp that won't ever be pronounceable by human vocal cords.

"That's the one."

"Please hold steady while the information is transmitted into your memory. You may experience some discomfort—"

Blinding pain slashes through my head and that's the last thing I remember for a good bit.

Kira

When I wake up, Aehako's in my face, a concerned expression drawing his brows together.

"Are you well, Sad Eyes?"

"I'm fine," I promise him as I sit up, his hand supporting my back. "I was just getting some languages, um, installed." I look over at Harlow and press a hand to my aching forehead. "How long have I been out for?"

"About an hour," she says with a grimace. "Three languages might have been too much at once."

My head throbs in response. "I think you're right." With Aehako's help, I get to my feet, though I'm wobbly. I lean against Aehako, glad for his comforting presence. "Any more signs of the Little Green Men?"

"Just the sound of the ship flying overhead," Harlow says. Her arms are crossed over her chest and it's clear she's worried.

"Again?" I look at Aehako with concern. "I think the aliens know we're here."

He rubs his mouth and considers. "What do their feet look like?"

That's a weird question. "Their feet?"

"Haeden and I saw tracks in the snow on the way here."

I gasp. "You didn't say anything!"

"There was no sense in worrying you when you are already beside yourself with fear." He touches my cheek, and my anger fades. "The tracks were unfamiliar to us." He spreads his fingers as if they're prongs. "Three large, spiky toes. Does that match your aliens?"

I shake my head, trying to remember. The orangey aliens with the pebbled skin had two toes, and the Little Green Men had small, wispy feet. "So now we have something else to worry about?"

"One thing at a time," Aehako tells me. "We should find Haeden."

As we head out of the mechanics bay, I turn to Harlow. "You think there are still guns on the ship?"

She gives me a shocked look. "Wasn't this a pleasure cruiser?"

"Surely even those would have some sort of defense system? We need guns if we want them to listen to us." Now that's a phrase I never thought I'd say.

Harlow looks worried at my suggestion. "I don't know how to shoot a regular gun, much less an alien one."

"Yeah, but the aliens don't know that," I tell her. If it comes down to it, we might have to bluff our way out of things. "If we look like we're armed and dangerous, then maybe they'll use a bit of caution when approaching us."

She nods, though she doesn't look happy. I don't blame her. I'm not thrilled about it, either, but we're low on options. All I know is that I'm not going back with them. Period. I rub my sore ear, thinking of my memories from being a captive on the ship. Harlow doesn't have the same memories I do. Of the constant terror. The rapes. Of being treated like you're less than an animal. That you don't matter.

Liz had joked that her dad had treated his farm animals better than we'd been treated, and she wasn't wrong. To them, we were nothing more than cargo.

Here, on Not-Hoth, I matter. To Aehako and the others, I matter.

So I clear my throat. "Computer, show me what functioning weapons are still on board this ship."

Two hours later, I'm bossing everyone around and trying to get things done. Haeden's been no help, so I have him sitting on the bridge, in charge of the single defense gun that the still-somewhat-functioning computer has. He has a bright red button he can push if things go to hell that will (hopefully) activate the single gun, provided it hasn't rusted over after all this time and the harsh weather. There are a handful of alien guns from the ship's security, but only one has any charge left. Harlow and I debate over who's going to handle it, but I win the argument.

I'm going to be the negotiator in charge, because I'm determined that things are going to work out.

And if they don't, I want Harlow, Aehako, and Haeden to get away.

The gun doesn't have a trigger like regular human guns. It's some sort of laser cannon that has a control panel that's voice activated and reveals—no joke—a button. And here I thought a trigger was déclassé. I'd feel better with one.

"What's the status of the alien ship?" I ask the computer as I practice aiming my laser cannon. "Is it still in the atmosphere?"

"Affirmative," the computer tells me. "Would you like a visual?"

"Yes, please."

The room's screen lights up and shows me the mountains in the distance, the ones that look like purple ice. Hovering just over the peak of one is the flat disk of the alien's ship, a black smudge on the gray skies. "Has it moved any in the last six hours?"

"Negative."

The sight of it is making me antsy. "Can we call it toward us somehow? I don't want it getting back to the others."

"I can relay a communication signal. Would you like to do so?"

"Not just yet," I tell it quickly, then look at Harlow. There are a few things I have to get done before we can proceed with our plan. "Can you do me a favor?"

The redhead turns toward me, curious. "What's up?"

"Can you go see how Haeden's doing? Make sure he's not going to get trigger-happy?"

She nods and heads out of the room.

I immediately shut the door behind her and flip the lock. I turn around, resting my back against the door. "Computer? I need a fail-safe."

"Query: what is fail-safe?"

"I need a secondary plan." I lick my lips, thinking hard. "A weapon I can smuggle on board the alien ship with me if I'm taken captive." After a moment, I add, "And I need a way to interface your computer to theirs."

The computer screen flashes with a variety of options, and I listen intently.

If they take me back with them, I'm bringing them down. If I'm not getting out of this alive, neither are they.

It's some time later that I emerge from the locked room to find the others. I've got a secret packet wrapped in a thin polymer film tucked into my hand, and new determination in my step. Unfortunately, my determination falters when I run into Harlow in the hallway.

"They're on the move," Harlow tells me. "The guys are at the front. Come on!"

We race down the narrow halls of the ship, heading toward the entrance. I guess Haeden's abandoned his post already, because when I arrive at the icy entrance, he's kneeling there in the meltwater with Aehako. My mate has his ear pressed to the door, listening on the other side. I want to point out that he's not going to be able to hear anything through the hull of the ship, but he gets to his feet the moment I arrive.

"Aehako," I say. "What—"

"Their ship has arrived," he tells me. He caresses my cheek and pulls me against him. "You and Harlow must stay here. Haeden and I will go out and speak to them."

I push away from him. "No, this is something I need to do."

"Kira," he says, a warning tone in his voice. "Let me protect you. You are my mate to take care of."

"That's sweet, Aehako." I reach up and pat his cheek. "But you are my mate, and I'm going to take care of you." I flick off the switch that covers the trigger button on my laser cannon. "Now, I'm going to go out and talk to those bastards."

"Talk?" Harlow's laugh is nervous. "You're kidding, right?"

"Nope." I'm tired of running scared. My heart's racing a

mile a minute, but inwardly, I feel calm. This is it. Once and for all, I'm not going to be scared of these bastards anymore. Because if the worst-case scenario happens, there's no longer anything to fear.

"You are serious?" Aehako's hand grips my arm. His voice is incredulous. "Kira, this is dangerous."

"I know." I look up at him. "So give me a kiss for luck, and make it a really good one."

He makes a strangled noise in his throat. "I don't want to kiss you right now. I want to throttle you for being foolish."

I shake my head. "This isn't foolishness. I've got everything under control. I promise."

The look on Aehako's face is pained and full of worry. I expect him to protest again, to tell me that I'm not the right girl for the job. Instead, he grabs me in a fierce bear hug and hauls me up to his face for a kiss. His lips brush against mine, surprisingly tender. His nose nuzzles mine. Then he closes his eyes and murmurs, "I will protect you with my life, you know that, yes?"

I'm overwhelmed by his sweet words. Hot tears threaten, and I fling my arms around his neck and kiss him like he should be kissed—wild and with utter abandon. This might be the last kiss I have with him, and I let him know how much I love him. My tongue slicks against his ridged one, and I kiss him so passionately and so fervently that Harlow clears her throat behind us.

Right. I have a mission.

I give Aehako one last peck. "I love you," I whisper to him.

"Be safe, Sad Eyes," he tells me. "Do not make me come out there to protect you."

"I won't." I force a smile to my face, like everything's okay. Truth be told, I have a really bad feeling about this. I look at

Harlow and the two hunters, both of whom are gripping their spears as if they'd do something against these aliens.

They'll be slaughtered. I can't let that happen.

I move toward Harlow and hug her. She seems surprised by my spontaneous gesture, and her arms go around me slowly. "Whatever you do, stay inside the ship," I tell her in a low whisper. "If I don't make it back, make sure Aehako and Haeden go back to the caves, all right? They can't come after me." I pull back and smile at her, pretending like nothing's wrong.

Wide-eyed, she nods at me.

I shoulder my laser cannon again and approach the door. I take a deep breath, and then furtively slip the small packet into my mouth, fitting it between gums and teeth. No one will know it's there, and I can barely feel it in my mouth. Perfect. "Computer, give me a visual on the aliens, please."

A wall panel off to my side lights up and displays the snowy wasteland outside. Only, instead of it being uninhabited, there are three figures off in the distance, heading in this direction. Two of them have rounded, burnt-orange heads that I remember have hard, pebbled skin. The one in the middle is smaller, rail-thin.

One of the Little Green Men, accompanied by his bodyguards. I need to stop them before they come any closer.

"Open the door," I say resolutely, then look behind me at the three. "Stay inside, whatever happens, all right?"

"This is madness," Haeden growls, clutching his spear.

Aehako puts a hand on his chest. "Let her do it."

The door slides open, and I take one last look back at Aehako's broad, blue face before I step outside. The air is crisp, the winds high. It's a beautiful day on Not-Hoth, ironically enough. There are no snowstorms brewing, and I can see far enough in the distance that I can make out the expressions on the aliens' faces as they notice me.

I hoist my laser cannon, aim, and fire at their feet.

"Hold it right there," I yell out in szzt. I can't make the sounds of the birdlike Little Green Men, but I can speak the other language well enough. "We have guns trained on you and we're prepared to shoot."

A little bluffing never hurt anything. I just hope they buy it. If they don't, well, I'm toast.

They pause, and I can see the slim green alien gesturing to the others.

"Guns down," I command.

They don't obey. But they do remain in place. They confer for a moment and then one of the basketball heads calls out, "Why do you shoot?"

"Because I know why you're here," I yell back. "You want your cargo back, and we're not coming back." I keep my laser cannon trained on them.

More conferring. Then, "You will be treated very well if you return with us," the basketball head translates.

Oh, bullshit. I know they're full of crap. "You can't take us off this planet. We've been infected with native symbionts and will die if we are removed. Your cargo is gone either way."

"Where are the girls that were in the stasis tubes?"

Nice to see we matter to them. "Gone. Infected as well."

More hushed whispers. Then, the alien guard speaks, his tone angry. "My masters are out a great deal of money with nothing to show for it. You have destroyed their property."

A gasp escapes me. "Property? They're not property. They're people! You can't just take them against their will!"

"And what of the animal skin you are wearing?" the alien growls at me. "Did you ask its permission?"

"That's different." I have a sinking feeling I'm losing this argument.

"The shipment my masters deposited here has been stolen from them," he says again. "They are out a great deal of money and have many clients waiting for their purchases. My masters are honor bound to return their property to them."

I grip the laser cannon tighter, a sinking feeling in my stomach. The aliens stare at me with black, calculating eyes. I notice one of the orange ones keeps eying my gun.

"Your ship is very old," one comments. He takes a step forward, his own gun held casually in hand.

"Stop or I'll shoot," I tell him, my voice wavering.

"I think you are lying," the one guard says, still approaching. The other two aliens watch him calmly, weapons in hand. "I think your ship is not armed. I think we will take you, and then you will lead us to the others."

"You can't! We can't be removed from this planet," I say desperately. "Look at my eyes! Our symbionts—"

"You lie," he says, and strides forward.

I lift my laser cannon to fire again, just as the alien in the distance lifts his gun. Something hot zings my hand, and the gun goes flying out of my grip. I'm smacked to the ground with a forceful blow, the air knocked out of my lungs.

"Kira," Aehako bellows behind me, and I hear the sound of feet slamming into the snow.

"No," I gasp as one of the aliens kicks my gun away. He steps on my wounded hand, pinning me to the ground. As I watch in horror, he raises his gun and fires, and I hear two shouts of pain.

"No! Aehako!" Ignoring the brutal pain in my arm, I twist around to see.

The two men are flat on the ground. Haeden's lying in a pool of blood, his leather tunic smoking. Aehako is facedown and unmoving.

My chest constricts with agony. "Aehako! *No!*"

The birdlike Little Green Man chirps a question. *Are they dead?*

The basketball head tilts his head, and as I watch, I see Aehako twitch and lift his elbow, trying to rise up off the ground. There's no sign of Harlow. I'm relieved. She's hiding in the ship like I told her to. "Not dead yet," the guard says and lifts his gun again. "I will fix that."

"No, wait!" I scream in the alien language. "I'll go with you. I'll take you to the others! Just leave them alone!"

The guard lowers his gun and looks over at his master.

An irritated chirp sounds. *They don't matter. Just bring her.*

The boot lifts off my hand, and a strong arm hauls me off the ground.

Aehako

I fight off unconsciousness as wave after wave of crashing pain moves over me. The intruders moved so fast. I barely saw them raise their strange weapons before Haeden and I were flattened on the ground. I hear Kira's cry of worry, and her frantic jabber in the strange language.

Then, silence. I try to sit up, but my body won't obey. It's like an invisible net has been cast over me. The blackness I've fought against so hard claims me.

One thought rings through my mind even as I succumb: they've taken my mate.

"Aehako?" A small, cold hand taps my cheek. "Wake up. Please."

Pain blazes in my side. I'm still facedown in the snow, and my entire body aches as if I've drunk three skins of sah-sah. With effort, I push against the earth and roll myself onto my back, squinting at the late afternoon sunlight.

A face swims into view. Pale, freckled, with a bright orange-red mane. Not Kira. I struggle to sit up, and her weak human hands try to assist. "Are you okay?" she asks in a tremulous voice.

"I am not dead," I grit out, though my ribs might complain otherwise. I run a hand down my side and pain stabs through me again. Punctured with one of their strange weapons, but not a fatal wound. It aches and bleeds but will not kill me. "Where is Kira?"

The girl's eyes fill with tears and she sniffs hard. "Gone. They took her."

Agony pounds in my chest. No. Not Kira. Not my sad-eyed, soft mate. I'm helpless and filled with rage all at once. "I must save her."

"Your friend . . . he's not doing so well."

I look around. Off to one side, Haeden's body is slumped. There's a dark stain under him that makes my chest clench with new worry. "Is he—"

"He's breathing, but I can't get him to wake up, and I can't carry him." She wrings her hands. "I don't know what to do. Kira told me to take you guys back to the cave—"

"She what?" I get to my feet with great effort, sending another wave of sheeting pain through my body.

The red-haired one—Harlow—wrings her hands again and paces. "She said that if they took her, I need to take you back to the cave so you can be safe. She doesn't want anyone coming after her."

"*She is my mate!*" I roar. I won't leave her. I'll get my spear, take off after their ship, and demand—

"They have guns!" Harlow cries. "And Haeden is dying!"

Haeden. My old friend. My truest friend. I stagger over to his side, clutching my wound, and roll him onto his back. His breathing rasps shallow in his chest, and the wound is in his gut. I can see the white of his innards in his wound, and there's blood everywhere.

He needs to get back to the healer, soon, or he will die.

I'm torn. I need to go after my mate, but it's clear that if I leave, Haeden will die. With a snarl of helpless fury, I turn to Harlow. "Why are you just standing there?"

"I don't know what to do!"

"Get something to bind his wound! Quickly! Or get poles for a travois!" With a travois, maybe even Harlow can take him back to the caves. I grab her arm before she darts off. "I must go after Kira. Can you take him back to the tribal caves if I make you a travois?"

Her face is pale but resolute. She nods. "Tell me the way and I will do it."

My heart sinks. She doesn't know the way to the caves. One slight storm, one wrong turn, and she will drag Haeden into the wild, where he will die. I press a hand to my forehead. The stink of blood is everywhere. We must do something soon, or predators will come after it to investigate.

I . . . cannot go after Kira. Not if it means leaving these two helpless ones to die. I close my eyes. *Forgive me, my mate. I will come for you as soon as I can.*

Then, I turn to Harlow. "Take a knife and cut two poles for a travois from the trees. I will find something to bind Haeden's wound."

"What about the ship? We can use it—"

I shake my head. I don't trust it. "We'll take him back to the healer. Hurry."

She nods and darts away.

Kira

One of the basketball head guards hisses at me as he hauls me up the ramp to the alien ship. "Walk faster."

"I'm walking as fast as I can," I mutter. Actually, that's not true. I'm dragging my feet deliberately. I don't want to go on the ship. I want to run for the hills, but I have to be brave. I knew this was coming if we couldn't scare them off.

And I have a plan B, the contents of which are still safely tucked inside my mouth, between gums and cheek.

I'm still terrified.

Nothing's in my control anymore. These things would just as easily take back my dead body as they would my live one. And I don't know if Aehako is even alive or dead.

I can't think about that right now. If I do, I'll totally break down. I have to think about my plan.

They drag me into the hold of the ship despite my deliberately slow steps. Instead of flinging me down into another hold like they did before, I'm taken to a sterile white room and dumped onto a narrow white board of a bed. Oh God. This looks like an operating room.

The guard that has taken me as his personal hostage looms over me, fingering his weapon. A few moments later, the door opens and another one of the Little Green Men comes in. He speaks, and his voice has a different timbre than the others.

This is the infected one that was mentioned? He tilts his head toward me, curious.

"Yes," the guard says in his growling language.

I try to chirp back to him, to let him know I understand his words. His head tilts again. *Is it trying to speak?*

"It's stupid," the guard says, and smacks my arm with the butt of his gun. "Want me to kill it?"

"I'm not infected," I say in the guttural language of the szzt. "I have a symbiont. A creature living inside me. But it can't be removed without killing its host."

A parasite? How very curious. I wonder if I can remove it anyhow. I should like to study this and see how long it can survive in an artificial environment, if at all.

They want to kill me just to see what happens? These guys are dicks, as Liz would say. "You can't do that," I say quickly. When they simply stare at me, I cast about for a logical explanation as to why they can't. "I'm worth more alive than dead."

The Little Green Man tilts his head and then reaches out to touch my ear. Even though I want to slap his hand away, I have to force myself not to react. *This is the one we implanted the translator in, yes? Her aural cavity shows markings of one, but I confess all these things look alike to me.*

"I had a translator," I tell him.

Where did it go?

"I had the ship remove it."

The ship on the surface? The creature's head tilts again. If it weren't for the fact that my life was in danger, all the head-tilting would be kind of hilarious. *It is not functioning.*

"It's not completely functioning. It doesn't fly, but I have a secret code," I bluff. "I know the access codes to the computers. I can give you the ship if you return me to the surface and never come after me and the other women ever again."

The thing chirps repeatedly, and somehow, I know he's laughing. *Why would I want an old ship that does not fly?*

"You can tow it," I tell him, staring into the enormous black eyes of the alien with what I hope is a confident expression. "I'm sure you have a way. And people always pay good money for"—I struggle to find the alien word for "antiques" and settle for—"very old and special things. That ship has lots of valuable equipment, plus all the valuables its passengers left behind when it was stranded several hundred years ago."

The aliens exchange a look.

We can simply take it with us, along with you, the one alien says.

"But if you take me from here, I will die. My dead body is of very limited use to you. Your employers won't pay as much for a dead girl as they would for a live one. I know this."

I don't know this. I'm guessing.

The black eyes of the Little Green Man blink slowly. *We will discuss this.*

I look over at the computers blinking on the wall. "Cool. You want me to just wait here?"

Put her in one of the holding cells.

The guardsman grabs me with a brutal hand, his rough skin tearing at my arm. I fight against him, but it's only playacting. It's what I think they expect me to do. In reality, a holding cell will work just as well as anything else for my plans. So I struggle and fight against the guard as he drags me down one of the narrow, metallic halls of the alien ship, and flings me into a dark hold. This time, there's no cage, just what looks like a storage room. Good. I skid to the floor and huddle against the wall, doing my best to look frightened. Granted, it's not that hard because I'm scared out of my mind, but I'm also thinking hard.

The guardsman looks down at me and curls his thick lip. He says something that I have no translation for, but is probably an insult, and slaps a panel on the outside wall. The door closes, and I'm alone in the dark.

Panic flutters in my chest. I have to remind myself that this is good news. This is what I want. I need to be alone.

Oh God, I need this to work.

I run my tongue along my gums, searching for the small packet I pushed there. Still there. I pull it out and rub it against my tunic to dry it, then press it between my lips to hold on to it while I look for the air filters to this room.

I noticed on the elders' ship that it had air vents much like my old apartment back on Earth did. That got me thinking about a game plan and what I could do against the Little Green Men. They have more technology than I do. They have guns and they have the numbers, so I have to be sneaky . . . and fearless.

I find a vent near the edge of the floor and dig my fingernails into it until I locate what feels like a fastening of some kind, and then rip it off. I tear a few fingernails, but that is a small price to pay. With shaking hands, I peel the thin layer of plastic off of the packet and remove half of the contents.

One part is a computer part, much like a USB drive, that will allow the elders' ship to access this ship, provided I can find a compatible slot to plug it into.

The other part is a small square of filter that I've pulled from the elders' ship. After hundreds of years of being in the atmosphere, it's filled with concentrated nalium. I know that this is the element in the air of Not-Hoth that makes it impossible for humans to survive for long. There are trace elements of it in the atmosphere, and within a week, we succumbed to sickness, our bodies growing weak and our minds disoriented. Our khui adapts us and allows us to live planet-side. Of course, planet-side, there are only trace amounts of nalium in the air. But after hundreds of years, the ship's filters are full of the element. And if I add it to the air supply in my room, I'm hoping it'll poison my guard.

The computer assured me that the tiny amount that I drop into the air filtering system is enough to do it, but the computer's also three hundred (and some change) years old. It could be wrong. This ship could be more self-sufficient than I hope.

A million things can go wrong. All I can do is cross my fingers.

I replace the filter cover and sniff the air. I don't smell anything. The air doesn't taste weird. I have no idea if it's working or not, if the poison is seeping into the air of my small chamber or throughout the ship.

I tuck my body against the wall and wait.

Hours later, I'm in a frenzy of worry. There's no difference in the air that I can tell, and all I have left is the small bit of computer I'm supposed to somehow interface to one that's three hundred years younger.

This is the stupidest plan ever.

Despair threatens to overwhelm me. I ignore it, because there is no plan C. This has to work. This has to.

A mental image of Aehako's fallen body flashes before my

eyes, and I clench my fists, determined not to cry. He's not dead. He's not.

I'd know if he was, wouldn't I? But we're not connected by khui. We're only connected by heart and mind and choice. We don't have that deeper bond. We never will because of my body—

Someone fumbles at the door.

I jerk to my feet, my stiff muscles complaining. My body's instantly on alert, my heart hammering in my chest. Did they decide to take my offer after all? The broken ship for our freedom?

Then again, what is to stop them from taking the ship *and* us? Or taking the ship and then coming back and snaring us at a later date? If they're into slavery, it's not as if they're upstanding people anyhow. They can't be trusted.

The door slides open, and the guard walks in.

No, he staggers. His steps trip, but he manages to catch himself, and he raises the gun. "Come on," he says. His words sound slurred.

My hands fly to my mouth.

Oh my God.

It worked. He's sick. I'm immune to it because of my khui, but it's affecting the guard. Maybe it's affecting everyone.

Hope flowers in my chest like a sunburst.

I get to my feet. He stumbles forward again, and I dart behind him. He turns groggily, and I kick the back of his knee. The guard falls forward, weapon clattering to the ground. I grab it, and race to the other side of my cell. There's a place to put the hand that's similar to my laser cannon, and I aim at my enemy and fire before I can think twice about it.

The gun blasts, shooting forth a bolt like liquid flame. It slices through the guard's head like butter, and he slumps to the floor, dead.

My throat closes and my nostrils flare as the hot smell of charred flesh saturates the room. I did it. I killed him. I'm not even sorry. These monsters don't care if I live or die, so I'm not going to waste a minute on regret.

I step over him, clutching the gun, and head for the door. It's slid shut again, and no amount of me slapping my hand on the panel will open it. Shit. This wasn't something I considered.

I turn and look back at the fallen guard. His arm is extended out to one side, his rough palm facing down. Oh, man. Swallowing hard, I lock the gun under my arm, aim, and shoot again.

The dismembered hand flies across the room.

Ugh.

I swallow hard and move to pick it up, then lay it across the panel. The door opens a moment later, and I step into the hall.

I'm one step closer to freedom. *You can do this, Kira,* I tell myself. *Just find the bridge, find a place to wire the two computers together remotely, and you're golden.*

There are two doors on one side of this narrow hall, and a door at the far end. I have no idea where I'm going, which means checking every door. I move quietly toward the first one, slap the dead guy's hand on the panel, and hoist my gun, ready to fire, as the door slides open.

It's a small room that looks like a storage closet. Of course it is.

Breathing a little easier, I pick up my extra hand and move down to the next door. This door leads to a cargo bay that makes me shudder with bad memories. It reminds me too much of my first time here.

It's also oddly empty. That makes me incredibly uneasy. Where are all the aliens?

The door at the end of the hall leads to another hall shaped like a T. I head directly across instead of forward, because I want to narrow down all possible ambushes. The last thing I want is to be close to freedom and then have it taken from me because I wasn't careful. So I explore the other wing of the ship. I find the medical bay again and resist the urge to use my gun like a flamethrower and burn everything to the ground.

I also find the dead body of one of the Little Green Men sprawled on the floor. My poison's working better than I thought. I push away the twinge of sadness I feel at killing them. They wouldn't have thought twice about me, and they aren't worth my pity.

Two doors over, I find a room with four small, strange doors lined up in a row. They're rounded, almost like bubbles in the wall, and I can't quite figure out what they are. I push my severed hand on one of the panels next to a bubble and speak in szzt. "Computer, can you open the door to one of these? What are they?"

"The doors in front of you are emergency deployment units."

"Escape pods?"

"They are alternate methods of egress, yes. Shall I ready one for you?" The computer's voice sounds as pleasant as the one back on the surface, despite the guttural tones of the language I'm speaking.

I get a wild idea. "Ready all of them." The panels light up, and then flash green. "How do I deploy them?"

"The unit can be deployed via an interior panel. Alternately, you can deploy a panel remotely from the control panel behind you on the wall."

I turn to the wall, and sure enough, there's a flashing schematic of four pods. Writing flashes across the screen, indicating the various system checks.

"What do I push to deploy?"

The computer gives me the instructions, and I press the sequence with the guard's dismembered hand. A door locks in front of one of the panels, and I watch as it moves backward down a tunnel, then shoots out into the air. Sunlight streams in from the place it once was, and I can see snow and the mountains far below.

Quickly, I deploy two more of the escape pods until just one is left. Then, I grab my hand and my gun and head off to figure out how to take over the rest of the ship.

My badass takeover of the ship ends up not being quite so badass. When I find the bridge, all the aliens are unconscious or dead. There's three Little Green Men sprawled on the floor and two more guards, and even though they're the enemy, I can't find it in myself to put my gun to their temples and kill them in cold blood. So I step around them and try to figure out how to interface with the chip I've so carefully smuggled on board.

It doesn't work, though. No matter what I do, I can't figure out how to get the stupid chip interfaced, and no amount of questions I ask the computer itself seem to help.

Frustrated, I slap the panels with the disembodied hand that is my key card to accessing the ship.

The world tilts.

I catch myself before I can tumble to the ground and stare at the control panel, alarmed. What did I hit that made the ship move like that? Through a little experimentation, I find that one of the panels is touch sensitive and acts a bit like a steering wheel. I tilt the ship downward, and then figure out how to make it accelerate instead of simply hang in the air.

Then, with one last slam of the controls, I push it into gear.

The ship groans and moves forward, and I watch as it begins to pick up speed. It doesn't move much at first, then slowly, it begins to descend, heading on a crash course for one of the far-away mountain peaks.

That done, I get my gun and hightail it back to the last remaining pod. I slide into the seat even as I hear the wind whistling and searing. It sounds like an airplane crashing—except I'm in the plane still. I slam the panel shut around me, hating that it feels like I'm trapped in a test tube. I push the alien's hand on the panel. "Release! Go! Go!"

"Where do you wish to go?" the computer asks. "Please input coordinates."

As if there were any question where I want to go. "Take me back to the surface." Back to my mate and my new people.

"Please enter in coordinates or access manual controls."

"Um, give me the manual controls, I guess."

Two joysticks spit out from the control panel, and I grab them. The moment I do, the pod detaches and slings backward at high speed, and my ears pop a bajillion times as the pod flings itself into the atmosphere, then hovers, waiting.

I watch as the alien ship tilts even more, listing to one side as it heads for the mountain. I wince, waiting for the collision. It doesn't seem like it's moving that fast, but—

BOOOOOOM.

The mountain—and the ship—explode in a fiery inferno. I sigh heavily and a weight feels as if it's been lifted from my shoulders. Those aliens won't bother us again.

Also, damn. I'm kind of a badass for taking down the bad guys. Who knew that little, shy Kira had it in her, huh?

Harlow

I need two poles for a travois. Okay. I can do this. Aehako's instructions ring through my mind, over and over. My heart races wildly in my chest as I sprint through the snow, looking for the thin pink wispy trees of this planet. Kira's gone, and both aliens are wounded. They need my help, and I can't let them down. My feet sink into the snow, but I trudge forward over a drift-covered hill, and when I see trees in the distance, I pick up the pace.

I have Haeden's knife, since he's too wounded to use it. When I get to the first tree, I touch the bark and wince, because it feels spongy and damp despite the chill in the air. It doesn't feel like a hard, woodsy tree at all. I have no idea if this will work, but I'll give it a shot. Kneeling down, I begin to hack at the base of the first tree. The knife sinks in with a squishing noise, and sap squirts out onto the snow. Ugh. I wrinkle my nose and keep cutting.

The snow crunches nearby, and I stand upright, surprised. It almost sounded like a footstep. "Hello?" I turn around and look. "Aehako?"

No one's there. I must be imagining things. Or maybe it's a rabbit. Or . . . whatever the rabbit equivalent on this planet is. I can't be a silly chicken and freak out at every little sound, though. I turn back to the tree and continue hacking at it.

I hear the crunch of snow again, and a moment later, a heavy thudding. No, not quite a thudding, a . . . purring? What on earth . . .

Something slams into the back of my head, and I pitch forward into darkness.

Even there, the purring follows me.

Aehako

There's no sign of Harlow. Damn the human for abandoning us.

I'm loading an unconscious Haeden onto a makeshift travois when a roaring sound comes from overhead. I look up and watch as the black smudge of the alien ship on the horizon approaches. My heart slams in my chest as I watch it slowly crawl across the sky. Is it leaving? Taking my Kira with it? Helpless fear burns a track through my guts.

The oddly shaped flying ship seems to be tilting to one side, continuing its slow descent. It flies overhead and I turn, then realize it's heading directly for the side of the nearest mountain. "No!"

My hoarse shout echoes on the lonely, snow-covered plains. It doesn't stop the alien ship from plunging headlong into the rocky slope, or the crash and fiery explosion afterward.

"KIRA!" I fall to my knees in agony.

No. My mate. My sweet, sad-eyed mate. The pain of loss is like nothing I've ever felt before. I've always been a lucky one, born into a large, loving family. We were spared when the khui-sickness hit the caves hard many years ago. I've never lost some-one I loved so intensely as I loved Kira.

The thought of going on without her staggers me.

I fall forward and press my fists to the icy snow, trying to contain my rage and grief. Haeden needs my help, even though I want nothing more than to chase down that black, smoking char of a ship and find any traces of my sweet Kira. Was she in fear when she died? Hurt? A harsh sob breaks in my throat.

She deserved better than this.

Dully, I look over at Haeden's unconscious form. It would be easy to just roll onto my back and wait for my own end to come. To give up and join my Kira in death. But Haeden is here, and he needs the healer, and for a moment I feel a wave of ugly re-sentment for my wounded friend, that he won't let me join her.

But that doesn't mean I cannot grieve for her.

I sit up on my haunches, ignoring the stabbing pain of my wound. I grab a fistful of snow and begin one of the mourning songs, the one for a mate. I have no ashes to pour over my horns, so I let the snow trickle down over my brow, and I give my dead mate the respect she deserves. I will have a better ceremony when Haeden is safe. I will give my horns the proper cuts, smear ash upon my brow, and chant songs of our love before I can go on without her.

If I can go on without her.

Right now, the thought seems impossibly cruel.

I pour another handful of snow over my brow and horns, my mourning chants growing louder. I'm so lost in my grief that I don't hear the noise around me until a shadow passes overhead. Then, I realize there's a thick buzzing in the air, a hum not un-like the elders' cave.

I wipe the snow from my eyes and watch as a pod, the same

dark color as the alien ship but much, much smaller, lands delicately in the snow nearby. There's a whoosh of air, and then a hatch opens, like an egg cracking. Something is immediately flung out into the snow, and the scent of blood and char touches my nose.

It . . . looks like a severed hand. An orange, alien hand.

Then, a small figure stumbles out of the pod and lands, face-first, into the snow. It's a human, with pale brown hair, dirty, torn leather clothing, and the most beautiful eyes I've ever seen.

"Aehako," Kira chokes.

"My mate," I growl, surging to my feet. I forget my wound. I forget the mourning rites. I forget Haeden, lying unconscious nearby. All I care about is that my Kira—my beautiful, delicate human Kira—is in front of me, alive and whole. I stagger toward her and sweep her into my arms, clutching her against me so tightly that I fear I'm going to crush her.

I can't let her go, though. She's never leaving my sight again.

"Aehako," she sobs again, and her voice is full of laughter and joy as well as tears. Her arms around my neck are the most beautiful thing I've ever felt, and when she grabs my face and begins to press sweet kisses to my mouth, I nearly explode from joy.

"Kira! Kira! My mate! How is this possible?" My fingers dig into her hair, and before she can answer me, I claim her in a rough kiss, my tongue seeking hers. The need to brand her as mine, to take her before she can be stolen from me once more, overwhelms me. I want to devour her whole, if only so she will never be apart from me again. It takes every ounce of my strength to stop kissing her long enough for her to draw breath, and when she looks up at me with a dazed, hungry look on her face, I kiss her all over again.

I will mate with her mouth for days on end now that she is

back in my arms. There is no part of Kira that will be safe from my hungry tongue. I will worship every bit of her.

Her breathless moans are utterly intoxicating, and I want to rip my loincloth free and thrust my throbbing cock into her welcoming cunt. I press her back into the snow, only to hear her gasp.

"I smell blood, Aehako—"

"It is nothing, my mate," I tell her between fierce kisses. "Let me mate your mouth with my tongue before I mate you with my cock."

Her hand pounds on my shoulder, and her outraged gasp echoes in my ear a moment later. "Aehako! You're bleeding!"

I sigh and simply hold her close, hugging her against me as her frantic hands move over my chest. Has ever a sa-khui male been so happy? I stroke Kira's soft hair and inhale her scent. Nothing else matters except my mate is alive.

"You're wounded!" Her cry of surprise screeches in my ears. "Aehako, stop! Let me look at you!"

I cannot stop smiling, cannot stop touching her. "My wounds do not matter, Sad Eyes. Where have you been? How did you escape?"

"Your wounds matter to me," she fusses, and it feels good to have my mate's small hands pulling at my clothing, determined to care for me.

I could die happily in this moment.

As she strips my tunic from me and binds my wound, she tells me how she escaped from the ship. Her eyes are troubled as she presses a thick piece of leather to my wound. "I killed them all, Aehako. I'm not even sorry about it. I just keep thinking of what would have happened if we went back with them. I couldn't let that happen."

"You protected your people, as fiercely as any chief," I tell her, caressing her cheek. "I am proud of you." Proud, and so utterly beside myself with joy that she is alive.

"I keep telling myself that maybe I should have negotiated more," she says in a soft voice, wrapping a long strip of torn clothing around my chest. "That maybe they'd have listened to reason and left us here. But I couldn't take that chance."

I say nothing. It's clear that she's working through this on her own. All I can do is support her and love her—two easy tasks.

"And I just thought—" Her thoughts stop and she looks around, then back at me. "Where is Harlow?"

"Gone," I say, unable to stop the irritation from flooding my voice. "Abandoned us and fled like a coward."

Kira's brow furrows. "I didn't think Harlow was a coward. I wonder what happened?"

"She left to get poles for the travois and never returned. She has run for the hills seeking safety from your aliens. She is foolish and has caused her own death, and possibly that of Haeden." I force myself to get up, even though I want nothing more than to remain here, seated in the snow with my mate as she fusses over me. "We must get him to the healer, and soon. I do not know if he will last another night."

Kira's eyes are wide. "But Harlow—"

"We must choose," I say gently. "We can wait here and hope she returns, and Haeden will almost certainly die. Or we can leave her to her fate and take Haeden to be healed." I leave the choosing to her. It is not my choice to make, because I will never be able to choose flighty, fickle Harlow over the man I have grown up with and whom I think of as a brother.

Kira's gaze moves to the travois, and then back to me. "Of course we can't stay," she says, her voice soft with sorrow. "I just thought . . ." She shakes her head. "I guess it doesn't matter. Poor Harlow. I hope she can find her way back to the caves at some point." She gets to her feet and then presses a hand to my bandages as I stand. "Let's get Haeden back safely. If he dies, I'll blame myself."

"Then we will not let him die," I tell her in a firm voice.

Kira

The return back to the caves is brutal. I worry about Harlow, who's gone missing. She's so secretive, though, I don't know if she's all right and just in hiding, or if something else has gone terribly wrong. Aehako is wounded, and Haeden is hovering at death's door, so there's no time to wait and see if she's going to return. We load Haeden onto the travois and pull it across the crisp snow.

For once, the weather holds for us, and the day fades into night with clear skies and not a bit of snowfall. We don't stop even when the sun goes down. We walk through the night, endlessly trudging back to the tribal caves. Aehako's weaker than he tries to let on; he has to pause and rest several times. I take the poles of the travois from him and drag it for a while to help out, though my strength is not even half of his. He kisses the top of my head and murmurs words of thanks at my efforts, though.

It's a long, miserable night. I make it by simply concentrating on putting one foot in front of the other. As long as I'm with

Aehako, it doesn't matter. Nothing matters. I wish I could hold his hand, but when he doesn't have the travois poles, I do. So I just tuck my hands into my fur cloak and imagine what life is going to be like when we get back to the caves.

Because I'm moving in with Aehako. He's mine and I'm not waiting any longer to claim him, khui or not.

Eventually, the sun rises. My feet feel heavy and cold as ice, but when we pause to check on Haeden, I can tell that Aehako's worried about him. He doesn't need to say anything; it's obvious that Haeden might not make it back to the caves. I bind his wound tighter, take off my fur cloak, and wrap it around his unconscious body, and then we continue on.

I'm utterly numb with exhaustion when I hear a high-pitched cry. It sounds a bit like a bird. I look over at Aehako, and his face lights up with joy. He cups a hand to his mouth and repeats the cry, adding a shrill yi-yi-yi at the end. "Hunters," he tells me. "Raahosh is near. They will help us."

"Oh, good," I breathe. Right now, I'd take a piggyback ride all the way home if it was offered.

"There," Aehako says, and points over a rise. Two fur-covered bodies are jogging toward us, one wearing snowshoes and a thick fur cloak, the other dressed in simple leathers and a loincloth. One horn twists up from his head where there should be two.

Sure enough, it's Raahosh and Liz.

"Marco," Liz calls, laughing as they approach.

I want to laugh at her joke, but I'm too tired. I lean against Aehako's arm as we wait for them. I could fall asleep on my feet right about now. Actually, I don't think I've slept in a long time.

"Yo, dude, you're supposed to say 'Polo,'" Liz says, hopping over to us before flinging her arms around me. Then, she blinks, takes in my pale face and the travois, and then looks at Aehako. "What's wrong? What the hell happened?"

"We were returning to the caves because we saw the alien ship," Raahosh says in a grim voice.

"Yeah, but it left again, so I thought everything was cool," Liz says.

"It didn't leave," I tell her. "I smashed it into the side of the mountain."

"We can tell you on the way back," Aehako interrupts. "But we must get Haeden to the healer before it is too late."

Raahosh's eyes narrow and he moves to the travois, ripping my fur cloak down and uncovering Haeden. A moment later, he gets up, replaces the blanket, and takes the travois poles from Aehako. "I will run it in. Stay with the women."

Aehako claps him on the shoulder gratefully, and we watch as Raahosh takes off like a racehorse, hauling the travois behind him with a speed and energy that makes me exhausted to watch.

"You okay, Kira?" Liz asks. "You look ready to faint."

"I'm fine," I assure her, though I weave unsteadily on my feet.

"I'd offer to carry you, but my muscles are kinda puny," she says, flexing an arm. She adjusts her bow, slung across her back. "But I'm happy to give you a shoulder to lean on if you need it."

"There is no need," Aehako interrupts, and in the next moment, he picks me up in his arms.

"You're wounded," I protest. "You can't carry me." I try to slither out of his grip, but Aehako only holds me tighter.

"You guys okay?" Liz asks, worried.

"I am fine. And you weigh nothing, Kira," he says, and then nuzzles my throat. "It is my honor and pleasure to carry my mate."

"Oh my God," Liz cries and claps a hand to her mouth. "You two resonated? Really?"

I shake my head, but Aehako interrupts. "No resonance. We have chosen each other."

"Aww, that's romantic, I think," Liz says, and there's a wrinkle in her brow as if she's not quite sure if she should be happy for us or not. I know what she's thinking—what happens if one of us resonates to someone else?

So I distract her as we start walking, heading down the path that Raahosh has cut through the snow. "You haven't seen Harlow, have you?" I ask her. "She was part of our group and ran off, and we can't find her anywhere."

"Jeez, I feel like I'm missing a big chunk of story here," Liz says. "Someone wanna fill me in between alien plane crashes, wounds, and a missing person?"

We do, and it takes a bit of telling. By the time the story is finished, we're striding into the mouth of the cave, me in Aehako's arms, and worried tribesmates swarm around us. I can practically feel the love and worry in the air, and it's a good feeling. For the first time, I don't feel like a lonely outsider.

Maybe it's because when Aehako sets me down, he refuses to let go of my hand and keeps me at his side. I like that.

Raahosh returns a few moments later and puts an arm around Liz's waist, possessive. He nods at Aehako. "Haeden is with the healer."

"I am glad you ran into us when you did."

"You need the healer, too," I point out. "You have a wound—"

"Hush," Aehako says, and presses a kiss atop my head. "My mother will pack it with herbs and that will hold me until the healer is ready. Come. We should tell her she has a daughter. She has always wanted one."

Liz giggles evilly. "Oh boy, meeting the in-laws. Have fun with that."

I cast a look back at her, but I don't protest when Aehako leads me deeper into the caves. His wound is first and foremost in my mind, not whether or not his mother likes me.

"Are you sure you're okay?" I ask, squeezing his hand.

"I will be fine. I don't wish to distract Maylak from the healing she is doing on Haeden. He needs all her attention." His brows furrow with worry and he casts a look at the healer's cave. "If he doesn't live . . ."

"He will," I reassure him. And when he hesitates, I gently steer him back toward his own cave. "Tend to yourself first, then you can see how he is doing."

He nods and tugs me along. I pass by Tiffany and Josie, who have worried looks on their faces. The loss of Harlow is one I'm not ready to talk about yet. I'm not even sure if I can grieve. It just doesn't feel real yet. How can we have possibly lost a human? There are too few of us as it is.

"My son," an elderly woman cries, and I see Sevvah emerge from her cave, holding out her arms for a hug. "What is this I hear about a wound?"

"It is nothing, Mother," Aehako says, and his usual grin resurfaces. "You worry too much."

"And you do not worry enough," she fusses, embracing him.

My hand slips from his as he steps into his mother's arms, and I remain behind, feeling a bit timid. I've talked with Sevvah plenty of times before. It's a small cave, and I like her. She's lovely, with gray braids looping around her horns, and is the same pale blue her son is. She looks regal and there are lines at the edges of her eyes from laughter, which is good. I shouldn't feel weird about walking right in and sitting down as she leads her son into their cave. I mean, she's invited me in for tea before.

It's just that the last time I was only one of many humans, not a daughter-in-law. A daughter-in-law that will never resonate.

I swallow hard.

"Where are you wounded?" Sevvah fusses. "Oshen, bring me my herb bags. Sessah, move away. Go play with Farli."

As I linger at the mouth of their cave, Sessah—a boy that can't be more than ten years old or so—bolts out of the cave, giggling. I always forget that Aehako has a much younger brother. I know he has an older one named Rokan, but the sight of Sessah's skinny body and twiglike horns makes me feel a curious kind of longing. Is that what Aehako's children would look like?

A tail flicks at the edge of my vision, and as I watch, Asha saunters into Sevvah's cave as if she owns it. I watch as the flirty female moves toward Aehako and puts an arm around his back.

To his credit, Aehako flinches away and looks for me. "Kira?"

I bite my lip and head in, though I feel like an intruder. Sevvah's giving me a curious look and Asha's shooting daggers at me with her blue gaze. Oh dear. I am really not good with confrontation, and this feels like confrontation.

Ironic that I took out the aliens without an ounce of anxiety, but approaching the man that loves me while his ex-girlfriend tries to slide in on my territory? While his mother watches? This is hard.

Meekly, I step to Aehako's side and lace my fingers with his again.

"Hold this?" Sevvah asks, and hands me a small bone bowl full of herbs and what looks like fluff. "Now, Aehako, tell me what sorts of things you have been up to, you naughty scamp." His mother's voice is loving, the affectionate tone of a woman who knows just how much trouble her son can be.

"Did you miss me?" Asha demands, pushing her way to Aehako's other side as if I'm not there.

He frowns at her and shakes his head. "I, no—"

As I watch, her hand slides to his tail and she grips it at the base. I gasp, because that seems incredibly sexual.

How dare that bitch touch my man?

My hand leaves Aehako's, and before I can even stop to think of what I'm doing, I slap her hand away from him. "Quit touching my mate!"

The words tumble out before I can stop them, and everyone in the cavern stares at us. Aehako's father, Oshen; his mother, Sevvah; Asha—they all look at me as if I've grown another head.

Then, Sevvah gasps and a smile breaks across her face. "My son! You resonated? And to such a lovely human!" She beams at me with matronly warmth.

"No resonance, Mother," Aehako says, and pulls me against his side, carefully steering me away from a gaping Asha. "I've chosen her as my mate, and she's chosen to be mine."

I wait for Sevvah to question this, but she only smiles. "Equally wonderful." She pulls at the laces of Aehako's leather tunic, but it's clear it's not going to come off like that.

I step back out of Aehako's grip. "Take off your shirt so your mother can see the wound."

He removes his clothing, and then hands his tunic to me with a wink. "Not back an hour and my mate's having me strip down. You see why I took her as my woman? She's demanding."

I blush.

Asha's still standing there, and I sneak a peek over at her. She is frozen in place, an unreadable expression on her face. It's clear she doesn't belong, and it's also clear she's making no attempt to leave. This is awkward. I feel bad for her. I know she's throwing herself at Aehako, but it's clear that she's miserable, all thanks to a khui that picked someone else.

Her gaze flicks to me and I offer her a tentative smile.

She scowls at me and storms away.

So much for sympathy.

Sevvah shakes her head and takes a handful of the wooly herbs out of the bowl I'm holding. "That one has a hard head. Perhaps now that you've taken a mate, she'll get it out of her mind that you should be together."

"One can hope," Aehako says drily. He hisses when Sevvah presses the bundle of herbs against the wound.

"This should be stitched," Sevvah tells him.

"Maylak can fix it."

"Maylak will be exhausted trying to save Haeden," Sevvah insists. "I won't have you bleeding out while you wait for her to recover. You have a pretty mate to take to your furs. The last thing you want is to spend your time moaning in pain."

"Not when I'd rather spend it just moaning, eh?" Aehako teases.

Oh my God, I can't believe he just made that joke with his mother. I stare at him, horrified and unable to laugh.

As if she can read my thoughts, Sevvah rolls her eyes, taps his cheek with her hand, and says, "Behave, you randy fool."

A giggle escapes me, and Sevvah flashes me a grin. Maybe the whole mother-in-law thing won't be so bad after all.

"So," Sevvah says as she readies an awl and a thick length of cord. As she pulls up a small stool, her husband, Oshen, retrieves a bowl from a shelf over the firepit and carries it forward with gloved hands. Hot water. He sets it down nearby and Sevvah dips a bit of leather into it, then dabs at the edges of Aehako's deep wound. "Where will you and your new mate be caving?"

"Caving?" I ask.

"What, you don't want us here, Mother? I am wounded."

My eyes widen. Sharing a cave with Aehako's big family? And trying to have sex while doing so? The idea is unthinkable. But there's no place else to go, either, and Harlow—and any hopes of a stonecutter—is gone. This is something I haven't even considered, and I shoot Aehako a worried glance. Does he really want us to live here?

But even as I look over, he winks.

Sevvah snorts. "The last thing a young mated pair needs are two old ones and two boys snuggled up in the furs nearby. Your mate will want more privacy than that." She dabs at his wound again, then looks at me. "Since there are so many newly mated pairs, there is talk of opening the caves to the south for the winter and splitting the tribes."

"Then we'll go there," Aehako says, wincing as his mother tends to him. "Kira and I will definitely need our own space."

"A noisy one, is she?"

"The noisiest," Aehako says proudly.

I'm so going to die of embarrassment.

I must drift off to sleep at some point, because the next thing I know, Aehako is kissing my brow and tucking me into bed. I should get up, but it's so warm and safe and I'm curled up next to him, so I just snuggle down closer and drift back to sleep.

It's heaven, pure and simple.

I wake up at some point because I feel like someone's staring at me. I squeeze one eye open and Sessah—Aehako's much younger brother—is gazing down at me. I feel a little awkward and shy under his scrutiny. "Good morning," I say in his language, since I know it now. The words feel fluid on my tongue, and I realize this is the first time I've been able to say more than just "hi" to the younger ones, who haven't been out to the elders' ship for the language dump. I decide to show off a little. "Am I sleeping funny? Is that why you stare?"

"You're Aehako's mate?"

"I am."

"But you didn't resonate. How can you be mates?"

Oh boy. Am I going to have to explain the birds and the bees to this kid? "Well, ah, sometimes when two people love each other very much, they want to be together all the time despite the fact that they can't have a baby."

He wrinkles his nose at the thought. "Does this mean you're moving into our cave? It's already crowded."

"I don't know. Um, is your brother Aehako around?"

"He is with the chief."

"Thank you," I murmur, and straighten my clothing before emerging from the bed. I'm still dressed, thank goodness, but my leathers smell like smoke and sweat and I kind of wish I had something else I could change into. Clothing's been at a premium with twelve new people to tend to, though. Maybe someone will have extras I can change into. I slide out of the furs, glancing around. I'm still in Sevvah's cozy cave, though this portion has been sectioned off with a strategic rocky outcropping and a large woven basket to give the illusion of privacy. Nearby,

I can still hear the heavy breathing of someone else sleeping, and the low murmur of Sevvah's voice.

Sessah's right. The cave is definitely small and crowded. I'm grateful for the bed, of course, but I think longingly of my loft apartment back on Earth that had seemed so small two months ago and now seems like unrivaled luxury. When the babies get here, we're going to be falling over each other with the crowding.

I . . . suppose that won't be a problem for me and Aehako. I feel a guilty pang at the thought. It was his choice to mate me despite knowing my flaws, so I can't worry about it. I tell myself this as I slide on soft boots, give Sessah a pat on the head, and then emerge from the private cave into the main interior of the tribal caves.

I yawn as I pad out into the main area and realize . . . I slept great. For the first time in what feels like forever, I slept without overhearing everyone having sex, the whispers picked up by the translator, everything. No wonder I feel so utterly refreshed. Even now, the cave is crowded but not overwhelming with voices. Instead, it's like a low, pleasant hum of conversation.

This is . . . awesome.

Of course, a small downside is that I have no idea where my mate is now. I can't follow the sound of his voice via the translator. I'll have to hunt him down the old-fashioned way.

Nearby, Tiffany and Josie are scraping skins stretched on frames. Josie gives a happy squeal at the sight of me and waves her gore-covered arms. "I'd hug you, girl, but I'm gross! I'm so glad you're back!"

Tiffany's the more reserved of the two, and she just smiles at me.

"I'm glad to be back, too." I rub my earlobe. "I feel so much better without the translator." I wonder how much they know about the ship returning and wanting to snatch us all again, or if that's being kept on the down-low.

"I almost didn't recognize you," Josie says in a sunny voice, then turns back to scraping her skin. "Maybe I should check out the old mother ship and see if it does breast implants. I'm feeling pretty inadequate around the other ladies." She shakes her small chest back and forth, trying to make what little she has jiggle.

"Oh, stop it," Tiffany says and nudges Josie with an elbow. "For real. No one's gonna give you boob implants because you're a skinny white girl."

Josie sticks out her tongue, and Tiffany returns the gesture before they both start laughing.

Yeah . . . I'm thinking they weren't told about the ship. They're entirely too happy. I gesture at the mouth of the chief's cave. "Is Vektal in there?"

Tiffany leans over to look at the entrance of his cave. "I don't think so? I thought I saw him walk outside with a few of the others earlier. You might check with the hunters if he's not in the furs with Georgie." She winks.

Oh, yikes. The last thing I want to do is run into them having sex. Lord knows I've heard it enough already. "Um, maybe I'll check with the hunters first."

"Good call," Josie cackles. "I saw more than I wanted to, once."

"These people need some damn doorbells," Tiffany says, and shakes her head.

I can't disagree with that. I give them both impulsive, one-armed hugs around their shoulders that they can't quite return because of their hands, and then trot off to find Aehako and the chief. Marlene is tending to a small fire where the cooked human food is prepared, and offers me a root-cake—not unlike a hash brown cake—for breakfast. I nibble on it as I walk. If there was some coffee around here, I'd say this cave was downright cozy.

I find Aehako and Vektal talking near the entrance to the cave. They're up on a rise, just far enough away not to be overheard. Georgie squats nearby in the snow, dry heaving as Vektal strokes her hair.

I cram my root-cake into my mouth and chew rapidly. Probably a bad idea to eat around the pregnant lady with morning sickness. Poor Georgie. She's been barfing ever since she got knocked up.

Of course, I'd gladly trade places with her. I'd barf every day for three years in a row if it meant I could have Aehako's child.

My mate looks up at that moment and sees me approaching, and a smile crosses his broad face. I bask in the warmth of his approval, so happy I could burst. The aliens are gone, my translator's removed, and I have the love of a sexy, delicious alien. Oh, it is so *tough* to be me.

Aehako kisses me on the mouth as I move to his side and then swipes at the corner of my lip. "You have grease on your face."

I scrub at my cheek, blushing. "I was trying to eat fast so I wouldn't bother Georgie." I look over at my fellow human sympathetically. "How are you today?"

"Not bad, actually," she says, and stands up, wiping her own mouth. She looks pale and tired, but gives Vektal a small smile of thanks as he hands her a waterskin. She rinses her mouth and then spits off to the side.

Vektal studies me, arms crossed. His tail flicks once. "I did not recognize you without your shell," he says, and gestures at one ear.

"I had the translator removed," I tell him, feeling awkward.

Am I truly so forgettable? But as I watch, his gaze devours Georgie, and my hurt feelings dissipate. I'm probably just another human to him, when Georgie's the only one that matters. It's clear that Vektal is obsessed and utterly in love with his human mate. I think it's cute, even if he still intimidates me a little.

Georgie leans against Vektal and his arm goes around her waist. "It's good that you arrived," she says. "We were just discussing things."

"How is Haeden?" I ask.

"Recovering," Aehako tells me. He takes my hand in his and twines his fingers with mine. "Maylak has worn herself out working on healing him, so I will stay wounded for a bit longer." He pats his stomach at the bandaged spot. "I guess you will have to be gentle with me in the furs, my Sad Eyes."

I see Flirty Aehako is back in full force. I snort and ignore his overt words. "And Harlow? Any sign of her?"

Georgie shakes her head. "I hate that she's just completely disappeared. Something about it stinks. She didn't strike me as the type to recklessly throw her life away." Then, she's silent again, and I know we're both thinking of Dominique. Dominique was another redhead who was captured and thrown into the hold with Georgie and me on the alien spaceship. The guards had raped her, and it had broken something in Dominique's mind. She'd survived the crash, but the moment she had the chance, she'd run away into the frigid snow wearing only a nightgown. She'd frozen to death.

The loss of her still hit hard, even after everything we'd been through.

"Harlow's smart," I offer, thinking of her quick mind as she'd pieced together parts for the rock cutter. "Maybe she'll find her way back."

"I think we should send hunters after her," Georgie says.

Vektal shakes his head. "The brutal season is coming on fast, and we have twelve—"

"Eleven," Georgie quietly corrects.

"*Eleven* new mouths to feed. And several of those are bearing young. We must think of the good of all of the tribe, and the hunters are needed every spare moment. If they are not leaving to hunt food, we cannot spare them." He touches her stomach. "I will not put you and our kit—or all of the other new lives to be born—in danger for one foolish human girl."

I don't like his answer, but as I look at Aehako, he's nodding. They know the weather of this place better than we do. If they're worried about not having enough food for the winter, then we need to worry, too, I suppose.

I can tell Georgie's not happy, either, but she shoots me a helpless look.

"She'll turn up," I say, determined.

We discuss the second spaceship and its demise. Georgie agrees with Vektal on this one—they don't want to tell the others. No one but us—and Liz and Raahosh, who were out hunting and saw the craft—will know about it. Georgie doesn't want the others to panic, not when they're just now settling in.

"And if they're all dead, there's nothing to worry about, right?" She gives me a determined nod. "Right. Which means we should talk about the tribe split."

"Split?" I look at Aehako, worried.

He nods. "When we were young kits, our caves overflowed and we had a second cave to the south that was also full of families. The khui-sickness took so many lives that we all moved to this cave system, but with the new families, I suggested to Vektal that we reopen the other cave."

"Only because you do not want to share a cave with another couple," Vektal teases. "You are like me and want your mate all to yourself."

Aehako gives his chief a lazy grin. "Is that such a bad thing? To want to be able to mate my female without the worry that Asha is going to show up and demand to join in?"

I make a choked sound. "Um, I'm for a new cave, too." The idea of Asha watching—much less trying to join—is utterly horrifying.

Georgie giggles. "You should see your face, Kira. Oh my God."

"If there is a new cave, all of the humans must remain with the healer."

"Is that fair to the others?" I ask. The last thing I want is to have the rest of the tribe resenting us.

"The humans are carrying kits," Vektal argues. "If they are not yet, they will be. They need to be with the healer."

I remain silent.

"I agree with Kira," Aehako says. "A cave full of elderly and single hunters will only breed dissent. It is fairest to split the tribe evenly."

"We only have one healer," Vektal growls. "She will remain with Georgie."

"Calm down, Vektal." Georgie pats her mate on his big arm. "I'm sure things can be divided in a way that's fair to everyone. What if we send the single humans to the new cave and keep the pregnant ones here?"

"What about Raahosh and Liz?" I ask.

"Their punishment remains," Vektal declares. "They will continue to hunt until Liz is too heavy to do so. But they can den with us when it comes time for Liz to have her kit."

"Then who will be in charge at the new cave?" Aehako asks. His hand tightens on mine.

For a moment, Vektal looks perplexed. "I was going to send you, but now that you have mated, this poses a problem. Kira will need to stay near the healer."

I bite my lip. I guess it's time to speak up. "Kira doesn't, actually. I can't resonate. I'm barren."

Georgie's face softens while Vektal looks confused.

"She cannot bear children. We have chosen our mating," Aehako declares, and hugs me close against him. "There will be no kit, but it does not matter. All that matters is that she is mine and I am hers."

His declaration makes me weepy.

"And if there is resonance to another later?" Vektal asks.

"Then we will handle that as it comes," Aehako says. "Until that day comes—if it should ever come—I belong to Kira, and she belongs to me."

Vektal nods and gives us both a look of understanding. "I would have done the same for Georgie, had she not resonated for me."

Aehako

It takes two full days and nights before we are allowed to go and visit the other cave system. Kira has taken to calling it the South Cave, and the name has stuck with me as well. We have said nothing to the others. If I am to be the leader of this small fragment of the tribe, I want it all decided and carved in stone before anyone is moved. Once we are in for the brutal months, the visits between the caves will be few and far between.

Balancing the tribes is a delicate matter and one that takes many days of discussion between myself and Vektal, and we include our mates, who are the voices of reason when it comes to the human women. If we do not balance things just perfectly, those moving to the South Cave will feel abandoned and useless. But if we take our strongest to the South Cave, then we handicap the tribe cave.

Back and forth, we argue about who should stay and who should go. Plans change hourly, until I'm ready to tear my hair out if Vektal puts his foot down and says no to my suggestions one more time.

He is the chief, and he is my friend, but he is also incredibly stubborn. A pain in the ass, as Kira says.

I'm short-tempered, myself. Haeden is still healing and Maylak, who is pregnant and must be careful with her own health, hasn't had time for my wound. It pains me, but not nearly as much as being unable to sleep with my Kira and not caress her.

She doesn't have to tell me that she's uncomfortable sleeping in the cave with my family around her. It's evident in the stiffness of her body as we undress for bed. Or at least, I undress for bed. Kira simply takes her shoes off and lies down, fully clothed and twitching with every small sound. Every hiccup Sessah makes, every snort my brother Rokan makes in his sleep, every murmur of my father and mother as they mate—Kira hears all of it, and it's clear she's bothered.

There will be no mating until we have our own cave and privacy.

Very well, then. I will just have to push things along. My need to claim my Kira again overrides everything. I hunger to taste her sweetness on my tongue, to mate her mouth with mine, to sink my cock deep into her cunt and hear her bellow with pleasure.

It's these thoughts that drive me to suggest a trip to the South Cave the next morning. Kira's nibbling on one of the root-cakes that she and the human women seem to enjoy so much and chatting with the others by the fire. Vektal is relaxing in the pool while Georgie braids his hair into a thousand tiny braids that stand up straight around his horns and look like a strange nest. Everyone's relaxed and enjoying themselves before starting the day—a perfect time to sneak away with my Kira.

When she finishes eating, I pull her aside. "Come with me today."

She dusts off her hands and nods. "Where are we going?"

"To see the South Cave. I want to take a look at how many caves make up the system before we decide who should stay and who should go."

Kira tilts her head and gives me a curious look. "You don't know the caves?"

I do, actually. I know them by heart and have been many times. But I'm itching to have alone time with my lovely mate, and this is the best way to do it. "I do, but I wish your feedback."

A brilliant smile crosses her face and my cock surges at the sight of it. We definitely need to get away from the others, or else they're all going to watch while I claim my lovely mate, because I'm not going to be able to resist touching her for much longer.

"Well?" I ask as she steps into the mouth of the South Cave. "What do you think?" I'm anxious to hear her thoughts.

She gazes up at the high ceiling. "You have stalactites."

"I do not know this word."

"The rock icicles," she says, and points at them. "They're not in the other cave. I think Harlow was right that the elders had rock cutters of some kind when they made your cave."

I admit I'm a little dismayed that her response isn't enthusiastic. If I'm in charge of this cave as Vektal wishes, she'll be with me. I want her to like it here. I want her to be with me.

"These caves are very different," I admit. "There is no bathing pool in the center of the cavern, for one."

She gives me a prim look. "That is not exactly a bad thing. The less I see of other people's junk, the better."

I chuckle. Her modesty is strange. She'll lose it eventually, but for now, I'll enjoy her blushes and her squirming. "Do you not wish to see your mate naked?"

"I see you naked plenty," she says, and her cheeks are pink as she steps past me, gazing around her. "It's darker in here, and colder."

I follow her. "The other cave is warmed by the underground spring, so it stays pleasant even in the brutal season. Here, we would need to rely on more fires."

"Fires aren't bad," she says, her expression thoughtful. "We still have a lot of people eating cooked food. And the ceiling is high, so the smoke won't be so bad." She heads toward one of the private nooks that are living quarters. There's still an old leather screen propped up in front of the cave mouth as a nod to privacy. And she gasps. "My goodness. It's so big in here!"

"Is it?" I feel a hint of pride return. "Do you like it?"

"As long as we don't freeze in the winter, I think there's potential," she says with a small laugh. She pushes into the private cave and looks around. I follow her. It's been at least fifteen full cycles of the seasons since this cave was inhabited, and I don't remember who it once belonged to. In the center of the room is a dug-out firepit with neat rocks circling it. There's a flat section off to one side that probably housed the bed furs, and a few withered baskets that have been chewed at the bottom. She walks past all this, and then flashes me a smile and sticks her hand out. "Show me which one you had in mind for us?"

I return her smile and take her small hand in mine. I love the feel of her cold fingers lacing between mine for warmth, and the urge to drag her to the floor of the cave and claim her is nearly overwhelming. I stare down at her, my cock hardening in my loincloth.

"Cave?" She squeezes my hand. "Aehako?"

My name falling from her lips makes my balls tighten. Somehow, I manage to focus and turn, judging the maze of small caves attaching to the bigger one. Whereas the tribal cave is built like a ring, this one is more like a horn, where the entrance is wide and open and narrows farther down into the side of the mountain. The caves at the front will be for the hunters, I have decided, and the fully sa-khui families. The humans are fragile and do not retain heat nearly as well, so they will need to be at the back of the cave, away from the snowy winds. There's one particular cave I have in mind, and I steer her toward it. It's smaller than a few of the others, but it has other charms.

There's a screen covering it as well, faded painted symbols dancing along the hide. Kemli had a sister once, Koloi, but she died with the khui-sickness. Koloi enjoyed painting, much like Kemli's daughter, Farli, now does. And her old cave still bears the remnants of her fanciful designs. I push aside the screen and duck to enter the cave, tugging Kira behind me.

Her pleased gasp tells me I've done well. "It's so dark in here, Aehako. But are those . . ."

"Designs, yes. The woman who used to live in this cave painted the walls. Do you like it?"

"It's so pretty." She steps forward, toward the firepit, gazing up where a trickle of light comes from overhead. "Smoke hole?"

I nod.

"That's handy." She gazes around again, and then points at the back of the cave. "What's that?"

I take a few steps into the shadows and recognition dawns. "It's the skull of a sa-kohtsk. There's no bathing pool here, so they would hollow the skull out and line it with waterproof hides to make a small bathing pool—"

Her shriek of excitement echoes. "It's a tub?"

I shrug my shoulders. I don't know the word. "I suppose?"

Kira hops in place and then bounds toward me, grabbing my hand. "I want this cave. This one's ours, right?"

I feel a sweeping sense of pride at her excitement. "Yes. This is what I picked for us."

Her arms fling around my waist. "This is wonderful!"

To think that my Kira would be so excited by a bit of paint on the walls and a makeshift bathing pool. My hands go to her back and slide up and down her spine. "I am glad you like it."

"I love it," she says. "I can't wait to move in. So much privacy will be wonderful. We'll have time to clean things up and make it cozy before the winter comes."

Winter is her word for the brutal season, so I simply nod.

She tilts her head back and gazes up at me, and there's a hint of a smile playing around her lips. I'm entranced at the sight of it. "There's one thing this place needs," she tells me.

"Oh?"

She steps back and pulls her bag off her shoulder. I know she's brought a waterskin and some of the root-cakes that the humans love for a meal, but I'm curious as to why we would need them now. She turns her back to me and moves toward the wall, toward the nook of the sleeping area. There's a bit of a shelf mixed among the spiky edges of the cave, and she places an object there.

I see it, and a bark of laughter erupts from my throat.

It's the courting gift I gave her—the replica of my cock, carved from bone. She's brought it and made the cave "ours" by placing it here. I laugh long and hard at the sight, and her happy laughter twines with mine. The sound of her carefree laugh— her happiness—makes my entire body react, and I pull her against me. "My sweet mate," I murmur, and drag my fingers through her hair. "Did you bring that so I could use it on you?"

Her expression changes to one of shyness and she averts her eyes. But instead of a protest, her hands slide to the front of my tunic and she tugs at it.

Aha. So my mate misses my body as much as I miss hers. Need surges through me. I dig my fingers into the silky strands of her mane and tug it back, exposing her neck. I rake my teeth over the cords of her throat, and then drag my tongue over her skin.

She shivers. "I've missed you, Aehako. I feel like we haven't had a moment alone in forever."

"Look around you, my mate. There is nothing but privacy here."

Kira tugs at the front of my tunic. "Then why are you still dressed?"

I nibble on her throat before releasing her. "So eager. It does a male's heart good to hear his mate is so anxious to join with him." I undo the laces of my tunic and then tug the entire thing over my head, leaving me only in leggings and loincloth. I spread my tunic on the dusty floor so my mate won't have to sit on the cold rock.

She immediately begins to undo the laces of her cloak, and I stop her. "I will undress you."

"Oh?" A smile plays at the corners of her mouth. "Are you going to unwrap me like a present?"

"Like a bit of organ meat hiding under the ribs of a fresh kill," I tease.

Her nose wrinkles. "That . . . sounds awful."

"Ah, but those are the tastiest, juiciest parts." I undo my loincloth and she watches me undress, chewing on her lip thoughtfully. I toss it down on the floor, and then my leggings, and soft boots. Then I am completely naked in front of her, my cock jutting hard, eager for her body. I clasp my cock in my hand and give it a teasing stroke, just to see her expression.

She gives a small gasp and her gaze locks with mine.

"Shall you watch me pleasure myself?" I love how startled she looks at the sight, and I pump my cock again, just the way I like, tightly dragging my circled forefinger and thumb from the base to the crown, and then giving it a small flex of the wrist.

"I'd say yes any other time," she whispers, unable to take her gaze off my movements. "But I really want you to touch me. Does that make me greedy?"

"If it does, then I am the luckiest male to have such a greedy mate," I tell her, and undo the clasp of her cloak at her throat.

She stands still, trembling with anticipation, and her eyes are huge as she gazes up at me. There's no fear or wariness in her face, just longing. She's so beautiful that it makes me ache to look at her. I am truly the luckiest male ever. I press my mouth to her strange, smooth forehead, and kiss her tiny, too-flat nose. She is perfect to me.

I bend down and touch her chin. I tilt her head back so I can kiss her mouth, mate our tongues in the slick, decadent way that the humans are so fond of. She leans into my kiss, her hands sliding to my sides and then resting on my hips, gripping me against her. My cock presses against her belly, hard and insistent. It wants attention, too. Soon, I remind myself. This is but the second time we will mate, and I must still be careful with her to make sure she is ready.

So I continue my slow removal of her clothing. I take the cloak from her shoulders and lay it on the ground, spread like a blanket. Her dress is made of the softest leather Kashrem creates, but the sleeve is torn and the garment is ragged and still has soot stains on the skirt from her capture. I frown at the sight of it, not only because the memory of her near loss makes my heart seize in my chest, but she needs warm, clean clothing. "You need a new dress."

"I forgot to ask for one." She shrugs. "It's not important."

"It is important to me. You are my mate. I want you clothed warmly."

"I'd like to make my own clothing," Kira says in a shy voice. "I want to learn. I want to be capable."

"I can show you how to make leather, but not nearly as fine as what Kashrem makes." I tug her dress over her head, and the moment I do, she grips my cock in her small hands, making the breath hiss from my lungs.

"Let's not talk about clothing right now?"

I chuckle. "So eager?"

The shy duck of her head tells me everything.

I sink to the ground on the furs and tug her down against me, pulling her into my lap. She settles on one of my thighs, her small, tailless bottom wiggling as she adjusts herself. I cup one of her breasts in my hand, admiring the softness of her skin and her gasp of response. "You are so soft all over, my Kira," I murmur, and lean down to take a taut nipple into my mouth.

She moans and her hips buck, and her arms go around my neck, clinging to me.

I lick and suck at her nipple, teasing it with the ridged tip of my tongue. Her soft cries tell me that she likes this, very much, and I can feel the wetness from between her legs seep onto my thigh. My other hand moves there to her cunt, to dip into her sweet honey. She's hot and soaked under the dark curls between her legs, her folds juicy and waiting for my tongue. My mouth waters at the thought.

And then I remember that she brought the courting present I made for her. Does she want to try it? I've not heard of such a thing, but humans are adventurous and I'm eager to participate. I did make it as big as my cock, and even though I want nothing more than to bury myself between her legs, I'm intrigued by how she'd react if I use the courting gift on her.

My fingers glide between her slippery folds. She's hot and

wet, and her hips move as I stroke her, encouraging me to push into her. A little moan escapes her as I lick her nipple, and that decides me. I want more of her moans, her cries, her wails of my name. I want to drive her wild.

I reach back to the shelf and pick up the courting gift, and hold it in front of her.

Kira inhales sharply, and her gaze flicks to my face.

"It's a good replica, is it not?" I admire my carving, right down to the veins tracing along the shaft. "You have no idea how many hours I spent staring at my own cock to get this right."

She giggles softly. "And you did that just for me?"

"Of course. You are my woman and I wished to please you."

She leans forward and her arms tighten around my neck, and she kisses me softly on the mouth. "You always please me, Ae-hako."

I drag it over her belly. "And now I want to please you with this," I tell her between kisses. I feel her stiffen, and her breath quickens, but she doesn't tell me no. Encouraged, I slide it lower, moving the head of it to her mound. "I think, like my cock, I will need to make sure it is wet with your juices before I slide it into you."

A whimper escapes her throat and her arms tighten around my neck.

"Spread your legs for me, my mate," I tell her.

She bites her lip again, but her legs ease open. I can see the gleam of wetness on her upper thighs, and I can smell the hot scent of her. It drives me insane with need. A growl forms low in my throat. The need to claim her is strong, but my curiosity and the titillation of the toy—as well as the thought of pleasing her—drives me. I push the thick head of the toy between her folds and it presses against her third nipple.

Kira cries out and her hips lift, her arms tightening around my neck. "Oh God!" The scent of her musk perfumes the air even thicker than before. Her body quivers.

I drag the head of the false cock through her wet folds, getting it slick. Every movement of it makes Kira react—she is climbing off my lap with her need, her fingernails digging into my shoulders. I push the head of the false cock into her, and she whimpers. I move no farther, because to do more, she will have to change positions, and I want her to ask for it. I want to know she's enjoying herself as much as I am. My own cock throbs with neglect, but for now, it is all about Kira and her need.

When I push no deeper, her whimpers increase, and her hips rise up, encouraging me. "Aehako," she pants, and her nails dig into my skin. "Please."

"Do you wish more, my mate?" I lean in and kiss her, and give the fake cock a little push to remind her of its presence.

She makes a soft, wordless sound, and then nods.

"Do you trust me?"

Again, she nods. Her eyes are huge in her face, her pupils dilated with need.

"Then lie flat for me." I pull the fake cock out, and when she simply stares at me, I lick the head clean of her juices. A low growl escapes my throat. She's delicious, and I want my tongue on her.

Kira shivers, and then nods. To my surprise, she flips over onto her belly and pushes her bottom up in the air, her legs slightly spread. Her stomach presses against my thigh, and I want to correct her . . . but stop.

Her bottom is smooth, no hint of a tail to interrupt the sweet curve. I realize that if I press the false cock into her, there is nothing to stop me from sinking it all the way inside her. Entranced by the thought, I push my fingers between her thighs to stroke her cunt, and she moans hard, pressing her face into the furs.

She's wet and slick and ready, and I remove my hand and push the head of the false cock at the entrance of her cunt. Her wriggle of encouragement is beautiful to see, and I press it deeper, inch by inch, until it's halfway into her. She moans as I begin to work it slowly, pushing deeper into her with each stroke. I'm fascinated by the sight of the cock—my cock—pushing into her and my own cock jerks in response.

"Aehako," she moans, and her hips wiggle as I push it deeper into her. As I do, the spur presses up against her backside, and she lets out a squeal. "What was that?"

"That was the spur."

"Oh," she breathes, and relaxes again. "Oh God, I don't know how I feel about that."

"Is it bad?"

"No, and that's the problem." She moans and pushes her hips higher again, encouraging me to give her more. I thrust it into her again, deeper, nudging at her bottom with the spur with every stroke of the cock.

And as she cries out, a stab of jealousy shoots through me. Stupid to be jealous of a carving, but I want her moans and cries for my cock. I want her cunt squeezing tight around me, her juices soaking my cock, not a bone carving.

I pull it out of her and toss it aside, ignoring her cries. But when I get up and adjust her hips, raising them into the air, her protests change to needy sounds, and she encourages me with her body. I run my hand over her smooth ass, my tail flicking. I never realized that a lack of a tail could be so . . . utterly erotic. I spread her thighs for me and sink into her in one fluid motion, watching as my spur penetrates her bottom.

Kira's cry of pleasure reverberates in the cave. "Yes!"

The growl escapes my throat and I grip her hips. It's been too long since I touched my mate and claimed her for my own. I can't hold back. I thrust into her again, rearing back and sliding deep into her once more, and Kira cries out her excitement. She can't contain herself. The more I stroke into her, the louder she gets, and the closer together her wails become until she's making one long keening noise as she comes. Her cunt clenches around me like a mouth, and then it becomes even more difficult to retain my control. I thrust three more times before I spill inside her, my entire body feeling as if it's emptying between her thighs. I don't stop pumping into her until I'm completely spent, and when I pull my cock from her body, I feel a slight sense of loss. Already I want to return.

But she sighs happily and collapses on the furs. "Oh, Aehako."

"Mmm," I say and lie down next to her, tucking her smaller body against mine.

"It should be criminal to be as happy as I am."

I chuckle. "Do we not deserve a bit of happiness?"

She's thoughtful as I pull the scattered clothing over her naked body to act as a blanket. I don't want her to get cold. "I don't know," Kira says after a moment. "I just worry that the other shoe is going to drop."

"You are not wearing shoes."

She laughs. "It's an expression. It means things are going so well that they are going to herald something bad."

I kiss her smooth shoulder. "You worry too much."

Her smile is soft as she looks back at me. "Maybe I do."

Kira

The move to the new cave is not what I expect, I suppose. In my limited experience between dorms and my own apartment, packing to move involves boxing up everything at a furious rate, and days of unpacking and placing items in their new homes. But the sa-khui people don't have as much junk as your average American girl does, and once it's decided who is moving to the new caves, everyone's packed and ready to go that afternoon.

It's a little shocking, but also exciting.

Aehako and I are taking the painted cave. I have to admit I'm excited to have my own cave, especially one that's already decorated and comes with a makeshift tub. Aehako loads his furs, his hunting tools, and his carving utensils, and he's ready to go. Me, I have even less than that. My worn leather dress, a pair of snowshoes, and my blankets. I think Aehako's mother, Sevvah, takes pity on me, because she fills his arms with a few baskets and utensils from her own cave, clucking over her baby bird finally leaving the nest.

Coming with us to the new cave is a mixture of old and new.

Maylak and her family will be staying in the primary cave, since she is the healer. Vektal and Georgie and all of the newly mated couples will also be staying with them, since no one knows exactly how a sa-khui/human pregnancy is going to go. Elder Kemli and her mate, Borran, and their young daughter, Farli, will be coming with us to the new caves. The elders—all men—will be coming and split into two of the caves. Tiffany, Josie, and Claire will be joining us, along with several of the bachelor hunters who now get to split the big, roomy caves at the front of the South Cave system. There's a bit of grumbling because the South Cave is full of the single and the elderly, but Vektal wants the elders to teach the humans the way of life here, and who better to do that than someone who's already lived a hundred turns of the season and is still going strong?

The only couple coming with us that Aehako's unhappy about is Asha and her mate, Hemalo. While they're a mated couple, they also don't have a small child, which means they're a natural pick to come to our cave, and all of the other caves back at the tribal complex are now back to their original uses. One of the hunter caves is now meat storage once more, and there's an empty cave that Vektal wants set aside in case Liz's pregnancy progresses faster than expected.

It's a good group heading to the South Cave, despite Asha's annoying presence. We hug all around—even though we're only a few hours' walk—and then set out. Claire's happy as could be, now that she knows Bek is also heading to the South Cave, and Tiffany's eager to learn more crafts from the elders. Josie's chattering happily to Kemli and Farli, even though neither can understand her. Haeden's coming to the new cave as well, and he looks rather irritated at Josie's talking. Part of me thinks that

Josie's blabbering is good for Haeden, who's entirely too self-contained and lost in his own thoughts most of the time.

When we make it to the South Cave, people exclaim with happiness, and for the next few hours, there's a lot of eager running around and exploring, checking out each other's caves, and setting up. A large fire is built in the central area, for lighting as well as to give the space a homey effect. It's nice and toasty warm for us humans, though I do notice that several of the hunters strip down due to the heat.

"Can't say that's a terrible side effect of things," Tiffany murmurs at me as I gawk at Aehako's brawny, sweaty chest as he sweeps a branch over the floor, ridding it of debris.

"No," I say, distracted as another near-naked hunter strolls past. "I can't say it is."

At that moment, Asha stomps forward and puts her hand on my mate. "I want to talk to you, Aehako. I don't like my new cave! It's too small."

Tiffany rolls her eyes. "Here we go. Princess is going to lobby for your cave, just you watch." She saunters away. And she's probably not wrong. It's clear that a long, long time as one of the few single women in the sa-khui tribe has made Asha rather spoiled and demanding. Of course, she's mated now.

Of course, I am, too. And she's touching my mate's arm and pretending to cry, and the sight of it irritates me. I watch as Aehako reaches out and pats her shoulder, trying to comfort her. "Your cave is one of the nicest. I promise."

"It's small," Asha pouts.

Oh, for Pete's sake. She doesn't have to share with anyone except her mate, which makes it twice the size it would have been if she'd had another mated couple squeezed on top of her.

I sigh with irritation as she takes Aehako's hand and tries to pull him toward her new cave, as if to give him a personal tour.

Enough of that.

I step forward, approaching Aehako's back. As I do, I notice his expression changes to one of horror as he stares down at Asha. Worried, I quicken my steps—

And hear the unthinkable.

Aehako's resonating and Asha's got her hand in his.

Shoe? Dropped.

PART SIX

PART SIX

Kira

I can't breathe. My heart's pounding in my chest so hard that my blood is thumping in my ears.

Aehako just resonated for another woman. I've lost him.

The shock and grief are overwhelming. I stare at their joined hands and look at my mate. He puts a hand on his chest, and I can hear it thrumming from over here.

He's resonating—his khui is reacting to the presence of his perfect mate.

And I'm not it. Asha is.

"I don't understand," I say. I can barely hear my own voice over the roar of blood in my ears. "Asha has a mate. You can't resonate to her."

You're mine, not hers.

It's too unfair. Aehako is the best thing that has ever happened to me and I'm going to lose him so quickly? A sob chokes my throat. My heart thumps a wild beat.

My handsome mate stares down at his chest, and then releases Asha's hand. "I'm not resonating for her." He turns to me, and his eyes seem unnaturally blue and bright.

The heartbeat in my ears pounds louder, faster. It keeps speeding up—

And then I realize what it is.

And I collapse with joy.

A moment later, Aehako's big arms go around me and he cradles me to his chest. "Kira," he murmurs, and holds my head tucked under his chin. "My Kira."

My own chest reverberates and thrums with resonance. That pounding that I was hearing? It wasn't my pulse. It was my khui, responding to his.

How is this possible?

Even as I wonder, my body changes. Intense feeling and need sweep over me, like a full-body flush. A sexual flush. I feel my thighs press together, and the ache to be filled settles deep inside me. My nipples feel oversensitive, and my skin aches even as my khui sings a humming beat along with Aehako's.

I cling to him, torn between hope and despair. "I . . . don't understand."

He laughs, and the sound is full of joy and wonder all at once. His mouth presses on my forehead, and he kisses me as we sit in the midst of the cave, collapsed around each other. "What is there to understand, my mate? Your khui simply needed more convincing."

I laugh, and my laughter turns to tears. "But . . . I can't—"

"Perhaps you can." He strokes my hair back from my face. "The khui adapts you to live here. Perhaps it changed more in your body?"

I stare at him in wonder. Maybe it did. Maybe the khui finds the broken parts in a body and mends them. All I know is that

I've always been told I could never have children. And yet here I am, resonating to the man I love.

"You are quiet," he murmurs, and his arms tighten around me. "Are you not pleased?"

I press my head to his chest, listening to the sound of his khui singing to mine. It's the most beautiful thing I've ever heard. "I am beyond joy. I can't even . . ." Hot tears well up. "I never imagined . . ."

More than a child, more than anything . . . Aehako is mine forever.

He growls low in his throat, and I feel the press of his cock against my hip. "Shall we go to our cave and please our khui?"

I choke out a laugh, clinging to him. "Yes, please! Please!"

Aehako gets to his feet, and I immediately feel bereft—and needy—the moment I'm no longer pressing my skin to his. But then he scoops me up into his arms, and I'm filled with such utter joy once more that nothing could break my happiness.

Nothing at all.

He heads toward our new cave and calls over his shoulder, "My mate and I will be busy. Do not bother us."

I should be horrified that he's told everyone what we're doing, but I'm too happy to even care. I peek over his arm and look back at the others in the cave. Tiffany and Josie are standing together, whispering, but they have smiles on their faces. Asha looks forlorn and lost. The other hunters simply laugh and call out jibes about Aehako and his prowess.

All the while, my khui sings and sings and sings.

Aehako carries me into the cave and gently sets me down on the pile of furs that will make up our shared bed. They're still bundled into rolls for transport during the move. We've been so busy overseeing the others that we haven't had time to set up our own cave. "Wait here," he tells me, and stalks to the entrance of our private cave, propping the stretched leather privacy screen in front of the entrance. All the while, I watch his ass flex under his loincloth, his tail flicking madly as he walks.

A tail has never been so sexy to me. But right now? It's driving me wild with need. Oh wow. I press a hand to my chest, and I can feel everything vibrating from the strength of the khui's song. It makes me want to reach out and touch Aehako . . . or myself. My thighs press together tightly, and I fight down the very real urge to flop back onto the blankets and stroke my clit until I come. I've never been this utterly sexualized. The khui is making it impossible to think about anything but grabbing Aehako and licking him from head to toe.

So, *so* hard to be me. So hard. Truly.

Instead, I reach for the rolls of the furs and work on untying them. We'll need something to lie on. My fingers, however, don't seem to want to work properly. My hands are shaking and I'm distracted. All I can think about is Aehako and sex.

Boy, they were right about this khui thing. It's like someone flipped a secret switch inside me and made me into an instant nympho. It's so strange. But I'm not unhappy about it—not in the slightest. I have to fight the urge not to cry out of sheer emotion, and my fingers pick at the leather knot uselessly.

I feel—rather than see—Aehako come and sit behind me. My khui's acutely sensitive to his, and our matched purring sounds feel strange and yet so right.

His hands come up from behind me and he cups both of my breasts in his hands and kisses my neck. "My mate. Truly mine."

The emotional tears I've been fighting finally burst free. I clutch his hands against my breasts and sob.

I feel his big body stiffen. "Why do you weep, Kira?"

"I just n-never th-thought it would happen for m-me," I babble. I'd resigned myself to being the only human amongst the others that couldn't have a baby when having children was so vitally important to the tribe. And Aehako had wanted them. I'd never considered having one myself.

It isn't until now that I realize how badly I want those things. And it overwhelms me. I weep even as he shushes me, and his embrace goes from sensual to supportive. He strokes my hair and murmurs as I cry against his chest. I'm not unhappy. I'm the opposite. And I have no idea why I'm so weepy, but I'm happy and so full of emotion I could burst, and I guess tears are the way it's coming out.

"Shhh," he tells me. "Everyone will think you are miserable at the thought of carrying my child."

A hiccupped giggle escapes me.

"It's true," he murmurs, and his hand slides down my arm, gliding over my skin. "They will say she is sorry that her khui has such poor taste as to mate a clever, beautiful girl with a fool like him."

I snort at that. No one could ever accuse Aehako of being a fool. "Don't be ridiculous."

"I am not. There are twice as many unmated males as there are the human women. Do you not think me the luckiest of males that I would resonate for you? I do."

I sigh, my tears drying because he's so sweet. I love this man so much. He's always seen me, even when no one else has. My flaws have never mattered to him—my smiles are the only things that do.

"I'm the luckiest," I tell him softly, and brush my fingers over the line of his jaw. He's so very handsome, my mate. I'm getting even more aroused just looking up at his big, broad face and his glowing eyes, and the smile that curves his mouth. I lean up and kiss him, and his hands immediately tighten around my waist, holding me against him.

"Kira," he says, and he sounds as breathless as I feel. His nose nudges mine before he takes my lower lip in his mouth and sucks on it. Oh God, he is way too good at kissing now. "When I take you this time, I will not be able to control myself. We will have long, tender nights of mating in our future. But I think now . . . if I do not sink inside you, I will lose my mind." He presses his ridged forehead to my flat one and closes his eyes. A tremor rushes through him and I realize just how close he is to losing his control. Oh wow.

My response to that? I slide my hand down to the front of his breeches so I can trace the outline of his cock. His breath hisses from his lungs, and I'm practically flung off his lap in the next moment.

Giddy with need, I expect to have him tackle me. Instead, I watch as he savagely rips the cords of the blankets with his bare hands, snapping the sturdy leather like it's nothing. He flings the blankets down onto the cave floor with unimaginable speed, and then turns to look at me, eyes blazing.

A shiver moves through me. He's so . . . brutal with his need. That is so damn sexy.

Then, he reaches over to me and grabs the front of my dress, then pulls me forward for a savage kiss. Hot prickles of need skitter through me and I moan against his mouth, my hands going to his neck.

"My Kira," he says roughly, and then pushes me onto my back, onto the furs. He jerks my skirts up around my thighs, and the next thing I know, he's facedown between my legs, his tongue seeking my clit.

A loud gasp of surprise escapes me.

He groans between my thighs, and I feel his tongue move over my sensitive flesh again. "You're so *wet*." He lifts his head and I see a feral gleam in his eyes as he licks his lips, shining with my juices.

Aehako rears back and rips at his loincloth. His cock emerges, a darker blue than the rest of him, the crown gleaming with pre-cum. I could stare at it for hours, but all I get is the briefest glimpse before he's on top of me, and his hand moves to my hair. His mouth captures mine—

And then he sinks in completely, thrusting into me in one hard movement.

My cry is swallowed by his lips and his seeking tongue. I cling to him, because, oh God, the sensation of him inside me is making my khui go into overdrive. It feels as if everything inside me is vibrating, and that only makes Aehako's cock feel that much better. I feel his spur rubbing against my clit, and my legs jerk, because I already feel like I'm about to come.

"Am I hurting you?" His voice is a gruff whisper against my jaw as he nips at my chin.

I manage a breathless shake of my head. "Feels good," I tell him. "Good" is perhaps an understatement, but I'm not sure that my lips will form around the words "earth-shattering."

His hips move and he pushes deep into me again. A moan escapes me, and my legs quake again. I'm going to come with just two thrusts, I know it. I raise my legs and lock them around his hips, just under his tail. Aehako growls again and thrusts once more, and I feel my khui hit a fever pitch with its humming. All I can hear is the song between us, and then as he sinks deep into me again, stars explode behind my eyes. I come, and come, and come . . . and I don't stop. It feels as if I come forever when he thrusts into me with powerful, needy strokes. Then he groans my name and his body stiffens on top of me, and he comes inside me as my body clenches and quivers around him.

Aehako drops on top of me, panting. He puts his weight on his elbows so he doesn't crush me, and nuzzles me with kisses on my neck and jaw as we try to catch our breath.

When my entire body no longer feels like it's about to splinter with sheer pleasure, I sigh heavily. "Wow." I'm pretty sure the furs are shoved up under my butt. I'm also pretty sure that was probably only three minutes or so of sex. I can't even be sorry about that, because I'm pretty sure I came harder than I ever have before.

He leans on his side and presses a hand between my breasts. "Your khui is pleased."

"Is it?" I place my hand next to his. The humming has gone down a bit, but it's still going strong. Even at those small touches, my nipples harden and my legs jerk, making me acutely aware that he's still inside me . . . and still hard.

And I'm still aroused.

"Um," I say, and stroke a hand down his arm. "How long does resonance last?"

"Until I plant a kit inside you." He kisses my jaw. "It might take many, many days."

Dear God. I will die of pleasure overdose. What a way to go. "But I'm ovulating right now, right? That's why I resonated?"

"What is ovu-lay—"

"Never mind," I say. That must be it. He wouldn't be able to make me pregnant otherwise, and all the others seemed to make it through their resonance all right. Wrecked, happy, but still whole.

His hips move, and I feel his cock drag in and out of me

again, the movement slow. I moan, arching up. "Oh God, are we going again?"

"We will go again many, many times," he tells me with a nipping kiss. "And then you will carry my kit." His hand goes to my belly. "This is mine," he murmurs. His hand slides lower. "And this is mine," he says, brushing a hand over where his spur grazes my clit. "Your cunt is mine and mine alone, sweet Kira."

I moan, because it feels like I'm about to start coming again. "All yours, Aehako."

"And then we will move back to the main cave so you can be near the healer—"

I shake my head even as he presses his thumb on the other side of my clit, sending ripples of pleasure through me. "I don't want to."

"No?" He sounds surprised.

"No," I say, and I'm confident. For some reason, I trust my khui. "I won't need the healer. Things will be fine. And this is where we're meant to be." I gaze up at the painted walls of my cave and feel a surge of joy. "We're home."

"My home is wherever you are," Aehako tells me.

I touch his face gently. "I feel the same way."

BONUS EPILOGUE

FUTURES

Kira

I take my time waking up.

It's not that I'm particularly tired. I've slept well, and with Aehako sprawled over the furs, he acts as my personal space heater. I'm warm and toasty tucked under his arm, and his body presses against mine from behind, reminding me of the solid, comforting presence of my mate. If I close my eyes, I can still hear our khui purring, though the sound is very muted now that resonance is satisfied. That's not the reason I'm lounging in bed, though.

Instead, I revel in the quiet. I wallow in the complete and utter lack of danger. Of stress. Of worry.

There's no translator in my ear to bother my sleep or to amplify the noises of my neighbors. There are no aliens chirping, reminding me that they're coming back to get us. The bad guys are gone, dead. The translator is removed. And me, who thought I would never resonate to anyone, I've resonated to Aehako, the man I love above all others, the man who fiercely declared me as his long before his khui decided to get on board. Now that resonance is satisfied, we've made a child between us, a human-alien hybrid that will be born to loving, excited parents. I'm not barren as I'd always been told. I'm carrying my love's baby.

Everything is perfect.

I don't trust perfect.

It makes me nervous. Ever since I arrived here, there's been something to worry about. Something to stress over. The alien people here are lovely and friendly, but there was always the worry that I'd get kicked out because I couldn't have children, or that Aehako would resonate to someone else right under my nose. Those worries are gone, and we've moved to a new cave with part of the tribe to start our life together.

I don't know how to do that. I'm a little terrified to move straight into "happy ever after." Part of me is waiting for the other shoe to fall, for something to go wrong and prove to me that I don't really get to be happy. Not really. That it's just a dream and I'll wake up and reality will hit me in the face once more.

They're stupid fears, but I can't help feeling them. I lie in bed and turn these thoughts over in my head as my mate breathes deep and easy, his breath fanning my hair. I don't even mind that Aehako has morning breath. I kinda love it, for the sheer normalcy of it. I love that his arm is pinning mine and I'm losing feeling in my hand. I welcome all of it because it means we're together.

So I lie quietly and just drink in the moment. I know exactly when Aehako starts to rouse. His cock presses against my backside, half-hard and prominent. He groans and nuzzles at my hair, then dips his head against my neck, his horn grazing my scalp as he kisses my shoulder. His arms tighten around me. "This is an excellent way to rouse," he murmurs, still sleepy. "How long have you been awake?"

"Not long," I lie. "Resonance is quiet."

"It is," he agrees, pressing another kiss to my shoulder. "I suppose we must rejoin the tribe now."

The amusement in his voice makes me smile. That's one of the things I love so much about Aehako. Whereas I greet the world with worry, he wakes with a smile. And instead of chastising me for being a worrywart, he feels it's his duty to spread those smiles to me. He never makes me feel like I'm a problem, or that I'm a bummer. He just loves me for me, and I pull his arm tighter around me. "I love you."

Aehako grunts. "You have my heart, Sad Eyes, but what brings this up? What troubles you?"

He's sensitive to my moods, this big alien man, and I feel guilty that I'm ruining things already. "I'm just worried that I'm too happy now."

He kisses my temple, then my ear, where I still have puncture holes from the translator. "Because all of your old worries have been resolved, your mind must create new ones?"

"That's exactly it. Silly, isn't it?"

"Not silly," he tells me. "We have had many storms recently. It is not foolish to mistrust the quiet."

"Then how do we get past it?"

He chuckles, and his breath moves over me, perfect and hot. "One day at a time, my heart."

It's the right answer. I wish there was a better one, perhaps, but I know he's right. I turn in his arms. "What are you doing today, then?"

Aehako rubs his big, blunt nose against mine. "I have traps near here that I have neglected. I was far too busy putting a kit inside you." His hand skims over my lower belly. "So I must check those and bring back any game. And tonight, I will let my mate bathe me in our new tub." He tilts his chin, gesturing at the big, decorated skull in the corner.

"Oh wow, I get to bathe you?" I tease. "How lucky am I?"

"You should know I am quite a prize," he tells me with a grin. "Asha will be most jealous."

I make a face at the thought of Asha. She's made it clear that she's not content with her mate and wants Aehako for herself. In a way, I get it. Asha is miserable, and Aehako makes everyone happy. But Aehako is mine and I don't want to share. "Maybe you should have Asha come and scrub your back, then."

"No," he says thoughtfully, pretending to consider my words. "She is rough with her hands—"

I smack his shoulder, and Aehako grins and tugs me down into the furs, kissing me until I squeal with laughter. We roll around like fools for a few minutes, until I'm breathless and aroused, and Aehako is giving me heated looks with his eyes. We pause, gazing up at one another, and then Aehako groans, pressing his forehead to mine. "Much as I want to stay in the furs and roll around, I must do my duty. It will not set a good example for the leader of the South Cave to stay in the furs all day long."

I give him a quick kiss. "You do what you have to do."

And I'll try to get over my strange, silly worry about how things are too perfect.

The moment I emerge from the cave I share with Aehako, Josie is all over me.

"This is wonderful!" she cries out, loud enough to wake anyone sleeping nearby, and flings her arms around me. "I'm so happy for you! Was it everything you dreamed of and more?"

Embarrassed, I endure Josie's enthusiastic hugging, trying

not to make eye contact with anyone else who watches us from over her shoulder. I was so wrapped up in resonance with Aehako—wonderful, wonderful resonance—that I forgot all the knowing looks we'd get when we emerged from our cave. Not that I'd change anything, but for someone as quiet as me, it's a lot of attention.

To make matters worse, my mate emerges from our cave a moment later, adjusting his loincloth as if we just finished. I know he's doing that on purpose to tease me. He *loves* to tease me. I still flush bright red and give Josie another squeeze. "It was . . . nice."

"Nice? Just nice?" She looks horrified and betrayed by my answer. "Kira! You just made a baby with the man you love! It has to be better than just 'nice'!"

Oh my God, why is she so very loud? "It was . . . nice," I manage to choke out. "Very nice."

Aehako moves forward to where I'm trapped in Josie's arms and leans in to whisper in my ear. "If 'nice' is all I get, I shall have to work harder tonight."

I blush, and Josie chortles even more. She's a whirlwind of excitement this morning, grabbing me by the arm and tugging me toward the firepit that's been established as the "community" fire. "I just made breakfast. You can come tell me all about it."

"About it?" I echo.

"Resonance," Josie agrees firmly. "I want to hear everything."

"Spare no detail, my mate," Aehako calls after me, grinning. "Fill her ears with how glorious I am. I do not mind."

Glorious. Right. He is pretty incredible, and I love him, but I'm not telling Josie any of that. I let her tug me along toward the fire, where Tiffany sits with Kemli, Farli, and Vaza. Farli and

Vaza are both sharpening their spears, and Kemli is sipping tea and talking quietly with Tiffany, who has a sewing project in her lap. Everyone of course looks up the moment I arrive with Josie, but their smiles are welcoming, at least. "Hi," I say quietly. "Good morning."

Josie practically pushes me into a seat. "You relax. I'll get you food and tea." She leans over the fire, grabbing a bowl and a cup, and gets to work. As she does, I admire how much the cave has changed since we arrived. When Aehako and I first scouted this place, it was nearly bare, as everything usable was taken to the main cave when it was abandoned fifteen years ago. Aehako and I have been squirreled away in our cave for days now, feeding the mating frenzy that is resonance, and so I haven't really been out to see the changes made here in the cave. I'm not surprised to see that it's smoky inside, a bit more than I'd like, but I'm willing to put up with that more than the cold. It's a little dark, but the ceiling here is high and stalactites dangle above like icicles. That I expected, of course, but I'm surprised to see that the lowest-hanging stalactites have had cords strung between them, with bundles of leaves and strips of meat hanging off to dry. Someone must have spent time standing on someone else's shoulders to get those done. The cozy firepit has seats with pillows settled around it, and baskets line the walls. Off in the distance, I see a stretched-out hide frame where someone has set up their skinning project.

It looks like a home, and it makes me happy, smoky or not.

Josie practically shoves a bowl into my hands. "Here! Try this! It's seeds and some of those not-potato things. I think it's delicious. Haeden says it tastes like dung-cakes, but then I asked him why he was tasting dung-cakes and he got all pissy and stormed off." She flutters her lashes, all innocence. "Here I was trying to be nice and make breakfast, and he had to be an ass about it."

I smile at her, taking the bowl. Josie knows as well as I do that the sa-khui people aren't big fans of the not-potato root that we humans have been obsessed with. My guess is she deliberately made food he wouldn't like. They love to prick at each other. I guess there's someone like that in every family, even on an ice planet. I take a big mouthful of the food and it tastes a lot like unflavored oatmeal. Not my favorite, but at the same time, it reminds me of home, and I decide I'm going to eat every bite. "So how are you settling in, Josie? Tiffany?"

Tiffany holds up her sewing project. "I'm making housewarming gifts. These are bowl cradles because those bone bowls get hot sometimes." She flips it inside out, showing me the stuffing she's putting inside. "It's like a pot holder but for your plate."

"Oh, that's awesome. You're so clever, Tiff." I smile at her. The sa-khui have work-roughened, tough hands, but our fragile human palms have been burned on a bowl or two before.

"Isn't she?" Josie sighs. "She's so smart. She thinks of all this good stuff and all I think about is resonance." She props her chin up on her hands, her elbows on her knees, as she sits next to me. "And, like, if I'm ever going to have it happen."

"It will come for you," Vaza says, giving Josie a friendly look. "It comes for all fertile females. Wait and see."

Tiffany makes a disapproving noise in her throat. "You make it sound like a plague."

Vaza chuckles, his gaze resting on Tiffany. "It is a great gift, make no mistake. But if you are not ready for resonance, there are others who would happily be a pleasure mate to you until then. All you need to do is ask."

Tiffany says nothing, simply stabs at her sewing a little more vigorously. I chew a big mouthful of food, feeling awkward at the tension here. Is Vaza . . . hitting on Tiff? Right in front of everyone? It's great to get a little attention now and then if you want it, but Tiffany has not encouraged anyone at all, and it's clear she doesn't reciprocate.

As if she senses the human discomfort, Kemli clucks her tongue. She gets up from her seat, abandoning her leaves, and smacks Vaza lightly on one of his horns. "Leave the human females alone. You are taking Farli hunting, yes? Go hunt, then. You will find no prey at this fire, you old rutting beast."

Vaza just laughs and rustles Farli's dark hair, mussing it. "Your mother has spoken. Are you ready to catch a fine hopper today?"

Oh, that reminds me. "If you get a chance, look for scythe-beak? That's Aehako's favorite and he says there's a lot of them near here." My mate has talked about roasted scythe-beak ever since I've known him. "If not, that's all right, too. I should probably learn how to hunt them."

"You can't go hunting," Josie protests, giving me a horrified look. "You just got knocked up! You have to give the baby time to settle in before you go running around."

"It's not going to fall out of her, Jo," Tiffany jokes. "I'm sure she's fine if she wants to hunt."

I shove another spoonful of food into my mouth since it prevents me from having to speak up. Fortunately, Aehako arrives with his spear in hand. He approaches me with single-minded intensity and presses a kiss to my head. I offer him my spoon, and he takes a mouthful of my breakfast, then grunts and tells me, "You taste better."

I make a strangled sound as Vaza chortles.

"Um, so are you hunting today? Can I go with you?" I ask.

After days together, entwined in the furs, it feels weird for him not to be at my side constantly. I'm probably going to turn into one of those clingy types obsessed with her man, but after years of being lonely, I feel like I'm allowed.

For a moment, Aehako looks stricken. He tugs on a limp piece of my hair, and I can feel his tail snake around my waist. "I would love it, Sad Eyes, but I need to check my traps and it's a long haul for human legs. We can hunt tomorrow, if you like?"

"Like there will be any hunting that takes place," Josie giggles, and Farli joins in.

"Tomorrow," I say softly, smiling up at him. "I'll figure out a way to stay busy here, then."

My big blue alien grins. "When I return, you can show me how much you missed me."

I wonder if I'm going to spend the rest of my life blushing around this man. Probably. For some reason, the idea doesn't bother me as much as it should. In fact, it sounds kind of fun.

Aehako

A short time later, I gaze out at the twisting canyons that hug the valley that the South Cave is located in. The air feels fresher today, the bite of the wind crisp and inviting. It does not matter that the skies are overcast and it smells like snow. Today is an excellent day.

Farli giggles at me as she heads past with Vaza. "You're still thinking about your mate, aren't you?"

"Always," I say with a grin. "It will make me hurry home once I have done my duty." Even now, I want to drag Kira away to our cave and press kisses on her skin again. I like to go hunting, and I enjoy a jog through the snows and checking my traps, but I also miss my mate. I know I have to do my part to feed the tribe, but it does not mean I will not lick my lips over and over again for a lingering taste of her. "I will not be able to bring home great amounts of meat like you, Farli, but I will hopefully bring back something."

"If not, I'm going to steal your mate from you and feed her," Farli teases back. "Since you cannot."

I chuckle, because I love such confidence in one as thin and gangly as Farli. She reminds me of my youngest brother, Sessah, who is back in the other cave. "I will work doubly hard, then."

"See that you do." Farli tosses her mane and gives Vaza a look. "Let us go, then. Kira wants scythe-beak tonight."

Vaza barks a laugh and gestures with his spear. "Lead the way, little one."

I watch as they go, Farli all swagger and Vaza her amused mentor. Rubbing my chest, I feel for the thrum of my khui. It is quiet without Kira's presence here, and it is strange, but I miss it. I have always said I did not need resonance, but now that I have it with Kira . . . I am addicted. I understand more than ever the dazed look on Vektal's face, or Raahosh's wild actions. I cannot think straight when my mate is near, because my thoughts are all hers. I panic at the thought of her being in danger again.

And to think I nearly lost her . . .

My gut clenches and I force the thought out of my mind. If I think about such things, I will never leave the cave—or Kira's side—again. I will be useless to all. Perhaps my mate's thoughts are affecting me. Kira does not know how to act when she is happy. I am looking forward to a lifetime of showing her just how to be happy every single day.

But first, I must check my neglected traps. Smiling to myself, I jog off in the opposite direction of Farli and Vaza, determined to enjoy the day.

After all, I have a pretty mate at the cave waiting for my return home.

Kira

I decide that if we're starting fresh, it's time to take the bull by the horns. I'm going to talk to Asha. She's here in the South Cave with her mate, Hemalo, and I was initially unhappy at the fact that they were coming with us. This is going to be our home, though, and the tribe is small. I'm determined not to let a single person destroy things. We're both adults—we can talk and hash things out like adults, and come to a truce of some kind.

Hopefully.

But because I don't like confrontation, I sit by the fire for a while first. Tiffany and Josie remain there, chatting, and we catch up on things. It feels good to talk with my friends, to look at their faces and know they're well. Josie is all enthusiasm. She hopes the new change will mean that her khui will resonate to one of the single hunters that joined us here. Tiffany is more reticent, and I notice she's quiet. Perhaps she likes this change less. I make a mental note to talk with her in private, once things have settled. "I haven't seen Claire," I point out to the others. "Is she all right?"

"Her and Bek were arguing this morning," Josie whispers. "She stayed with him last night and I heard them snapping at each other first thing."

Ah. Another problem, but not one for today. Bek is one of the more overbearing hunters, and Claire is a meek, sweet thing . . . until she gets pushed. I can't blame her for wanting to find a bit of security, but I do worry that if they're arguing this quickly, it's not a good sign for the relationship. She won't appreciate me interfering, so I'm going to stay the heck out of it. "No resonance between them?"

"Nope," Tiffany says. "I'm staying out of it."

I nod. Wise words.

When Josie heads off to find Hemalo and work on skins and Tiffany finishes her project, I decide I can avoid it no longer. I get up from my spot by the fire and dust off my leathers, heading for one of the caves farther back in the winding tunnel of the South Cave. I don't remember which one Asha was in, just that she was complaining about it being small. I move toward the back caves, and as if she senses my presence, Asha ducks out of her cave's entrance and straightens.

We make eye contact, and I'm struck again at how beautiful Asha is.

She's tall, as all the sa-khui are. Her horns curve gracefully against the thick black waves of her hair, and her eyes are bright and thickly lashed. Whereas my Aehako's features are blunt, Asha's delicate blue features seem to be carved by a master sculptor, with full pouty lips, high cheekbones, and a perfectly straight nose. She's gorgeous, though that gorgeousness is usually marred by her shitty attitude. Her gaze flicks over me, resting over my chest for a brief moment. "Resonance is fulfilled, I see."

"Yes," I say, and I'm surprised at how calm my voice is. "And I wanted to talk to you."

"I am sure you have plenty to say to me," she says in an arch, cold voice. "You need not worry. Once resonance takes a male, he has no interest in another." She shrugs and holds a pouch out to me. "This is for you."

This . . . isn't what I expected. A gift? I take it from her and peek inside. It looks like . . . leaves. "Thank you?"

She puts her hands on slim hips, her tail flicking behind her. "It is a tea. For mornings. When you carry a kit, a great many things can sour the belly. I found that this tea helped me quite a bit."

I gape at her. She's giving me pregnancy tea? Here I came over to give her a piece of my mind and set firm boundaries, and she's being . . . nice. I suddenly feel like the world's largest asshole. Asha's surrounded by people resonating and getting pregnant. She's the only one in the tribe who has resonated and has no baby to show for it, and now she's estranged from her mate. Of course she's struggling. Sure, she tried to sleep with my mate, but resonance has soothed away any hurt that might have lingered there. Asha's offering an olive branch, and the least I can do is take it. "Thank you. I'm really touched. I'm sure this will come in handy."

"It is not poison." Her mouth curves into a tight smile. "Coming from me, I am sure you had your doubts, but I know what it is like to be pregnant. I can at least help on that front."

"Of course," I say softly. I try to think of something to say. Something that won't come across as awkward as she watches me expectantly. Then, the perfect idea hits me. "I wanted to talk to you." When the look in her eyes grows wary and shuttered, I charge on ahead. "You mentioned that your cave was small. There are other caves here, right? Not all of them are full. We can get you a different one, and I'll help you move your stuff."

Her wary expression softens, as if she was expecting me to lash out. Maybe Asha's been waiting for the other shoe to drop as well.

"I would like that," she says, and smiles.

Aehako

I am a fool, I decide, as I gaze down at the half-dead dvisti snared in my trap. A fool to set traps this far away, even if they always produce results. I scrub a hand down my face and contemplate the sheer size of the creature. Most dvisti are agile, lean things. This one is older, with a head so shaggy it looks like two dvisti piled into one. The hooves are enormous, and it lies on the ground like a sodden lump, my snare trapped around one shattered leg. I thought the thing was dead until it twitched as I approached.

It is a lot of meat. A lot. I rub my jaw, considering. The nearest cache is brimful, and if I decide to cache the creature, I will have to dig to the side of the pit, making it wider. I cannot lay my meat atop the cache and simply go on my way. Too close to the surface and it will draw the attention of metlaks, who can scent out fresh meat from a great distance. I squint at my surroundings. I am a good distance from the South Cave, and if I take the meat back with me, I will not return until late.

If I dig an addition to the pit, I will return late.

I put my hands on my hips, glaring down at the dvisti. "You had better not taste stringy, my friend. Already you are more trouble than you are worth. I have a mate to return back to." A mate that has consumed my thoughts all day long. A mate that I long to see again, as if we have been apart for a very long time. I want to see Kira's smile, her beautiful eyes when she gazes up at me. I want to drink in her scent and rub my face on her soft, soft mane. I have been looking forward to my return home. My other traps were full of meat as well, a few fresh hoppers and one trap that had been cleaned out by metlaks before I could return. It happens, but now I am presented with an abundance of meat and not enough time left in the day to handle it all.

If Kira were here . . . she would give me a patient look and blink quietly, waiting for me to come to an answer. I would tease her, make her blush, and then we would share the burden, with me carrying the dvisti and her handling the hoppers. It would not matter how late we were out, because we could simply stop at a hunter cave for the night and spend our time alone, in each other's arms.

The last thing I want is to stay at a hunter cave tonight, though. Now that I have a mate, I want to be with her. I want to feel her body under mine. I want to hear Kira's cries as I stroke inside her. My cock rises just thinking about it.

Cache it is, then. I will dig more out, skin and dump the old dvisti, and then head home to my pretty mate and spend tonight between her thighs, licking her cunt until she wakes the entire cave. Grinning to myself at the thought, I bend over the dvisti to cut the creature's throat. What will Kira say when I show her the shaggy, ridiculous pelt of this thing—

One of the big hooves kicks the moment my knife sinks into the creature's throat. It connects with my ankle and sends me tumbling to the ground with a bellow of pain.

I roll on the snow, clutching my leg as the white-hot pain throbs through it. When it finally subsides into a dull ache, I want to laugh at myself for being such a fool. I am so besotted with my mate and imagining her smiles that I did not back away from the dvisti's legs like I should have. The other hunters will laugh uproariously at me—and deservedly so. It is a move that only the newest of young hunters makes.

Wincing, I run a hand down my leg. The skin is broken from the contact, blood making the leather of my boot stick to my skin and crust up with the cold. My ankle is starting to swell, and I test putting my weight on it. Another lance of hot pain shoots through me, and I groan, falling backward.

Experimentally, I wiggle my toes. Nothing broken. Hurts, yes, but nothing is snapped. I need to stay off of it for a bit, let my khui mend my leg, and then limp back into camp with my tail tucked between my legs at the foolish thing I have done.

"Looks like you and I will be here for a while," I grunt to the now-dead dvisti as I shift my weight on the snow, getting comfortable. So much for seeing my mate this night. I will wait here tonight, endure the cold and bitter night, and then try my ankle in the morning.

I hope Kira does not worry too much. She will laugh at me when I return, but I worry her eyes will be sad until I am safely home, and I do not like that at all.

Kira

It's a long day without Aehako nearby, but I do my best to keep busy. I spend the morning with Asha, and we consider all the empty caves. The others all have flaws—ceiling too low, this one catches all the smoke, this one feels damp—and finally she decides she will stay in the one Aehako picked out for them. "I suppose this one is best," she says with a sniff. "If we must make do."

"If you're sure." I give her a patient smile. "You know everyone wants you to be happy here. This is your home as much as anyone else's."

She flashes a smile at me, all fangs and bright white teeth. "I do not love it, but perhaps I can grow to appreciate it as long as *someone* does not spread his mess everywhere." She glares at someone over my shoulder, and I inwardly wince to see it's mild, sweet Hemalo, who ignores his mate entirely. He picks up a tool from a basket and leaves the cave once more without saying a word to her.

Yeah, that's uncomfortable. I murmur my excuses and escape, spending the rest of the afternoon working on sewing proj-ects near the fire. As Aehako's mate, I'm expected to make his clothes for him. Hemalo has always made his clothes for him in the past—as he and Kashrem have done for all the unmated males—but since we are mated now, that duty falls to me. It feels a little . . . sexist, but I remind myself that I can go hunting with him in the future, and I can show him how to make his own damn clothes.

And . . . he has been looking a little raggedy. So I get to work on a leather kilt for him, piecing together bits from different leathers and making belt loops at the waist. His leather belt has been looking rather sketch as well, so I talk to Hemalo about making a new one for him. It's one of my first times to actually chat with Hemalo and I'm surprised at how sweet he is. He's an attentive listener, and kind. He shows me a few strips of leather that he's been working patterns into, and I pick one out for Ae-hako. It needs a carved bone loop at the end, but my mate can handle that part.

Even when he's not here, Aehako seems to be consuming my thoughts. I suppose it's normal for a recently resonated couple, and I kinda like it. I like having my mate on the brain. It makes me feel less alone, like he's just in the next room. Obsessive, maybe, but I don't care.

Since I haven't done my share of the chores around the cave lately thanks to resonance, I take over the evening stew from Sevvah. I chop bits of not-potato into it, stir in a truckload of herbs to go with the meat, and let it simmer, occasionally adding a few bits of root here and there for flavor. Working on a big batch of stew helps my mind stay occupied, and I watch the en-trance of the cave, waiting for Aehako's return. I can't wait to see his big smile, to hear his easy laughter. I can't wait for him to kiss my cheek and make some sort of innuendo that'll leave me blushing and excited for alone time with him.

The others come and go from the fire, teasing me about where my big, strong mate is. I take it all in stride, because I know Aehako is loved by everyone and a resonance is a happy occasion. By the time the stew is almost gone, I feel as if I've seen every hunter make their way in from the cold. Even Haeden, who is moving slower due to his recently healed wounds, has returned from hunting with a kill, and Farli and Vaza return, too.

"Any sign of Aehako?" I ask Vaza as I give him a bowl of food.

Vaza just shakes his head. "He probably went far. Aehako always did like setting his traps a good distance away from the rest of us. Now it is biting him in the tail." He grins and gives me a knowing look. "He will return home soon enough, knowing that you are waiting for him."

Sevvah swats Vaza with her tail as she walks past. "Do not embarrass her. This one is shy, you old fool."

"How can she be shy? She is mated to Aehako. He is the loudest of us all." Vaza is all innocence as he begins to eat.

I sit down with my bowl and pick at my food. If I peek outside, I can see the twin suns are going down, the snows outside turning purplish with twilight. Exactly how far out were his traps? Should we be worried?

When it gets dark, I start panicking. I clean up, frantic as I scrub snow in the stew pouch, making it ready to use for the next person. I'm seconds away from tears, but if I have something to focus on, I won't lose my shit. Not quite yet.

"You okay?"

I look up to see Claire and Bek heading in, both of them dressed in heavy fur cloaks. They went out for a walk after dinner and now they're coming back because it's dark and my mate is still missing and what if he's in a canyon dead and I won't know until we find his frozen corpse a year from now and—

I burst into tears, sobbing.

"Oh no," Claire exclaims. "What did I say?" She moves to my side, rubbing my shoulder. "Kira, what is it?"

I swipe at my face, feeling foolish for bursting into tears. "Aehako went out hunting early this morning and hasn't returned. I'm worried."

Bek crosses his arms, frowning. He's a hard one to get to know, since he makes it a point to only really talk to Claire. Bek's one of those people who is perfectly content having one friend alone, unlike Aehako, who wants to be everyone's friend. "Sometimes hunting can take longer than expected. He might be staying in a hunter cave tonight."

"Fresh off resonance?" Claire asks.

Bek grunts. "It does not seem likely, no." He gestures at the cave. "You go inside, Claire. I will go looking for him."

"At night?"

He will? I straighten, desperate and so damn glad that Bek is volunteering. "Can I go with you? Please?"

They exchange a look.

"I'll keep up," I say desperately. "I'll run the entire time if I have to. I just need to see him." The other shoe has dropped, just as I expected. Maybe the universe isn't going to let me be happy after all. But I'm going to fight every step of the way if that's the case. Aehako is mine and I'm keeping him. "If you won't let me come with you, I'm going to go on my own."

Bek makes an irritated noise. "Are all you humans so stubborn?"

"Yes," I say at the same time Claire does.

"Come on, then." He gestures at me. "Dress warmly and wear heavy boots."

We race through the darkness, the snow crunching under our boots. Bek has his spear in hand and we carry no torch, because he can see just fine in the dark. He leads the way and, at Claire's suggestion, holds one end of a strap. I hold the other end, staggering along a few paces behind him. The strap allows me to follow behind him in the darkness without getting lost. There's not much light—the skies are cloudy with no sign of moonlight—and something howls in the distance. I'm not afraid, though. At least, not of that. I'm terrified for Aehako, and my only thought is to get to him, and quickly.

Thank God for Bek. He moves swiftly through the darkness, and I don't care that he's not chatty in the slightest. He's fast and efficient and isn't slowing down for my sake, which I'm thankful for. I don't bother making conversation—I save my breath for desperate gulps as I trot after him, exhausted but determined to keep going.

Aehako is somewhere out here. I know he'd come home if he could, because he can't leave me behind. Something has happened. We'll find him, I tell myself. Just keep one foot in front of the other. Just keep one foot in front of the other. Just keep—

I plow into Bek's back, then fall to the ground.

"Hsst," he says, lifting a hand in the shadows. "I hear something."

I stare up at Bek, a little dazed from crashing into him. The snow is cold under my butt, and I fell in an awkward position, but I remain utterly still, straining to hear. For the first time, I wish I had that stupid translator device sticking out of my ear again, because it amplified sound. I wait, and wait, hearing nothing.

Bek suddenly cups a hand to his mouth, tilting his head back. "*HO!*"

A distant voice calls back, "*Ho!*"

I burst into ugly, snotty tears at that. I know that voice. That's my Aehako. Swiping at my face with my sleeve, I sob as I get to my feet, and when Bek changes directions and starts climbing the slope of the nearest hill, I follow behind gladly. "We're coming!" I shout, unable to stay quiet. "We're coming, Aehako!"

"*Kira?*" He sounds closer.

"Quiet," Bek hisses at me. "Do you want to call every metlak in the mountains to our sides?"

"Sorry," I say, but I'm not sorry. My heart is pounding in my chest and I'm so relieved that Aehako is near that I want to choke with tears all over again. I'm desperate to see him. I need to run my hands all over my mate and know he's safe. Hot tears leak out of my eyes as I scramble up the hill behind Bek, but they're tears of relief at this point.

At the top of the hill, there's a few of the whiplike pink trees, and one thwacks me as the breeze picks up. Hair flutters around my face, but I'm not sure if it's mine or Bek's. He's paused at the top of the hill, scanning the area.

I get impatient that he's not moving. "Do we—"

"Hsst!" Bek glares at me over his shoulder. I can't even be mad at that. He heads off again, and we stumble through the darkness a little longer, and then I see the most beautiful sight ever.

It is my mate, leaning against a rock wall. He is covered in a filthy, shaggy fur, the horns sticking out the only reason I don't mistake him for a metlak. As we get closer, he grins with enthusiasm. "You brought my mate to me! Such a good friend you are, Bek."

"Where have you been, you fool?" Bek says by way of greeting as we approach. "Your female was worried sick."

I drop the tether that kept me on Bek's trail and race forward toward my mate. The heavy snow clings to my boots, sucking at my feet and keeping my movements slow, but I don't care. I surge my way forward, another sob escaping me as I fling myself into Aehako's arms. "You didn't come home," I weep. "I was worried."

"All is well, Sad Eyes," Aehako tells me, his hands roaming over my face and shoulders. "You should have stayed home."

"Fuck that," I exclaim. "I had to come looking for you! What happened?"

"I was distracted with thoughts of my pretty mate," Aehako says, his easy grin on his face as he tucks me against his chest. "I got too close to the foreleg of a dying dvisti and it kicked me right in the ankle. Nothing is broken, but it hurts to walk. I was going to wait until morning to put weight on it, but I thought of my lovely Kira in our furs alone and decided to chance it anyhow."

Bek makes a dismissive sound in his throat. "You should pay more attention."

"I should," Aehako agrees. "You have my thanks for coming to retrieve this foolish, foolish hunter."

I snuggle against Aehako's chest, suddenly exhausted. All of the worry I've been carrying for the last few hours has crashed, and I'm left depleted. Relieved, but depleted. I pull away from my mate and adjust the fur around his shoulders. "Let's get you home. You—" I pause as I touch the fur. "Why is this wet?"

"It grew cold and the dvisti fur was just sitting there, so I skinned it as best I could." Aehako chuckles. "I am going to need a good bath when we get home, Sad Eyes. Are you up for it?"

I fight back a shudder of revulsion at the realization he's wearing a bloody pelt. He did what he had to in order to survive. I can't judge.

"Where is the meat?" Bek asks.

"Gone," Aehako replies. "Metlaks. I let them have it and they left me alone."

Bek grunts. "There is a hunter cave not too far from here. I'll lead you both there. It can be shelter tonight, and you can move on to the South Cave tomorrow."

That sounds like heaven to me. I move to Aehako's side and slide his heavy arm over my shoulders. "Lean on me to walk. Bek can lead the way."

Aehako

I should not be surprised to see my mate out in the snow with Bek, looking for me. My Kira is fiercely protective of those she loves. I ignore the pain that shoots up my leg with each step, doing my best not to lean on my mate's smaller form too much. Bek would be a much better choice to help me walk, but he needs to guard us and lead the way. The metlaks that stole my skinned kill might come back, so I pretend to lean on Kira and take each step of pain as my due. I want to hold her close and caress her, to reassure her that I am fine. To tease a smile back onto her face.

But mostly, I am just glad to see her. To hold her against me and know we are together, and that is all that truly matters.

We move slowly, far slower than I want to. The night is cold for a human, I imagine, but Kira does not protest. She does not drag her feet or try to get away when I accidentally lean heavily against her, or protest when Bek climbs up another hill and I am forced to use her help more than I would like. At the top of the hill, the hunter cave is tucked into the rock, the entrance narrow.

I know this spot, have stayed here many times before. It is a tight fit for two hunters and will be downright cozy for the three of us.

Bek pulls the skin aside and heads in to check it out while Kira and I limp toward it. He emerges a moment later with a nod. "It is safe and undisturbed."

"My thanks, brother," I tell him with a grateful smile.

"I will tell the others you both will be returning in the morning," he says. "I have no wish to share furs with you and your mate when my female is waiting for me." With a nod in my direction, he turns and heads off into the darkness.

Kira pauses. "Oh. He's not staying?"

"I do not think he wants to share warmth with us inside," I tease. "Humans have cold feet."

"You hush," she tells me, tapping a hand on my abdomen in mock reproach. "Let's get you inside and off that foot."

I like that idea very much. "And make a fire," I add. "In case the metlaks are lingering."

"Fire first," Kira agrees.

We squeeze our way inside the narrow opening of the cave. It is difficult for me as I try not to use my bad foot, and it makes balancing awkward. Inside the cave, it opens up a bit more, and I hop toward the rolled-up furs in the back, grabbing one and shaking it out. I hear Kira stumbling in the darkness behind me, her hands reaching out.

"You might have to lead me to the firepit," she says, breathless. "I can do my best in the dark, but it might take me a moment."

I have forgotten that humans have poor eyesight at night. Wincing, I drop to my knees, ignoring the throb of my injury. "I will start the fire and you can feed it, yes?" At her agreement, I get to work, and after a few moments of piling tinder and preparing the firepit, I find the pouch of fire-making tools left here for hunters. To my relief, they are spark rocks and not a bow and drill. Spark rocks are much faster, and I have no desire to do things the hard way this night. A few bangs of the rocks and I get a flare of light. I blow on it, making it eat the tinder, and then Kira is at my side, adding a fuel-cake to the side of the flame.

"Go relax," she tells me in a gentle voice, her lovely, strange human face lit up in firelight. "I have it now."

I stagger back toward the fur and lie back, hiding my wince as the movements send more pain up my leg. To think that the healer is back in the main cave. Maylak could fix this in mere moments. Now that she is not here, I will have to endure the twinges of my foolishness for several days. Ah well. At least I have good company. I put my hands behind my head, watching my mate as she leans over the flame, pursing her pink lips as she blows on the fire. Even though I am in pain, it is quite an enticing view. I watch as she continues to tend the fire, making it grow. She has learned a lot in the short time she has been here, and I am proud of my Kira. "You did not have to come after me, Sad Eyes," I tell her. "I would have made it home in the morning and we would have had a good laugh at my tale."

She sits up, and the look she gives me is miserable. "I was worried something happened. That you wouldn't be able to come home at all." Her breath hitches. "That the other shoe had dropped and I'd lost you."

"Why would you lose me?" I keep smiling, but I ache at the misery in her voice.

"Because the universe won't allow me to be happy!" Her eyes are full of tears. "I keep thinking something is going to happen, some change that will remind me that I don't get you. I don't get our baby." Her hand goes to her middle, pressing against her leathers. "That it's all going to come crashing down on me and then I'll be alone again."

"Kira," I say gently, pulling her toward me. "I promise you, I am not going anywhere."

She allows me to pull her close, tucking herself against me. "You can't make that promise. You don't know."

"I do know. I am a good hunter, at least most of the time. Today I was distracted, hurrying to return to you." I chuckle, rubbing her back. "It was a good lesson, because it taught me that I need to pay attention, even when my thoughts are determined to fill with visions of my pretty mate taking down her courting gift because she misses me."

Kira smacks my chest lightly. "I would not."

"Shame," I tease. "But I know how to hunt, my heart. I know how to take care of myself. There will be some hunts where I return late. There will be some where it will take me away for several nights, but I will always come back to you. I promise you this."

My mate sighs heavily. "Everyone has to do their share of hunting," she says, her voice reasonable. "I know you can't just stay close to the cave and, like, pick only small game."

"We cannot hunt much in the brutal season," I point out. "That is when all the meat is needed, and I will be by the fire so often you will be ready for me to head out on the trails for several days again." I rub her back once more. "But until then, I must hunt as much meat as possible. There are a great many more mouths to feed now, and I do not wish for anyone to go hungry."

"I know." She shifts against my chest. "Can I go with you sometimes? I want to learn how to hunt, too. Or not that I *want* to learn, but I should probably do it anyhow."

"Of course. I would enjoy that greatly. We will stay out for many days and get a great deal of hunting done, and at night we will share furs and I will make you cry out over and over again, until we have scared every metlak from these hills."

Kira sits up, giving me an annoyed look. Her expression changes, and she wrinkles her nose as she studies me. "You are positively gross right now. What's all that dark stuff on you?"

She is just now noticing? She must have been distracted indeed. "Blood from the skinned dvisti, I imagine." I swipe at a sticky spot on my brow. "I did not have time to scrape the pelt."

Making a gagging sound in her throat, Kira moves back. "You need a bath."

"Now this sounds like a hunter's welcome home," I tease, giving her an enticing look. "You are going to wipe me down?"

"I am," she declares. "And when you're clean, I'm going to get on top of you for sex, because I won't have you hurting your ankle more than you already have."

This sounds . . . excellent. I relax in the furs, lying back. "Have your way with me, my stern, disapproving mate. Show me how naughty I have been, allowing myself to get wounded."

The look she shoots me is withering, but only for a moment. Then she breaks into a smile and leans forward, planting her hands on my face and kissing me sweetly. "I'm just really, really glad you're okay."

"You know I would not abandon you." I smile at her. "Not now, not ever."

"Big talk," Kira says to me, pressing a kiss to my blunt nose and then moving away. She heads for the fire, setting up a tripod with expert hands and then hanging a cooking pouch. "You seem to think you are invulnerable."

Does she truly think that? I chuckle to myself, and as she

heads out to the front of the cave with a carved bowl, I call after her, "I can assure you, after limping on a bad foot for half the night, the last thing I think I am is invulnerable."

My mate just gives me a long-suffering look as she fills the pouch with snow and waits for it to melt. When there is enough water, she dips a bit of fur into it and begins to wash me clean of the mess from the quickly skinned fur.

She is quiet. That means her mind is working. While I love her cleverness, I do not like when it is turned against me. "Are you angry, my heart? Or do I need to tease you out of your sadness?"

Kira shakes her head and continues to tenderly cleanse my skin, wiping away dried blood. "I'm not mad. I'm just trying to reconcile all of this with how I feel. I know you have to hunt. I know you have to put yourself in danger. I know this world isn't a safe place. At the same time, I don't like it. So I'm trying to wrap my head around the concept that some nights you won't come home, and I just have to assume you're fine and nothing is wrong."

I do not point out that I thought I had lost her recently. That when she went after the aliens, I was convinced I would never see her again and grief wracked me. She knows this. I suspect part of her anxiety over my injury right now is due to her recent brush with death, and the loss of Har-loh. It will take both of us some time to get over what has happened. So I consider all of this when I think of a response. "You did not have such fear when I went out hunting before we were mated. You did not stay up all night then, worrying over me. I am the same hunter I was a few weeks ago, Sad Eyes. Nothing else has changed except our khui have decided to bond us."

"More than that has changed," she says, and touches her stomach.

Ah. Our kit. Yes, that does change everything. It is not just Kira and Aehako. She continues to wash me, her mouth pressing into a firm line, and I can tell she is stewing. "There is no winning this argument, my heart. I do not even know why we are arguing."

"We're not," Kira says. She wets the fur again and then wipes down my shoulders. "I'm just trying to come to terms with having my heart outside of my chest like this. It's terrifying."

"You think I do not know this?" I capture her hand in mine and press a kiss to her wet knuckles.

She softens, giving me a little smile. "I know you do. I guess this is payback for when I went after the aliens, right?"

Payback? I frown at that. "What is this pay-back?"

"You know. I scared you, so now it's only fair that you scare me?"

Oh, my sweet mate. I pull her into my arms, ignoring the throb of my ankle when I shift my legs. "My Kira, there is no payback. This is not a game between us. We are mates. If I could figure out how to keep you from worrying when I go out to hunt, I would. But I must hunt. It is my duty to help with the tribe. It is my duty to make sure all mouths are fed."

"I know." She puts a hand on my chest, gazing at me thoughtfully. "I really do know, Aehako, and I don't want you to change for me."

"Then we compromise," I tell her. "When my ankle is better, we will go out hunting together, you and I. You will see what a skilled hunter I am, and if there is anything you are concerned about, we will address it. And I will teach you how to hunt, so I will not worry that you are helpless, either."

Kira's face brightens and her smile is wide. "I think that is an excellent idea. Thank you, Aehako. I love it."

I slide my hand down her flank. Covered she may be in furs, but she is still as enticing to me as if she were utterly bare. "Do not be so thankful yet. I might be a harsh teacher, impossible to please."

She responds to the tease in my voice and her expression grows heated. "You? A hard teacher? Does that mean you plan on spanking me if I don't obey?"

I am puzzled. "Why would I do that?"

"A sexy spanking?" she clarifies, then shakes her head. "Actually, just forget it. We'll talk about sexy spankings tomorrow." Her hand moves lower and tugs at the worn leather belt I wear to keep my loincloth in place. "I have other ideas of what to do tonight, since we're alone."

My grin turns into a groan as she lifts her hips and slides her hand between us, stroking my cock. My precious, perfect mate. So eager to touch me, so hungry in her need. I pull at her leathers, dragging my fingers through laces. "You said you wished to be on top, yes?" At her nod, I give up on unlacing her tunic and move to her leggings. "Then I will let you do all the work."

"You just lie back and enjoy," she agrees, a purr in her voice. Her khui is humming its pleasure at our joining, mine singing along with it. I love the feel of her slight weight over me, her hand on my shaft as she frees me from my leathers. She slides her leggings down her legs with quick, anxious movements, until they pool around one ankle only. "Close enough," she mutters, and then she seats herself over me, guiding my cock into her hot, wet warmth.

The breath hisses from my lungs as my shaft presses into her channel. So good. So very good.

"I love you," Kira breathes as she rocks her hips over me. It is not quite the same as when I thrust into her, but I like her on top of me. I like to see her bounce her weight atop my cock, to see the focused look of attention on her face as she works herself over me. "I love you, Aehako."

"My mate. My Kira." I grip her hips, helping her in her motions, and dragging her down with force when she falters. "Never be afraid of the future, my heart. No matter what happens, it is a future we will greet together, every day."

"Together," she agrees, leaning forward to kiss me. "I like the sound of that."

ICE PLANET HONEYMOON

AEHAKO & KIRA

Kira

I wake up to the sensation of the baby kicking my bladder. With a grimace, I get out of my warm bed, next to my sleeping mate, and make my way out to the designated "bathroom" area for the South Cave. The setup here isn't as nice as the main tribal cave, but we make do. It doesn't bother me most times . . . just when I have to wake up in the middle of the night to pee.

Which happens a lot more lately, come to think of it.

My toes curl on the cold stone floor and I get my business done as quickly as possible, then pour a bit of water into a bowl used for washing hands. It's cold this time of night and the water is turning into icy sludge, so I'm shivering by the time I make it back to the cave I share with Aehako. We had chamber pots in the cave for a while, but the concept makes my stomach turn, and with being pregnant, I can't have one in the living area. I just can't. I'll endure cold feet.

And so will my mate, I think impishly as I slide back under the covers and immediately stick my cold feet on him.

Aehako groans and grabs me, tucking me against his bigger body. "Cruel female."

"Don't you want to warm my toes for me?" I tease, snuggling up against him. Aehako is massive—bigger than a lot of the other sa-khui, who aren't a small people. I have to be the little spoon every time, but he's a sprawler and sometimes I wake up with him stealing all the blankets in his sleep. So he gets to warm my cold feet. Those are the rules.

He tucks me against him, brushing a hand on one of my cold feet as I curl it against his thigh and lie on my side once more. He tucks his arm around my waist, his lips against the top of my head.

The baby kicks again, this time doing an impressive kick instead of a slight flutter. I suck in a breath, surprised at the ferocity of it.

Aehako loses all of his drowsiness. He immediately stiffens against me, his hand splaying over my belly. "Are you well?"

"I'm fine," I promise him. "It was just a kick."

"But you drew in breath. Does it hurt?"

"It was just surprising. That's all. Go back to sleep." I cover his hand with mine and close my eyes, pretending to go back to sleep myself. All the while, the baby in my stomach has decided that it is most definitely not sleep time. It flips and kicks and moves around, and I can feel the tension brimming in Aehako's big body. He doesn't go back to sleep. I know he doesn't, because I know him. And so I wait.

It doesn't take long.

"Kira?"

"Mmm?"

"Are you asleep, my mate?" His lips brush over my hair, pressing a kiss there.

The baby kicks again, and even though I just peed, it feels

like I need to get up again. I knew being pregnant wouldn't be a barrel of fun, but sometimes I wish this kid would pick somewhere to sit other than my bladder. "I'm awake."

"Do you think the kit is well?" His hand caresses my belly, and I can hear the worry in his tone.

My heart squeezes. My Aehako is always laughing and so carefree, so easily confident. Yet lately, as my belly grows, so does the worry in his eyes. This isn't the first night he's been unable to go back to sleep, and I suspect it won't be the last. He's not going to sleep well until I have this baby . . . and that's months and months (and months) away from now. "I'm sure it's fine. Go back to sleep, love."

"But it is very active tonight."

"Sometimes it does that."

His hand slides over my belly. "What if it is trying to get our attention? What if something is wrong?"

"Nothing's wrong," I reassure him.

He doesn't sound convinced. "How is your stomach?"

I have the occasional bout of nausea thanks to strong smells, and every time I do, Aehako panics. It's like he can't stand the thought of me sick or hurting, which is kind of sweet. In the middle of the night, though? It's also kind of irksome. I remind myself that he's just worried. This is our first baby together. It's natural for him to be overprotective. "It's good." I make my voice sound as sleepy as possible. "Go back to bed, love."

Aehako just tugs me closer, burying his face in my hair. "You would tell me if it was not, yes?"

"I absolutely would, I promise."

He grunts and gets quiet, but I notice his hand stays protectively over my belly, and he twitches every time the baby kicks again, as if it's punching his insides and not mine.

My poor Aehako. It's strange, because normally out of the two of us, I'm the worrier. I'm the one that stresses over small things and tries to take the weight of the world on my shoulders. He's the lighthearted one, the laughing, teasing one that makes me forget all of my worries. When it comes to this pregnancy, though, our roles are reversed. I'm the one that takes everything in stride, and it's Aehako that has the sleepless nights and the constant fear. It's Aehako that hovers over me as if I'm fragile glass and won't let me do a thing around the cave that might disturb me.

He's making himself crazy. At some point, he's going to snap, because I don't think he can take another six months of this, which is what it sounds like I'm in for.

The baby shifts again, and I fight back a groan of irritation, because now I really do feel like I have to pee. But if I get up again, Aehako's going to panic.

There's no winning this.

"He is stressed," Kemli tells me as she hands me a cup of tea later that morning.

"Do you think so?" I take a sip, trying not to worry.

The elder sits across from me with her own cup, her expression wry. "All males get touchy when their female is with kit. It is not just the body that changes, but she gets tired. Her feet hurt. She craves strange foods." Kemli shrugs. "My Borran fussed and hovered with each of my kits. You would think a female had never had young before, the way he acted." Her mouth quirks, and then she sobers. "You must also remember that you are not with the healer, here in the South Cave."

"But . . . I feel fine," I protest. "There's no need to bother Maylak when I feel fine."

"I have known Aehako all his life," Kemli says wisely as she stirs her tea with a fingertip, pushing the leaves around. "He is all humor and charm, but he is also very protective. When he worries, he cannot hide his feelings behind a smile. Do you know that I offered to make bone broth with his last kill, and he looked outraged that I even suggested it?"

I gasp, shocked. "What? Why?"

"Because it was one of the fanged hoppers with a long tail, and you know how strong they smell if cut wrong. He worried it would smell in the cavern and he did not want your stomach upset." Her mouth twitches again. "It was just a simple suggestion, but the next thing I knew, he'd decided to take his kill out to the cache. I suspect he hid it so I would not make broth without him knowing. He's been making others cook at the far end of the cave, too. As far away from you as possible."

I'm surprised. I had no idea this was going on, though I have noticed that there haven't been a lot of cooking scents lately. I thought maybe I was just not noticing them. "Oh, but—"

Kemli waves a hand in the air. "He is to be a father for the first time. Everyone puts up with it. We are all excited to see your little one be born." Her smile grows warm, and she looks at my belly as if she can see the barely noticeable bump underneath my thick clothing. Her voice lowers and she leans closer to me. "It has been a while since kits crawled around these caves. To think that there are new kits on the way. It is like the tribe is waking up from a long sleep. We are all very eager to have more young born."

"Even so," I protest. "Everyone has to cook. You can't live

your lives tiptoeing around me just because I'm pregnant and will be for a while. I'm just one person."

"Ah, but you carry hope in your belly."

"Well, so do Georgie and Liz—"

"But you are here," Kemli points out. "They have the healer with them. You do not. And Asha is here in this cave."

Oh, I know all about Asha. My mood sours as I think about the annoying woman and how she used to hit on Aehako. It's been months and I still haven't gotten used to her being around. Every time I see her, I want to punch her in the face with jealousy, so we stay apart.

Kemli's weathered blue hand covers my smaller one. "Be kind to your mate. The last kit to be born was Asha's and it did not live. You must forgive Aehako if he worries more than he should."

God. I immediately feel like the world's biggest jerk. That's why Kemli says Aehako's worried. It doesn't have to do with Asha's flirting but the death of her baby. "Of course," I manage, touching my belly. "I really do think everything is fine, though."

"I imagine it is," Kemli says with a chuckle. "You are human, but still strong and healthy."

"Thanks?"

She pats my shoulder. "It will just take time for him to get used to fatherhood."

"How much time?"

Her eyes twinkle. "How much longer until the kit is born?"

I groan. "That long, huh?" I sip my tea and try not to grimace at the flavor. It's a mixture I always liked before, but now that I'm pregnant, the taste feels a little too strong, a little too bitter. I don't want to turn it down, though, because I'm acutely aware of how much effort goes into every bite of food and every sip of water. Nothing here comes from a spout or a grocery store. Tea leaves have to be gathered and cleaned and stored, and even the smallest cup of tea shouldn't go to waste.

But if I drink it, I'll barf, and then Aehako will flip his lid, and then the rest of the day will be shot and—

Kemli drains her cup and smacks her lips. "I do love strong tea. Is yours to your liking?"

"It's great," I say, holding it up. "Thank you so much."

She lifts her chin, indicating my drink. "Shall I finish that for you?"

With a sheepish smile, I hold the cup out to her. "I think the baby doesn't like strong flavors."

"When my belly was full of my youngest, I hated the taste of red meat." She waves a hand in the air and rolls her eyes. "That was a very long three full turns of the seasons."

I'll bet. A lot of the diet here is red meat. I can't imagine living three years on fish and roots. I chuckle at her expression. "So what did you—"

"Human," a voice hisses, and an all-too-familiar woman stomps into Kemli's cave without bothering to scratch a greeting. "Come and get your mate!"

"Asha," Kemli says in a dry voice. "Come in. My cave is always welcome to visitors."

Asha tosses her thick, dark hair and glares at both of us. I get to my feet, feeling just a little fat and awkward in her presence. The female sa-khui is utterly gorgeous, her skin a lovely shade of flawless blue, her eyes bright and snapping fire. Her stomach is lean and hard and reminds me that my belly is starting to distend and my ankles have a tendency to swell lately. She's magnificent and she knows it.

She's also kind of an arrogant ass. She looks down her flawless nose at me, her expression imperious. "Do you not think we have enough to put up with right now? Can you not make Aehako behave?"

"Make him behave? I don't understand." I rub the slight bulge of my belly as I get to my feet. "What's he doing?"

Her gaze goes to my stomach, and for a moment, pain flickers in her eyes and I feel like the biggest jerk. Then, the sneer returns to her pretty face and Asha looks at me with such disdain. "He is harassing Hemalo over dye. He says it will upset you, and Aehako now says such things are not allowed in his cave while his mate is pregnant."

I wince. "Oh boy. I'm coming."

"Good," Asha says viciously. "Are we all supposed to sit and stare at the fire until your kit is born? Because that is what Aehako will reduce us to."

"This is his first kit, Asha," Kemli says mildly. "All males lose their minds when their female is pregnant."

"I do not *care*."

"I'll talk to him," I say to the women. While it's sweet that Aehako is so, so protective of me, Asha also has a point. The entire cave can't tiptoe around while they wait for my baby to be born. I don't know if I'm going to be pregnant for nine months or twenty, because the sa-khui carry for so much longer than humans. Either way, Aehako needs to learn to cope, and I do, too.

We're not the only ones that live here. It's an entire cave system full of people and they can't cater to one pregnant lady.

So I follow a huffing Asha out of Kemli's cave and to the back of the South Cave, where the storage areas are set up. Sure enough, Hemalo is set up in the one cave set aside for hides—cured, uncured, dyed, and undyed. He's in front of a stretched skin, a bowl of pungent junk at his feet, and I can smell the concoction even before he comes into view.

I smile brightly even though the scent of it makes my eyes water and my gag reflex rise. "Hi, guys, what's going on?"

Aehako immediately comes over to my side, all big protective body and flicking tail. He's got a slight frown pulling at the edges of his normally smiling mouth. "You should not be in here, Sad Eyes. The smell will make your stomach upset."

"I'm fine," I tell him, keeping the fakely cheery smile on my face. "I heard you and Hemalo were fighting?"

The big male behind Aehako gets to his feet. Of all the people in the tribe, I would think both Hemalo and Aehako would be last on the list of fighters—my mate because he doesn't take much in life too seriously, and Hemalo because he just seems all soul and art. He's not a warrior or a hunter like the others. He's a creator and loves nothing more than fussing with leathers.

Hemalo gives me a mild smile, his soulful eyes full of apology.

"We are not fighting," Aehako says, his voice surprisingly tight. "I am simply telling him that he cannot dye leather with you so close by." Even now, his big hands—though gentle—are steering me toward the entrance of the cave, as if he doesn't want me anywhere near the tanner. "In fact, you did not sleep well last night. Perhaps you should take another nap."

If I take another nap, I'm going to fall asleep out of sheer boredom. "Aehako," I protest, letting him pull me along. "I'm not tired."

"You are," he insists.

"No, I'm not."

"Yes, you are." He takes my hand in his, and when I plant my feet, he just grabs me and carries me away.

"Aehako!" I protest. "Stop this!"

"I know what is best for you, Sad Eyes. Do not be stubborn."

I want to grab his shoulders and shake him, but his movements are making my stomach churn a little. Either that, or the smell of the dye really is affecting me. I twist my hands in his warm tunic, holding on as he carries me in his arms back to our cave as if I'm nothing more than a naughty child. He eventually sets me down oh-so-gently in the middle of our quarters and then looks me over.

I put my hands on my hips, annoyed at his high-handed actions. "That's it. We need to talk."

"Are we not talking right now?" He gives me a ghost of his usual playful smile and touches my cheek. "Or do you want me to do other things with my mouth?"

He gives me a roguish grin as if he didn't just pitch a tantrum at one of his tribemates. I stare at him, aghast. "Don't get flirty on me. What's eating you?"

The lighthearted smile on his face fades immediately into a scowl. "Nothing."

"You yelled at Hemalo—"

His eyes flare and suddenly my playful Aehako is gone. In his place is a wild-eyed, teeth-baring, snarling man. He stabs a finger at the ground. "*Because he is* not *doing as he is told! Hemalo is not thinking of you and our kit!*"

I stare at him, aghast.

"He is being selfish!"

"Will you listen to yourself right now?" I shake my head. "Aehako, love, they live here, too. They can't just tiptoe around for the next year because I'm pregnant."

He flings his hands wide. "Why *not*?"

I'm worried about him. We were both a little anxious when I got pregnant, because we knew that I shouldn't have been able to get pregnant. That the khui fixed the problems that had led to me being sterile, so we were cautious at first. But as time has gone on, I've become more and more comfortable with being pregnant, and it's clear Aehako has . . . not.

"You need to calm down," I tell him in my most levelheaded, soothing voice. "You're stressing yourself out, and you're making me worry about you. I love you, Aehako, but I don't love how you're acting right now."

My big alien mate drags a hand over his face. "I . . . My apologies, my mate. I just saw him at work, and it made me angry." He drops to his knees in front of me and pulls me into his arms, nestling his head against the slight swell of my belly. "I think only of you and our kit."

I put my hands on his head, run my fingers lightly over the short hairs of his scalp. "They live here, too," I say gently. "If the scent bothered me enough, I'd talk to him. Do you really think Hemalo would do anything deliberately to try and spite us?" Hemalo is so kind and gentle, I can barely imagine him with Asha, much less doing anything to be cruel. "He's just working on his leathers because he likes to. It's nothing to do with you or me."

Aehako sighs heavily, his cheek pressed to my belly as I massage his scalp. "I just . . . worry."

I want to ask if it's because of Asha and Hemalo's empty arms, but if their loss isn't on his mind, I don't want to add another worry to the pile. "You're supposed to be the carefree one, remember? I'm the 'Sad Eyes,' and you're the happy one." I trace my fingers down his scalp, caressing one ear lovingly. "I hate that you're so upset, love. Talk to me about it. Don't take it out on others."

His arms tighten around me. "I . . . have had bad dreams."

"About?"

"You and the kit." His words are thick, reluctant. "That terrible things happen to you both and I am helpless to do anything about it." He buries his face against my tunic, as if he can't bear the thought of even remembering those dreams.

I chew on my lip. "Like . . . Rokan type dreams?" I ask hesitantly. His brother Rokan has a strange connection with his khui, and always seems to "know" a bit more than he lets on. If Aehako has the same . . .

"No. Nothing like that."

I let out a sigh of relief. "So just bad dreams that make you wake up in a terrible mood." I caress his head as he rubs my belly and nods. "I understand. They're just dreams, though, love. I promise you I feel fine and I'd let you know the moment I didn't."

"I know." His big hand cups my belly even though it's nothing but the slightest of bulges. "I just wish that the healer was here. I would feel better knowing she checked you and said everything was fine."

It's a brilliant idea, and one I immediately latch onto. If seeing the healer will make him return to his laughing, carefree self, I'm all for it. "Great. Let's go see her, then."

Aehako looks up at me in surprise. "What?" He shakes his head. "It is the brutal season. You should not leave the caves."

"I don't care," I say, smiling. "It's a half a day's walk to the main caves, right? I can walk for half a day."

"It will take longer with bad weather," Aehako admits.

"Then we walk for a full day. Look, if it'll ease your mind, why don't we do it? I think it's a great idea."

He frowns, running his hand over my belly again. "I cannot take my mate out in the brutal season."

I let out a frustrated puff of breath. "Why not?"

"It is cold."

I chuckle. "It is always cold, love. I'm not going to snap like an icicle the moment I go outside." He looks alarmed at my choice of words and tugs me a bit closer. "Besides, I'd like to see the healer, too."

"You said nothing was wrong?" Aehako blurts immediately.

"Nothing is wrong," I quickly reassure him. "I just would like to see Maylak. I'd like to see Georgie and Liz, too. We can compare notes about human-sa-khui pregnancies." I touch his cheek gently, running my thumb over his high cheekbones. "I want to visit with my friends. I want to relax in the heated pool in the center of the cave and not come out for days. And we can visit your mother and father. That'd be lovely, wouldn't it?"

The more I think about the idea, the more I love it. Maybe we need a vacation. Just to get away from everyone else in the South Cave for a few days. Because it's the brutal season, everyone's underfoot and getting on each other's nerves, and Aehako is more stressed than I've ever seen him. Being the leader is an extra burden, and he'd probably do well talking to Vektal, too.

It'll be wonderful for both of us, and I'm willing to put up with a little snow and a terrible day's walk there to do it.

But my stubborn mate shakes his head. "It is too dangerous."

I'm not deterred by his refusal. "Is it really? You and the other hunters go out in the brutal season when the weather is decent. It can be done, but it's just unpleasant, right? I can live with a little unpleasant."

Aehako traces his fingers over my belly. "It is also far, far colder—"

"Then we bundle up."

"The weather might blow up and catch us by surprise—"

"Then we bring extra supplies and stick close to the hunter caves. If it takes us three days to get there because we have to keep pausing at hunter caves, I'm fine with that, too."

He gets to his feet and gazes down at me, his face so full of frustration. He smooths my hair back from my face, troubled. "It is a lot of walking and you are carrying my kit."

"I don't mind walking—"

A thoughtful look crosses his face. "Though we *could* make a sled."

"To carry our stuff?" I ask eagerly.

"For you to ride on."

"Oh." It's not my ideal situation—I'd much rather walk—but he's the expert. If he says it's too nasty in the brutal season for me to walk to the main cave, then it's too nasty. It doesn't matter. I'll ride in a sled if it means we get a chance to visit the healer and just take a break from things. "We can do all of that," I tell him. "If we have a sled, we can pack it cram-full of extra supplies so we know we're totally prepared for anything that comes up."

Aehako still looks doubtful. "I will need a few days to prepare everything. And we must wait for good weather."

"I'm fine with both," I say, grabbing his hands. "This will be wonderful."

He squeezes my hands. "Are you sure you wish to do this, my mate? It might be best for you to stay here, curled up by the fire. I do not want you to push yourself just for me." His gaze is a mixture of worry and relief both.

"It's not just for you," I reassure him. "It's for me, too." And for the rest of the cave, because I'm pretty sure Aehako will snap before the brutal season is over. "As long as we go in totally prepared and take our time, I'm not worried about anything. You know this land. You know the paths, snow-covered or not. I trust you."

Aehako smiles at me, and then drops to his knees to press

another kiss to my belly. "Then it looks like we will be taking a journey. I will let the others know."

I beam at him. I hope this is enough to take his mind off of all the stresses. Right now, my poor love is driving everyone crazy with his good intentions. And if this doesn't help . . . we'll figure something else out.

Aehako

For the next several days, I barely sleep. My mind is too full of preparations. I must ensure that everything is perfect and that we are ready when we finally step out into the brutal season snows. I will not risk my mate in the slightest.

So I work. I build a sled out of sa-kohtsk bones and thick hide, and some of the other males, bored with their confinement in the caves as the snow and wind roar outside, assist me. Eventually it is big and sturdy enough that it will glide over the snow with ease, and has plenty of room for my delicate mate, her growing belly, and the mountain of supplies we are going to take with us to ensure that we are prepared for any and all situations. I strap extra bone runners and leather to the sled, just in case it breaks. I pack bags of trail rations, even though there are caches scattered throughout these valleys and I am familiar with all of them. I prepare additional waterskins. Tea. Medicinal roots for my mate's belly in case she wakes up ill. Extra clothing. Extra boots. Extra furs. Blankets. Tools. Knives. Spears.

Kemli's mate, Borran, takes one look at the growing pile atop the sled and laughs until his entire body shakes. I do not care. I will be prepared for *every* situation.

My Kira says nothing about my enthusiastic packing. She just smiles at me and rubs a hand over her small belly, a sweet expression on her face.

It takes me two handfuls of days before I feel we are ready to go. I can think of nothing else to add to the sled, now bulging with its contents. I head out into the driving snow and practice pulling it, rebalancing things to ensure that the sled will not tip with my precious mate sitting atop it.

And then, finally, a day comes when the skies dawn clear and snow is not angrily flooding from them.

It is time to begin our journey.

"Today?" my Kira asks as she wakes up.

"Today," I agree, and my belly is filled with dread and determination both. More than anything, I want to take my Kira to see the healer, to reassure us that all is well . . . but I hope this is not foolish. I hope this is not a mistake. I frown, thinking of the bags I have packed. "Perhaps I should get one more pouch of trail rations before we go."

"How many do you have?" Kira asks, yawning as she crawls from the furs and begins to straighten things.

I think for a moment. "Eight."

She sputters, turning to look at me with wide eyes. "We can eat off of just one bag for a week. Eight seems excessive."

"I want to be prepared," I tell her with a grin, and decide to quietly add one more bag. Just in case. "Now, come. I have extra furs for you to wear while we travel."

"Oh no."

"Oh yes." I cup her cheek and smile down at her skeptical little face. "I will take good care of you, never fear."

"Oh boy. Should I put my boots on?"

"I have boots for you."

"*Oh boy*," she says again. But Kira puts her hand in mine and lets me lead her out of the cave.

I have our sled and supplies waiting at the entrance to the cave, so I begin bundling my mate after she says a quick goodbye to the tribe, most of whom are watching us prepare to leave. I layer one set of leathers on my mate, and then another, and another, belting them to keep the clothing tight against her body so no wind can cut through and chill her. After a few more layers, someone snickers quietly nearby.

I study my mate, and then add another heavy fur vest, one of mine that hangs to her knees on her and nearly wraps around her twice. I belt it tight and then start to add another layer, just in case.

Kira sputters. "Aehako, how many layers do I need?"

"All of them," I tell her cheerfully.

She giggles, and when I pick up a cloak, she touches my hand. "Enough, love. I can barely walk in this."

"You do not need to walk at all. You are going to be on a sled."

She shakes her head, bouncing her arms against her well-padded sides. "I look like a snowman."

I have seen the rounded figures the humans sometimes make out of snow at the cave entrance and . . . she is not wrong. It is adorable, though. I lean in and give her small nose a kiss on the tip. "I bundle you because you will be sitting instead of walking. Trust me when I say you will be cold enough to be grateful for all these layers."

Kira gives me a skeptical look, but nods. "All right, then. You're the expert."

I get her seated on the packed sled, then pile furs atop her and swaddle her like a kit, until she's laughing at my protectiveness. Perhaps I am overdoing it a little, but I do not care. She is more than precious to me, my mate, and I do not mind looking foolish if it saves her a moment of discomfort. When I am convinced she will be warm enough, I toss on my own wraps and loop the strap for the sled around my waist, harnessing it to my body. Even if I should drop the leather ropes, she will not slide away from me.

With a cheerful wave goodbye, I haul the sled out into the cold. The day is mostly clear, a thick cloud cover hiding the suns from sight and keeping the temperature icy. The wind is high, biting at my exposed skin, so I tug a wrap higher around my nose and make sure that Kira's covers most of her face, and then set off.

We set a good pace, the snow thick on the ground, and I choose a path that will stay close to the cliffs but will not entail dragging the sled up the steep slopes of the nearby rocky surfaces. The farther we get away from the South Cave, the more concerned I am that it is perhaps far too cold for Kira. Her human skin cannot take the cold like mine can. She is sitting, which is bound to make her colder, and the clouds look as if they are growing thicker by the moment.

A short time later, I spot the trail to a hunter cave. I immediately head in that direction, moving toward it. The privacy screen is up to protect the cave's contents, but no one is inside. I pause, considering the skies once more, and then turn to my mate.

"We are stopping here for the day," I announce, unstrapping myself from the sled.

Kira pulls off the thick fur covering the lower half of her face like a mask and gives me an odd look. "We haven't gone very far, have we? It's not even been a few hours."

"I will not chance getting caught in a snowstorm with you

and our kit," I tell her, moving to her side and taking her hands to help her to her feet. "You said you did not care if this took many, many days, right?"

Her mouth quirks in a hint of a smile, but she nods at me. "I did say that."

I help my mate waddle into the cave (perhaps I did wrap a few too many layers of furs around her) and start a fire so she can warm herself while I unpack. As if the skies have decided to agree with me, large flakes of snow ride the wind, and the day grows dark despite that it is midday.

"You see?" I tell Kira as I haul our packs inside. "Your mate is always right."

"I'm gonna ignore that," she teases, holding her pink hands toward the fire to warm them. "Do you need help?"

"If you go near the front of that cave, I will spank you like a naughty kit," I promise her. "Sit and warm up."

I work on unpacking the sled that I just packed not too long ago, and by the time I am done, the snow is easing up. I wait for Kira to point this out, but she says nothing, feeding bits of fuel to the fire and setting up a tripod and pouch so we can make tea. She has stripped most of her extra layers off and created a nest of furs in the back of the cave, and when I put the privacy screen over the entrance to block the wind, she straightens and smiles at me.

"All done?" she asks, a smile on her face.

I nod, taking the food satchel out of her hands. "I know you think I am overprotective, but I would rather be cautious than caught out in the cold with you and the kit."

"Did I say anything?"

"I could hear you thinking it," I tease her. "You think very loudly."

"Not loudly enough, it seems," Kira says, moving to my side. She unties the belt holding my clothing to my body, letting it slide to the ground. She pulls at my clothing, peeling one layer off and then another. "I was just thinking that there's nothing wrong with us taking our time. Spending a little quiet time together, just you and me. I think you could use a vacation."

"A vay-cay-shun?"

She nods. "It's where humans take a little trip to get away from their worries."

"You think I have worries?"

She tugs on another thick layer of furs over my chest, smiling up at me as she leans close. "Or maybe you just need to get away for a little bit." She lets the fur slide to the ground and then I am in nothing but a vest and my leggings. Kira moves behind me, her hand sliding across my backside.

"Are you seducing me?" I ask her. "Should I expect a courting gift?"

"No courting gift. But . . . would it be so bad if I was seducing you? Should I stop?" She presses her cheek to my arm and hugs me from behind, her hands on my stomach. "Is it so bad if I like touching my mate?"

"It is not bad at all." My breath quickens, and the press of her smaller body against mine makes me hungry for more. I ache to touch her, to fling her down onto the furs and just rut into her welcoming body . . . but she is carrying my kit. We must be careful. "Are you tired?" I ask instead. "Should you lie down and rest?"

"Rest? From sitting in a sled all morning?" She lets out a derisive little snort and one of her hands slides to my cock. "I'm feeling pretty good, actually." Her fingers graze up and down the front of my leathers. "It seems you feel pretty good, too."

I groan at her featherlight touch. Just that small caress is enough for my cock to harden, and I pull my mate tighter against me. I tilt my head back, giving my body over to her touch. "It is because I have the finest mate in both caves," I tell her. "Just knowing that she is mine makes me impossibly hard."

"It's a wonder you're not hard all day," she teases, rubbing her mouth against my bare arm and then biting me lightly. "Just wandering around the hills of snow, your dick standing up for all the world to see."

"How do you know I do not?" I tease back, because I like her silly mood. "How do you know I do not stop every few feet and just stroke my fine cock while I think about my mate?"

She chuckles, coming out from behind me. "Because every time you come back to the cave, you're so excited to see me. If you'd been playing with your cock all day long, you wouldn't be able to last for nearly as long as you do." Her cheeks flush with a hint of color. Even after many turns of the moon as mates, my Kira still gets shy when she says bold things, as if she expects to be rebuffed.

Impossible. I will never rebuff her, especially not when she is eager for my touch. It is the greatest of gifts. "You are saying I have great stamina, then? I am pleased, my pretty mate. Sometimes I wish to last longer, just to please you." I pull her mane free from its braid and let my fingers glide through her soft locks.

"If you lasted any longer, I might fall apart," she teases me.

"Such flattery."

"You love it."

"I do indeed."

Kira smiles at me, and then she tugs on my vest, pulling it off. Her hands go to my leggings next, and I let her undress me, though I draw the line at my boots because I do not want her bending over more than she has to. She rolls her eyes at my insistence and strips off her own clothing.

I will never get over the joy of having a mate, I think. Of watching her eyes brighten with anticipation as I stand naked before her, of seeing the familiar curves of her body reveal themselves as she pulls off her clothing. I help her along, letting her lean on my shoulder as she kicks off boots and leggings, and then we are both undressed before each other. I have mated with Kira more times than I can count, but each one is as fresh and as joyous as the first. I will never tire of her smile, of the sight of her hips, or the flush on her cheeks when she comes. I will never tire of her, ever.

My khui has chosen so very well for me.

As I stand there, smiling at my mate like a lovesick fool, my poor female shivers, her full teats pricking in response to the cold air. "Let's get under the furs."

"I thought you would never ask," I tease.

We go to the bed of furs, and instead of lying down first, Kira puts her hands on my chest and mock-pushes me toward the nest. "You first. I want to play with you for a bit."

"You do? Truly, I am the luckiest of males." I eagerly lie on my back, adjusting a roll of fur under my neck so my horn tips do not press uncomfortably against the cave floor. My beautiful, nude mate slides her leg over my body and then descends, settling her bottom against my hips. My cock brushes up against her backside, my spur teasingly close to her soft folds, but she does not sit fully against me. Instead, she leans forward and runs a hand over my chest.

"God, I love looking at you," Kira sighs, her fingers brushing over my flat teats and dancing across the plating of my chest. "Just seeing you like this makes me want to bite you all over."

I shift underneath her, because my cock likes the thought of her biting me very much. "What is stopping you?"

She lifts her head and gives me a surprisingly mischievous look. My Kira is normally the somber one, the one that needs encouragement to laugh. She is the serious one and I am the tease, the lighthearted one. Seeing her like this, though, it makes my heart pound.

I love it when she takes control.

Kira sweeps her long hair over her shoulder, then leans down and nips at one of my teats. Her small teeth are nothing but a graze against my much-harder skin, but I shudder anyhow. The sight of her actions alone is enough to make my cock harden painfully. She nips at me again, tiny bites up and down my pectorals, and then lifts one of my arms and nibbles up the soft inside, sending shivers of longing up and down my spine.

"Lean back," I rasp. "Seat yourself on my cock."

"Soon."

"At least rub yourself on my spur," I cajole. "Wet it with your cunt. Slide over it. Take me in your body."

"Soon," she promises again, and nips at a vein on my arm.

I groan again.

Kira flexes her hips, teasing her bottom against my cock as she brushes her lips over my skin. I want to put my hands all over her, force her down onto my length, but she is fragile and carrying my kit. I fist my hands at my sides instead, determined not to touch her and interrupt. I flick my tail up and down her creamy thigh, though, unable to stop from touching her in some way as she nibbles and bites her way over to my opposite arm.

"You're so big," she says with a happy sigh. "Big and strong and just looking at you turns me on."

"Does it?" I manage. "Show me how much."

She gives me a playful look and then takes my cock in her hand. She lifts her hips and rubs my length up and down her folds. "Do you feel how wet I am? That's all because of you."

I groan, fascinated at my mate's aggressiveness. I love how Kira can be both shy and yet hungry for my touch at the same time. Truly, I am the luckiest of males to have her as my mate. My khui has chosen so very well. "Come and sit on my face," I entreat her. "Let me lick you until you come."

"Not today," she promises, breathless as she rubs my cock through her folds again. This time, she fits the tip of my cock at her entrance and lets out a little gasp of sheer delight when I buck my hips, thrusting lightly into her. "You're not playing fair."

"Does it matter?" I ask. "Come ride me." I give up on holding my hands at my sides and cradle her waist instead, dragging her down farther onto my cock. Her sheath is slick with her arousal, and we both groan as she takes me to the hilt. When her hips are flush to mine, she wiggles against me, rubbing herself against my spur, and I love the way she gasps. Her nipples are taut with her excitement, and I let my tail slide over to one, teasing it as she begins to ride me.

I love watching her as she presses her hands to my chest, her eyes closed as she bounces atop me, using my cock to pleasure herself. She sets the pace, and it is clear to me that she will not last long. It seems like no time at all before her movements become jerky, her cunt clenching tighter with every rocking motion, and Kira becomes more frantic, bouncing quicker. I encourage her with teasing words, grinding her hips down upon me even as I thrust upward, and love the squeal of pleasure she makes when my spur hits her just right.

Then she is clenching and coming atop me, and I gently roll our bodies over until she is beneath me and I can claim her for my own release.

When we are both spent, I slide free from her body and press a kiss to her soft mouth, then rest my head on her belly. "Did we wake my kit?" I ask, rubbing a hand over her naked belly. I cannot be more content than this moment, I think. Not ever. I have everything I have ever wanted right here in my arms.

"Sleeping, I imagine." Kira yawns. "You know . . ."

I lift my head, giving her a curious look. "What is it?"

She gets an innocent look on her face and shrugs. "I was just thinking we could always go looking for Harlow while we're out."

Not this. As gently as I can, I pull my mate into my arms and stroke her hair. "I love you, my Kira, and I love that you have never given up, but look at the weather outside, my mate. If your Har-loh managed to live when she wandered off, do you think she could live through this?"

"I don't know." She sniffs, and I hold her tighter. I hate that she still thinks of her lost tribemate. "I just . . . I feel like we should have looked harder. That maybe if we turned the right corner, we'd have found her."

"There are always those that walk into the snow and never come back," I say, stroking her mane. "It is hard to accept, but it is part of life. Risking your life—and that of our kit—to find her body will not do anyone any good."

"I guess," Kira says with a small sigh. "I just . . . I hate that we lost her. I feel responsible."

"You are not. You did not force her out into the snow. You could not have known what was to happen." I press another kiss to her brow. "Is this why you wished to go on this journey? To look for her?"

"Actually, no," she admits, her hand sliding up and down my side. "I'm selfish, I guess. I thought it might be nice if we got away from the others for a while. Had a little 'you and me' time."

"We have 'you and me' time in our cave every night," I reassure her.

"No, I mean, time alone. Together. Just the two of us. Like Georgie's honeymoon. It's time for us to just spend together, bonding. Reconnecting."

"Do we need to reconnect?" I gently thrust my hips at her. "I am ready."

"Not like that." She ducks her head against my shoulder. "Pervert."

I just grin. I like her smiles more than anything in this world. "So what you are telling me is that you do not mind if our trip to the other cave takes a great many days because we can spend them alone together?"

"Yes." Her voice is muffled against my skin.

"This is a good thing," I promise her. "Because I intend on stopping at every hunter cave along the way to ensure we are not caught in a storm."

She chuckles, pressing a lazy kiss to my skin, her fingers tracing patterns on my hip. "Exactly how many are there between here and there?"

I consider the path in my head, one I have traveled a great many times before. "Six."

"Six?" she sputters. "What, are we going just across the hill and stopping for the day?"

"Possibly. Is that a problem?" I reach up and cup one of her teats, toying with the sensitive nipple. Her teats have grown larger, I think, the nipples darker. I decide I like the change, just like I like the way her hips and bottom are spreading larger. It is just more of her to enjoy. "I thought you wished for us to reconnect. I have lots of parts that need connection to my mate. Very, very frequent connections."

She just rolls her eyes at me and settles in against my side. "Your hand feels good," she admits after a moment when I keep rolling her nipple.

"Another connection," I promise. "Shall I connect my mouth to your nipple and feast?"

Kira lets out a dreamy sigh, rolling onto her back. "God, yes."

Six days of connecting with my mate. I like this idea a lot. Even as I nuzzle my way down her soft skin toward her teat, I wonder if I can find more caves along the way to extend our trip.

As long as we are safe from the weather, after all, what is the harm?

Kira

It's so odd to me how our roles have reversed, Aehako and I. In my pregnancy, I'm the easygoing one, the one that never worries about anything. Aehako is the one that stresses over the smallest of things. When we get ready to leave the hunter cave the next morning, a thick snow starts to fall, so we unpack our things and stay for another day.

And then another.

It takes three days before the weather lets up enough for us to travel some, and it takes another four days before we approach the valley that holds the main cave of the sa-khui.

"Well," I tease Aehako as he hauls the sled through the snow, the smoke from the main cave on the horizon. "You did say it would take several days."

"It might take one more," he admits to me, pausing and looking up at the gray skies. "I do not like the sight of those clouds."

If we stop right at the finish line, that just seems silly. "I bet we can make it," I tell him cheerfully. "I can get off and walk—"

Before I finish the thought, he tugs the sled along, hustling through the snow at a breakneck pace. I smother a giggle behind my thick glove.

Really, even if we stopped for another day, it'd be all right. The "vacation" away from the South Cave has been good for us. I didn't realize how much stress that being leader was putting on Aehako, in addition to my pregnancy. He worries all the time if his decisions are correct ones, or if the tribe would not be happier back at the main cave. He worries some—like Hemalo and Asha—are displeased with his leadership. He worries he is not as authoritative as Vektal, because he is usually a more laughing sort.

And me, I had no idea my mate was holding all this in. I thought he'd taken to leadership the way he takes to everything—with enthusiasm and a big smile. Turns out he's been hiding his fears because he didn't want to burden me.

The guy thinks I'm more fragile than glass, apparently.

So we talk, a lot. We organize supplies in each cave we stop in, and refresh what we need. I start sewing a blanket out of fur scraps just to give my hands something to do, and we talk more. Aehako laughs so much on this vacation that I realize he hasn't been laughing much in the last few weeks, and I've been too preoccupied to notice it.

I vow to make him laugh more often.

So I start sewing something else with the scraps. I tell him that it's just another blanket, but I make a small, fuzzy loincloth instead, and I stuff the backside full of more scraps so it'll make the wearer have a massive bubble butt. Another idea occurs to me, and for a moment, I shake my head. That's not who I am, making obscene things out of leather . . . but it'll make Aehako laugh. So after smothering a few giggles, I go ahead and make an "attachment" for the front of the loincloth, too.

All of this happens under Aehako's nose as we laze about in the hunter caves. He takes naps, so many of them I worry he's been losing sleep, and he puts his hands on my belly and talks to our kit for hours on end. It's so nice to be away, just the two of us, that I secretly hope for bad weather on our return trip, too.

After all, we're in no hurry to get back, are we? Everyone's an adult. The South Cave can manage itself for a few weeks.

The sled jerks ahead, making me yelp as Aehako picks up the pace. Sure enough, a thicker snowfall is starting to pour from the skies, but Aehako has apparently decided to sprint the rest of the way instead of pausing at another hunter cave. I cling to the packs as we zoom over the snow, and the distant cave comes closer and closer to view. The sight of the large, triangular opening of the main cave fills me with a curious sense of . . . not exactly homesickness, but a wistful sort of pleasure.

This was my first home here on Not-Hoth. It'll always hold a special place in my heart.

"Ho," someone cries, and a fur-covered figure jogs toward our sled.

"Ho!" Aehako pants, not stopping even as the other hunter pulls up alongside us. "We are heading in before the weather hits."

"I see that! And you brought your pretty mate!" The hunter lowers his hood and it is Zolaya, who grins at me. "My mate will be glad to see the both of you. I suppose I can put off checking my traps for a day or so."

"Go check them," Aehako tells him with a friendly shout. "We will be staying for several days yet. Feed your mate's growing belly!"

Zolaya claps a big hand on Aehako's shoulder and then nods at me. "Perhaps I shall!" He jogs off again, passing us by, and then we are almost at the cave.

"Ho!" cries another voice. "Visitors!"

My eyes brim with happy tears as more people crowd at the entrance of the cave, and I see humans mixed with friendly blue faces. I didn't realize how much I'd missed everyone until just now, and I'm filled with a wild, impatient sort of joy as we approach.

I can't wait to hug all my friends again.

Aehako finally stops his endless jog and pulls the sled directly in front of the cave entrance. His shoulders heaving, panting, he moves to my side and helps me climb out of the massive pile of supplies. Immediately, I'm met with happy squeals. Marlene—ever exuberant—flings her arms around me and Ariana bursts into tears and hugs me, too. I see Georgie, standing next to her mate, and Nora, and it's all too much. I get weepy, too, and then Georgie and I collapse on top of each other and sob, much to Vektal and Aehako's chagrin.

"Pregnancy tears," I explain to my mate as I wipe my cheeks. "I'm happy. I really am."

My mate looks uncertain, but he's quickly distracted away as his mother and father arrive. Sevvah and Oshen are enveloped in bear hugs, and then his brother Rokan is there, a faint smile on his face. Sessah—a much tinier, younger version of my mate—is there, too, and he beams up at his grown brother, so small and adorable that I realize that our child might look just like him.

And I start crying again. Before Aehako can ask, I blubber, "I swear I'm happy!"

Sevvah just clucks at me, tugging me into her arms. She's so regal, his mother, with her looping gray braid and the only hint of her age the lines around her eyes. "Of course you are happy, dear heart. You are carrying a kit. If he has not seen you weep at least once a day over nothing at all, then he should count himself very lucky." She smooths her fingers over my face and then beams down at me. "Come, I will make you something to eat."

"Now I'm hungry," Georgie mutters at my side.

"Then I will feed you, too," Sevvah says easily. "Come sit by the fire while my Aehako greets his friends."

Sevvah fusses over me for a while as Aehako meets with Vektal, and then is pulled away for one thing after another. I get it, though. He's leading the South Cave and everyone's going to want to know what's going on there. He's going to be busy all day, even though he casts several worried looks toward his mother's cave as if he wants to come and hover all over me.

"His father was like that the first time I carried," Sevvah says with a rueful smile. "He was at my side so much that I wanted to shove his head into the snow if he did not give me space to breathe."

I smile at her. "When does it wear off? When does he relax?"

"He does not." Sevvah chuckles at her own joke. "If he is anything like his father, he will be the most attentive of fathers— sometimes annoyingly so."

That's all right with me.

Georgie shows up at Sevvah's cave entrance just then, and peeks inside. "Knock knock."

"Come in," Sevvah tells her. "I was just about to prepare this evening's meal."

My friend looks at me, then holds up a soft wrap. "I was actually going to take a dip in the bathing pool and wondered if Kira wanted to join me."

It sounds like a gossip session, and it's been so long since I've had a long chat with Georgie and Liz and the others that I immediately get to my feet. Then I hesitate, looking over at Sevvah.

"Go on," the older woman says, squeezing my shoulder. "Food will not be ready for a while yet, and if you are out in the open, Aehako can quit casting worried looks in this direction." She rolls her eyes.

"All right." I head toward Georgie.

As we approach the main part of the cave, I see Aehako glance over. He's talking with Rokan, his expression grave. A twinge of worry hits me, and I squeeze Georgie's arm, letting her know that I'll join her shortly. I head toward Aehako, and when I move to his side, he and Rokan immediately stop talking.

Well, if that's not alarming, I don't know what is. "Hello, Rokan," I say easily. "How are you?"

"Very well." He smiles at me. "It is good to see you and my brother again. I like how happy you have made him."

"We're both very happy," I agree, and Aehako runs his hand down my hair affectionately. I glance up at my mate. "What were you two talking about?"

"Nothing important," Aehako says, perhaps a bit too brightly. "Maylak is napping so you will not be able to see her until later tonight. Kashrem says her kit is big in her belly and makes her very tired."

"I know what that's like," I murmur, caressing my belly. It already feels enormous . . . and I'm tired all the time at the halfway point. Just more to look forward to, I suppose.

Aehako puts a protective hand on my shoulder and bends down, peering into my face. "Are you tired? Do you need to rest? Perhaps you should rest—"

"I'm fine," I tell him firmly. I lean in and give him a quick peck on the nose. "And I'm going to go relax in the pool with Georgie and the others. I promise I'll take it easy."

He hesitates, and then nods, rubbing his knuckles along my jaw. "Speak if you need anything."

"I will." I smile at Rokan, and then head over to the center of the cave, where the large bathing pool steams and calls invitingly. Megan and Nora are already in it, both of them naked. Georgie joins them, sliding into the pool, and I loosen my wrap and outer layers, folding them neatly before I set them on a nearby rock seat. I ease myself to the edge, wearing nothing but a leather loincloth and a breastband. No one will think twice if I get completely naked, but I'm still a little awkward about nudity, and my changing body isn't helping things. I slide into the water, and then the delicious warmth of it hits me like a freight train. I bite back a moan of pleasure as the comforting heat soaks into my tired body. "Oh boy, I missed this."

"I can imagine," Georgie says. "No pool at the South Cave? You heathens, you."

"We have a sa-kohtsk skull in our cave that I can put water in, but it never gets very hot or very deep, because getting rid of the water is such a chore. This is . . . different." I close my eyes, leaning against the ledge. "This is bliss."

"I'm in here almost every day," Megan agrees. "It helps with my fat ankles. Or at least, I tell myself that it does."

"You just missed Liz, by the way," Nora says. "She and Raahosh set off yesterday. She'll be so bummed she missed you."

I'm bummed I missed her, too. I love her brash mouth and wish I could see how she's handling her pregnancy. If Raahosh is letting her go hunting with him, I'm guessing he's not as hover-y as Aehako is. "We're staying for a few days. Maybe they'll return before we leave."

"I hope so." Megan rubs her belly, which looks twice the size of mine, complete with stretch marks. For all that we're only a few weeks apart, she looks way more pregnant than me, and I'm briefly envious. Does that mean she'll have her baby sooner than me? Or is she just naturally carrying larger? I wish we had more answers, but we're all going to be the first ones to have "hybrid" babies. This is uncharted territory for all of us.

I glance over at my mate again, but he's deep in discussion with his brother, neither one of them looking over here. I wonder if anything's amiss. Wouldn't he tell me if it was?

"So," Megan continues. "Give us all the gossip at the South Cave. How's Josie? Tiffany? Claire?"

I settle in and talk about my tribesmates for what feels like hours: who is up to what; Tiffany's latest craft projects; Farli and her new pet, Chompy, who poops literally everywhere in the cave, much to Kemli's chagrin; and the latest hunting mishaps. I don't think of myself as a chatty sort, but I find that I'm talking for hours about the smallest details of our life at the South Cave, and Megan and Nora and Georgie all share their own stories with me. There's a tale of a hopper that got into the storage rooms and destroyed a ton of roots before anyone realized what was happening, and Megan talks about her latest macramé projects. Nora talks about sex—being Nora—and how she and Marlene are trying to design better underwear.

"Where is Marlene?" I ask, curious.

"Probably having sex with Zennek again," Georgie comments, dragging her hand through the steamy water.

"She's been insatiable lately thanks to the pregnancy. Me, I get swollen ankles," Megan complains. "She gets a kicked-up libido."

"I'm pretty sure Marlene was born with a kicked-up libido," Nora giggles.

"Like you're one to talk. We hear you guys going at it every night." Georgie rolls her eyes. "Your voice in particular echoes *really* loudly."

Nora just giggles again. "Can I help it if Dagesh has incredible stamina? Or that he's turned on by my big pregnant boobs?"

"Ew?" Megan teases. "Did I want to know that?"

"About as much as I wanted to know about your foot thing?" Nora replies sweetly.

Megan groans.

"Foot thing?" I ask, my face scrunching in confusion. "You mean like Cashol has a foot thing?"

"No, like Megan does." Nora wiggles her brows. "You should hear her go on and on about how veiny Cashol's 'strong feet' are."

Georgie makes a mock gagging noise.

Megan just groans again and lowers herself under the water's surface, as if that can hide her from the good-natured laughter in the cave. I try not to giggle too much, but the happiness in the cave is infectious. It's so nice to see my friends again. I love everyone in the South Cave, but half of our family is here.

It's nice to come home, even for a little while.

I towel off and sit near the pool, chatting with Georgie while I wait for my hair to dry. It's been the laziest of afternoons, but I've enjoyed every moment of it. Tomorrow, I'll pitch in and help Sevvah around the cave, or Maylak, or sew with Georgie— whatever is needed. Today, though, I'm being a lazy, indolent slug and loving it.

Sessah trots over to where we sit. He's Aehako's younger brother, just a small scrap of a boy, but I could swear he's shot up by several inches in the last few months. He's got a serious look on his face that reminds me a bit of Rokan, but when he approaches me, his grin is all Aehako. "Mother told me to come and get you," Sessah says. "She made a meal just for you."

"I'll be there soon," I promise him, glancing at Georgie. "Where's Aehako?"

"He's talking with Rokan." Sessah gives me a toothy grin. "Did you bring me a present?"

I reach out and tweak the long braid over his shoulder. "Your brother might have been making something for you," I say, knowing full well that there's a carved slingshot for him in Aehako's packs. "What are they talking about, your brothers?"

"Dreams." Sessah's answer is cheerful.

My blood runs cold. I think of Aehako's worried confession from a few days ago. "Dreams? What kind of dreams?"

Sessah shrugs, already bored. "I'll tell Mother you're coming."

"Be right there," I whisper, my gut churning as he races away. The baby in my belly flips and I absently caress it, fighting the panic rising inside me. I think of how serious Rokan and Aehako looked. How they quickly changed topics when I approached, guilty looks on their faces.

Aehako assured me that he didn't have the "knowing" dreams like his brother does. But . . . what if Rokan is having bad dreams about us, too? What if something's wrong with the baby?

What if I'm not meant to have one after all?

I feel cold all over.

"Kira?" Georgie asks as I get to my feet. "Are you okay? You just got really pale."

I nod absently. "Uh, just gas." I pat the small swell of my belly. "You know how it is."

"Boy, do I ever." She gets to her feet, slightly awkward. "Come hang out after dinner if you're not too tired? I've missed talking to you." She squeezes my hand and gives me a warm look.

"Will do." I turn toward Sevvah's cave, but I can't concentrate on anything. I can't concentrate on Sessah coming back out to retrieve me, holding my hand in his smaller one. I pick at the delicious root chowder with chunks of fresh fish in it. Normally I'd devour two bowlfuls, but I have to force myself to eat tonight. My stomach is too upset, and after dinner, I claim fatigue and that I want to lie down. Sevvah helps me set up a bed and a fire in one of the storage caves so Aehako and I can have privacy, and I curl up in the blankets, watching the fire crackle as my thoughts churn and churn.

I keep thinking of Aehako's guilty expression. Of how he and Rokan both looked uncomfortable when I showed up. How quickly they stopped speaking.

Dreams, Sessah said.

I touch the rounded bulge of my belly. Here I thought all of my dreams were coming true. What if I'm wrong, though? What if this is just another one of life's cruel jokes?

Do I . . . need to prepare myself for the worst? Just the thought makes my breath catch. I . . . can't. I just can't. If something happens to my baby or to Aehako, it'll break me. I've been strong through so much, but I can also only take so much. I need to see Maylak and have her tell me what's wrong, but the thought of finding out those answers frightens me even more.

I don't want to know. If avoiding her means I can prolong the inevitable, I'm going to hide in this stupid cave for the next few days and beg Aehako to take me home early. I can't handle bad news about my baby. I can't.

I put my hands on my stomach and cradle it gently, too terrified to even cry. Under my hands, the little one kicks my bladder and spins, and I've never been so glad to have to pee in my life.

I must drift off to sleep at some point, because I wake up when Aehako slides into the blankets beside me, and the fire is out. The cave is chilly, and he puts his hands on my warm body, rubbing them up and down against my bare arms. "I thought you were going to come and get me when you went to see the healer," Aehako murmurs against my ear, spooning my body with his bigger one. "What did she say?"

I can hear the hurt in his tone. Does he think I would go without him? He doesn't realize that I'm in here, hiding from the world. "I haven't seen her yet. I'll go in the morning."

He leans over and kisses my cheek, holding me tight against his chest. "Are you feeling well? Is everything all right?"

You tell me, I want to scream. But I don't. I can't be mad at him. If he's talking to Rokan behind my back, it's because he's afraid of upsetting me. He wants to try and "fix" whatever he can without alarming me. It's sweet, and it makes me love him all the more.

I'm everything to him, just like he's everything to me. Him . . . and the baby.

I roll over and face him, studying his handsome, broad features. He doesn't look devastated or stressed—at least, no more so than usual. Is he trying to hide it from me in all ways? My heart aches with such love for him. I don't know how I managed to end up here, planets and planets away from my own, to land in the arms of this man, but I'll be forever thankful for it.

Whatever happens in the future, we face it together.

I cup his face and kiss his mouth fiercely.

Aehako groans in surprise at my initiative. He licks at the inside of my mouth, the ridges of his tongue sending hot flutters through my body. His tail wraps around my ankle, and he slides his big hands over my ass, kneading my muscles. "On your knees, my pretty mate," he murmurs between kisses. "Let your male take care of you."

"Yes," I whisper. I want that. I want him to take care of me. I need it. His touch is like a drug, and I want it to send me spiraling. I bite his lower lip hungrily, and then turn, getting on all fours. With my belly growing, this is becoming our position of choice, and just putting my palms on the blankets makes me get all hot and bothered. Maybe Marlene isn't the only insatiable one lately.

"Love how needy you are," he murmurs, tugging my leather leggings down and pushing my tunic up to expose me.

Am I needy? Maybe I am. I need to connect with my mate. I need to feel his touch. I need him to make me forget all my worries.

A little gasp escapes me as he glides his hot, aching length through my folds from behind. I'm wet already, but that erotic touch makes me even wetter. I love the drag of his ridges through my pussy, love how big he feels, how invasive against my spread folds. I lean forward a bit more, pressing my cheek to the furs and arching my back.

"So beautiful," Aehako murmurs, lightly raking his fingers up and down the backs of my thighs and my buttocks. The touch sends little frissons of shock through me, my nipples tightening. So good. How does he always know how to make it so good?

Then he's pushing inside me, so big and thick that I can't stifle my moan of pleasure. He grunts as he sinks deeper, his hands tight on my hips, and I know what's coming next, but I'm still not entirely prepared for when his spur pushes into my back entrance, pressing in the most exquisite and deliciously unnatural sort of way. It shouldn't be nearly as amazing as it is, but having sex like this makes me completely and utterly crazed with need. "Move," I whisper, my fingers curling in the furs. "Please, please move."

He does as I ask, retreating slowly, and then in the next moment, his hips slam into mine. His spur invades me again, and it just makes everything ratchet up to eleven. I gasp with every thrust, whimper every time he pulls back, and within minutes, my toes are curling and my calves feel tight with the onset of an orgasm.

"Please," I choke out again, and the way he breathes my name on his lips does something to me. The shudder of it starts low in my belly, and the next thing I know, I'm coming, my entire being tightening in a wild, impossible release that feels exquisite and is somehow exactly what I needed.

Aehako thrusts into me, his movements careful and precise until I clench tight around him, and then the breath heaves from his lungs and he's coming, too, his release making our bodies slide wetly together even as he thrusts deeper. I moan one last time as he covers me, his heated skin pressed to mine, and then he collapses in the furs, his arms tight as he drags me with him.

I squirm on the blankets with him, because his spur is still buried in me from behind, and it's . . . not the most easy-to-ignore sensation. Now that he's sated and relaxed, maybe I can get him to tell me what's going on.

"So . . ." I begin quietly. "Is there anything you want to tell me?"

Aehako

I flex my hips against my mate's backside, loving the feel of my cock—and the tip of my spur—seated in her body. Even after several turns of the moon, the eagerness for mating that resonance brought to us feels unabated. I can see her flick her mane, and I get hard. She looks at me through her lashes and I get hard. She snores and puts her cold feet on me . . . I get hard.

Truly, I am the luckiest of males.

So when she pats the arm I wrap around her waist? I get hard. I lean in close and brush my lips against the curve of her small ear.

"So. Is there anything you want to tell me?" Kira asks.

I try to think, but it is near impossible with the hot clasp of her body holding my cock. "I . . . love you?" Humans like to hear the "love" word often, so I try to tell it to Kira many times a day. Sometimes she is moody because of the kit, though, and needs to hear it more often. I think for a moment and then add, "You look very beautiful today?"

She slaps my arm and then wriggles out of my grasp. My

cock leaves the warmth of her body and then she moves away from me on the blankets, grabbing new furs as if she is going to make a nest for herself. "You are impossible. Just tell me already!"

I sit up, confused. "Tell you what?"

Kira meets my eyes, and to my surprise, she looks as if she is about to weep. "Don't do this to me, Aehako. Tell me what's wrong with the baby."

My heart seizes in my chest. It is my worst nightmare coming true. "What is wrong with our kit?"

"You tell me!" She bursts into tears. "No more secrets! You can't withhold secrets from a pregnant woman!"

"I do not know what you mean, Sad Eyes." I slide across the blankets, moving toward her and trying to take her in my arms, ignoring her feeble slaps. "Tell me what is wrong with our kit. Did you feel something bad? Did something move that is not supposed to move?" A new worry hits me. "Did I hit it with the head of my cock?" Sometimes when I tilt her hips just right, I get so deep that I worry about such things, even if it cannot be true. Unless . . .

She makes a noise that is half snort, half sobbing. "Don't make me laugh! I'm mad at you!" Her small fist smacks my chest.

I want to be relieved—so I did not jab my son, or daughter, with my cock—but she keeps crying and my heart will not slow down in its fevered, frightened pounding. "Kira, I am very confused right now."

"You said you would tell me if there was a problem with the baby, but I caught you talking to Rokan and you changed subjects and had this look on your face—"

"What look?" I sputter.

"The guilty look!"

I have a guilty look? Wait. What does this have to do with my brother? "Is there something wrong with our kit?" I ask again, trying to stay patient.

"You were talking to Rokan about dreams," she cries, swiping at her cheeks. "You tell me. What do the dreams mean?"

I stare blankly. I still have no idea what she is talking about.

At my expression, she continues. "Sessah said you were talking to Rokan about *dreams*. You told me your dreams weren't like his! That you didn't have the knowing sense!"

Dreams. Dreams. I think hard, trying to remember what it is I talked to Rokan about that would have had me look guilty and dreams and . . . oh. "I told Rokan that you and the kit were all of my dreams coming true."

Her tears ease, a little. "You . . . what? You did?"

"Yes. And Sessah heard that, I assume." I am going to throttle my little brother for scaring my mate.

"But then why did you look guilty when I came up to you?" She stabs a finger at my chest. "I know you. That was a guilty look. You wear it every time I say I'm tired and then you pretend you just want to cuddle. It's *never* just cuddling."

I am caught. She *is* right. It is never just cuddling. I try to think of what else I spoke to Rokan about . . . and then I know what it must be. "We talked about moving back to the main cave. Me and you. I spoke with Rokan about it." I hesitate. "I did not want to say anything to you because you are very stubborn about making the South Cave our home, but I do not want to be a half a day's walk from the healer if you need her." I reach out to touch the small swell of her belly. "And now I am convinced that we should if there is something wrong with the kit."

"Wait. Wait. I thought you said you didn't talk about the kit."

"I did not. You are the one saying something is wrong—"

"But you just said—"

"I do not know what I am saying," I exclaim. "All the blood is in my cock still, and you are trying to talk serious things when my mind is soft. All I know is that I am taking you to the healer—right now—and we are going to get answers."

When I reach for her, though, she grabs my wrists, a puzzled look on her face. "So you didn't talk to Rokan about the baby?"

"I told him I was excited and scared. I think I might have used the words 'pissing myself with fear,' but he said every new father feels like that." Now I am even more terrified, though. I place my palm against her belly, and I cannot feel anything moving. Now, I am starting to panic. "When was the last time you felt the kit move?"

"Do you really want to move back?" She looks startled.

"I want to know how the kit is doing." I can think of nothing else right now. I touch her stomach for a moment longer, but nothing moves, and a sliver of fear pierces me. I jump to my feet and wrap a blanket around Kira's shoulders. "We are going to see the healer right now."

"You're naked—"

I scoop her up into my arms and carry her out of the cave.

"We just had sex, Aehako," Kira hisses at me, struggling to get out of my grip. "At least let us clean up before we go visiting—"

I hesitate, but only because she struggles in my arms so. I set her down gently. "Hurry, then."

A few breaths later, Kira and I are clean enough, and she throws one of my tunics over her body, grumbling when I pick her up again. "It is the middle of the night," she protests again. "If there's really not a problem, we should wait until morning."

At this point I do not know if there is a problem or not. I only know I am terrified for my mate and my kit. I do not care if I wake up Maylak. She will understand. All I care about is making sure my Kira—and my child—are all right.

Kira makes another protest as I cross through the cave. "If you didn't talk to Rokan about the baby . . . I think we've just freaked each other out."

"It does not matter," I say stubbornly. "We are going to the healer now. We are getting answers."

She sighs but does not struggle. I have no doubt she wants to see the healer, too, but she worries she will be too much trouble. There is no such thing as "too much trouble" when it comes to my mate and my kit, though. It does not matter how much trouble we are, only that all is well.

The privacy screen is to the side, but Kashrem sits up as I storm into their cave, rubbing his eyes. "Aehako?" he asks, his voice low. "Is all well?" Maylak is curled up at his side, her pregnant belly enormous. On her other side, her young daughter, Esha, is curled up against her.

"I need Maylak to check my mate and my kit," I say.

"Please," Kira adds in a sweet voice. "We're very sorry to wake you up in the middle of the night."

"No, we are not," I say, equally sweetly. "We are just worrying ourselves stupid."

Maylak rubs her eyes, waking up as we talk to Kashrem. She yawns at my words, hiding her face behind her hand . . . or perhaps she is hiding a smile. "Come sit," she says, patting the blankets. Her belly seems enormously swollen, but her smile is easy. Kashrem takes Esha into his arms and hugs her, heading out of the cave with the sleepy little girl.

I feel a little guilty at waking the kit. Only a little, though.

"Sit, Kira," I say to my mate, and when she shoots me a fierce look, I kiss the top of her head. "Please."

She makes that little sound she always does when she is irritated with me, but I ignore it. All I need are answers. She can be mad at me later, and then I will kiss her frowns away.

"Do you need a blanket, Aehako?" Maylak asks calmly as she puts a hand on Kira's belly.

Comparing their pregnant bodies makes me realize just how much more Kira has to go before our kit is born, and I begin to sweat. Our kit must be so very small inside my mate, and I do not know how I will handle it if the child comes early . . .

"Aehako?" Kira asks, her brows scrunched as she looks up at me.

"Eh?"

"You're naked, love. And you're eye level with poor Maylak."

"And hovering," the healer adds. "I have seen everything before but that does not mean I want it in my face."

I find a fur on the floor, wrap it around my hips, and discreetly adjust myself. "Do you feel the kit? Is all well?" I drop down next to Kira and take her hand in mine, nervous. "If something is wrong, can you tell what it is? Should we stop mating? Does my mate need to eat more red meat? What—"

Kira pulls her hand out of mine and covers my mouth. "Hush, love."

Maylak closes her eyes, putting both her hands on Kira's stomach, and concentrates. I can hear the gentle thrum of her khui. It purrs, but not like it does when there is resonance. It is a different sort of reaction, one that happens when she uses her healing senses.

I hold my breath.

Maylak eventually opens her eyes. "From what I can tell, the kit is fine and healthy, and growing much faster than mine." She pats her distended belly. "Humans must breed so fast."

"Nothing's wrong?" I echo. "You did not sense any pain? Any problems?"

"No pain," the healer reassures us. "No problems. How do you feel, Kira?"

My mate lets out a long, shuddering sigh. "I've felt great, but I think my imagination's running away with me. Aehako was worried, and his worry made me worry. I freaked out and then he freaked out and that's why we're here. I'm so sorry, Maylak."

I touch my mate's belly, wanting to shove my ear against her skin so I can listen for the kit. "But you are certain there is nothing wrong?"

"Nothing," Maylak reassures us. "I would feel it if there were. Small things would sing . . . wrong. They would be evident when I touched you, like a snarl in a mane that catches the fingers." She strokes Kira's belly again. "But all is well. Why are you so worried?"

"Because she is small and human," I say.

Kira snorts.

"And she is everything to me. Her and the kit both. I would give anything for them." I hesitantly touch my mate's belly, and sure enough, there is a flutter of response. "They are my everything and I am the luckiest."

"Shit," Kira mutters, and starts to swipe at her eyes. She is crying again.

"I cannot help worrying," I admit. "Sometimes I worry I am too lucky, and it is all a dream."

"Never say the word 'dream' again," Kira sniffles. "And I love you, Aehako, but we can't keep freaking out. Either one of us. I swear I aged ten years tonight."

My pulse hammers. "You did?"

Kira groans. I swear Maylak does, too. "You know what I mean," Kira says. "We've got to calm down."

"I will never calm down. This is my first kit!" I smile with relief when the child kicks against my hand once more. "The little one just moved."

Maylak just chuckles. She gives Kira a knowing look and yawns. "I can check you again in the morning. When you leave, will you send Kashrem and Esha in?"

"Of course," my sweet mate says, and offers her hands to me. "Help me up, Aehako?"

I do, and when Kashrem enters with Esha asleep in his arms, her skinny legs dangling, I think that might be a good way to carry my mate, too. But before I can suggest such a thing, Kira drags me away from the healer's cave and then taps the top of my chest, her signal that she wants to kiss me and I need to bend down.

I do so, gladly.

She cups my face, shaking her head at me. "You're an idiot sometimes. I am, too. We have to promise to stop freaking each other out, all right?"

"I cannot make such promises," I tell her sheepishly. "I will always worry about you and our child."

"I know. I worry, too, but we really can't make ourselves crazy like this." Her soft fingers skate over my face, and she studies me, all serious expression and sad eyes. "Do you truly want to move back?"

"Will it make you feel safer?"

"No."

I am surprised at her answer. "No?"

"I already feel safe, Aehako." She shakes her head at me.

"I've felt fine. Better than fine. If I get sick every now and then, that's just part of being pregnant. Kemli's at the cave and she's had lots of children. And we truly are only a sled ride away from this cave and the healer. I'm not worried about anything. But when you worry, apparently I pick up on it."

"Are you telling me to calm down?"

"Do you think you can?" A hint of a smile plays at her lips.

"I know one thing that helps me relax," I drawl, and she rolls her eyes. I love making her chuckle, and it feels like a gift when she does so right now.

"I can only guess that it involves your cock and my body."

I give her a sly look. "Perhaps Rokan is not the only one with a knowing sense."

"You're impossible."

"But you love me anyhow?"

She leans in and kisses me. "I do. But let's relax for the rest of our vacation, all right?"

"You know what relaxes me?"

Kira mock-groans. "You really are the most impossible mate." But she is smiling as she says it, and I know if I suggest cuddling, it will turn into touching, and mating . . . because it is never about just cuddling. Never.

And Kira loves that it is never just about cuddling, too.

My mate reaches up and caresses my cheek. A wicked smile curves her mouth. "Remind me to show you the new loincloth I made you in the morning."

I can tell from the look on her face that it is going to make me laugh long and hard . . . and then we will probably end up mating afterward. "In the morning, then."

She wiggles her brows at me.

Truly, I am the luckiest.

AUTHOR'S NOTE

Hello there!

First of all, let me say thank you a thousand times to everyone who has bought the new editions of Ice Planet Barbarians. I'm so fiercely in love with these illustrated covers, and I hope you are, too. The artist is Kelly Wagner, and she's done such an amazing job of bringing the characters to life in her style while managing to make books about cave-dwelling blue barbarians look light, fun, and trendy. I'm seriously in love and am using all the exclamation marks possible to express it. I jokingly call these my "Lisa Frank" covers, but honestly, how can you look at one of these beauties and not be happy?

This book, *Barbarian Lover*, was the first one I didn't write as a weekly serial. Both *Ice Planet Barbarians* and *Barbarian Alien* were put out as weekly installments, with me compiling the "final" story and then selling it once the serial was done. I truly love the serial format, as I grew up reading weekly comic strips and buying up every comic book I could get my hands on. In my college years, I watched soap operas with the ladies in the lunchroom at my retail job (I went to school part-time and then kinda just stopped going—don't be me, kids!). So I knew how a serial story worked, and I both loved and hated the format. I loved it for the tension it brought, the constant OMG, WHAT HAPPENS NEXT WEEK? feeling of excitement. I also hated it for the same reason (heh). It ended up being really, really fun to write.

However, and this might come as a shocker to no one, fans really didn't like it! I know! Imagine! No one liked having literary blue balls for six weeks in a row! Go figure! So for book three, I decided to try something new: Kira and Aehako's story would be put out in a single novel, and the entire thing would be available from the get-go. I figured if it failed, I could go back to serials.

It, of course, did incredibly well. So you have those early readers who sent me angry emails to thank for my discontinuing the serial format. (I'm kidding, I'm kidding, I actually enjoy feedback like this because it helps me figure out what readers are into. Sometimes "fun" for the author is not fun for the reader, like when we kill beloved characters. Authors *love* doing shit like that, and readers are less enthused.)

Just like I knew book two would be the combative Liz and Raahosh, I knew book three would be quiet Kira and not-quiet Aehako. I tend to pair like with like in a lot of stories, because in my opinion, it's easy to fall in love with your best friend. But reading about two people as low-key and quiet as Kira would have been like watching paint dry, and two people like Aehako together probably would have been a headache. So I paired flirty confidence with someone who exuded Eeyore vibes. As a cheery person who is married to someone on a more somber wavelength, I'm aware that we feel the need to make that other person smile. I like to think it's a good pairing, but I'm biased.

This is the first time I actually explored infertility in the books. Ice Planet Barbarians has been referred to as a "breeding" series, but I actually didn't intend for it to go that route, oddly enough. I wanted the emphasis to be on soul mates and finding that missing piece and living happily ever after. It's just that the soul mates are driven together by the khui and biology, and, well, the next thing you know, the tribe is swimming in babies. I don't hate it. ☺

But infertility was a topic I wanted to play with. How would it factor in when there's such a focus on finding mates and making families? Kira is reluctant to show favor to anyone because she feels as if she's taking away a future choice from someone who opts to be with her. I knew going into the story that Kira and Aehako were going to resonate, which meant I was going to have to "fix" her infertility. This is a plot device that can actually really bother me if handled improperly. I hate the idea of the hero's magic dick fixing everything that was wrong with the heroine's lady-business. To me, it implies that she's broken, and infertility is not you being "broken." I just think of it as, well, a laptop. (There I go with my horrible analogies once more.) You can be a perfectly good laptop and not have a USB port. It doesn't make you a bad laptop. It just makes you a laptop that has slightly different capabilities than one with a USB port.

Anyhow. I knew going in that Kira was going to have her infertility "fixed" by the khui, so I researched what sort of infertility could be caused by sickness or other factors that the khui could swoop in and take care of. The reason in the story is a legit one, and I've actually had readers contact me and say they had the same medical issue, which is a neat way of fiction intersecting with reality. The khui fixed the "damage" to Kira's reproductive system, because it saw the changes in her body as something that needed to be corrected.

(On another note, I've had readers ask me why the khui wouldn't "correct" a character who's postmenopausal and make her fertile again. That's a naturally occurring function of the body, and the khui wouldn't recognize it as a problem. The khui keeps the host healthy and "fixes" issues it finds. Someone aging out of their fertility years? Not an issue.)

But enough about uteruses!

In this book, I also wanted to dig a little more into the world itself and some of the plotlines I'd left hanging. Were the aliens coming back? What do people eat on an ice planet other than meat? And how exactly do aliens court? This book actually grew slightly "legendary" for the courting present Aehako gives Kira. To this day, I get people sending me messages with pictures of dildos and telling me it made them think of book three! And then, of course, once the "courting gift" came into the story, I had to use it! Chekhov's gun was absolutely in play, and the first Ice Planet Barbarians sex toy was made. I like to think that it'll sit proudly on a shelf, and in later years, Aehako will tell his children about it and thoroughly embarrass both kits and mother.

Thank you so much for reading. I hope you enjoyed this story almost as much as Aehako enjoyed giving Kira her courting gift.

ALL BEST,
RUBY

THE PEOPLE OF
BARBARIAN LOVER

THE MAIN CAVE
THE CHIEF AND HIS MATE

VEKTAL (Vehk-tall)—Chief of the sa-khui tribe. Son of Hektar, the prior chief, who died in khui-sickness. He is a dedicated hunter and leader, and carries a sword and a bola for weapons. He is the one who finds Georgie, and resonance between them is so strong that he resonates prior to her receiving her khui.

GEORGIE—Unofficial leader of the human women. Originally from Orlando, Florida, she has long, golden-brown curls and a determined attitude. Newly pregnant after resonating to Vektal.

FAMILIES

RAAHOSH (Rah-hosh)—A quiet but surly hunter. One of his horns is broken off and his face scarred. Vektal's close friend. Impatient and rash, he steals Liz the moment she receives her khui. They resonate, and he is exiled for stealing her.

LIZ—A loudmouth huntress from Oklahoma who loves Star Wars and giving her opinion. Raahosh kidnaps her the moment she receives her lifesaving khui. She was a champion archer as a teenager. Resonates to Raahosh and voluntarily chooses exile with him.

ARIANA—One of the women kept in the stasis tubes. Hails from New Jersey and was an anthropology student. She tended to cry a lot when first rescued. Has a delicate frame and dark brown hair. Resonates to Zolaya. Still cries a lot.

ZOLAYA (Zoh-lay-uh)—A skilled hunter. Steady and patient, he resonates to Ariana and seems to be the only one not bothered by her weepiness.

MARLENE (Mar-lenn)—One of the women kept in the stasis tubes. French speaking. Quiet and confident, and exudes sexuality. Resonates to Zennek.

ZENNEK (Zehn-eck)—A quiet and shy hunter. Brother to Pashov, Salukh, and Farli. He is the son of Borran and Kemli. Resonates to Marlene.

NORA—One of the women kept in the stasis tubes. A nurturing sort who was rather angry she was dumped on an ice planet. Quickly resonates to Dagesh. No longer quite so angry.

DAGESH (Dah-zzhesh; the *g* sound is swallowed)—A calm, hardworking, and responsible hunter. Resonates to Nora.

STACY—One of the women kept in the stasis tubes. She was weepy when she first awakened. Loves to cook and worked in a bakery prior to abduction. Resonates to Pashov and seems quite happy.

PASHOV (Pah-showv)—The son of Kemli and Borran; brother to Farli, Salukh, and Zennek. A hunter described as "quiet." Resonates to Stacy.

MAYLAK (May-lack)—One of the few female sa-khui. She is the tribe healer and Vektal's former pleasure mate. She resonated to Kashrem, ending her relationship with Vektal. Sister to Bek.

KASHREM (Cash-rehm)—A gentle tribal tanner. Mated to Maylak.

ESHA (Esh-uh)—Their young female kit.

SEVVAH (Sev-uh)—A tribe elder and one of the few sa-khui females. She is mother to Aehako, Rokan, and Sessah, and acts like a mom to the others in the cave. Her entire family was spared when khui-sickness hit fifteen years ago.

OSHEN (Aw-shen)—A tribe elder and Sevvah's mate. Brewer.

SESSAH (Ses-uh)—Their youngest child, a juvenile male.

MEGAN—Megan was in an early pregnancy when she was captured, but the aliens terminated it. She tends toward a sunny disposition when not abducted by aliens. Resonates to Cashol.

CASHOL (Cash-awl)—A distractible and slightly goofy-natured hunter. Cousin to Vektal. Resonates to Megan.

THE UNMATED HUNTERS

EREVEN (Air-uh-ven)—A quiet, easygoing hunter.

ROKAN (Row-can)—The son of Sevvah and Oshen; brother to Aehako and young Sessah. A hunter known for his strange predictions that come true all too often.

WARREK (War-eck)—The son of Elder Eklan. He is a very quiet and mild hunter, with long, sleek black hair. Warrek teaches the young kits how to hunt.

ELDERS

ELDER EKLAN—A calm, kind elder. Father to Warrek, he also helped raise Harrec.

THE SOUTH CAVE
FAMILIES

AEHAKO (Eye-ha-koh)—A laughing, flirty hunter. The son of Sevvah and Oshen; brother to Rokan and young Sessah. He seems to be in a permanent good mood. Close friends with Haeden. Has recently resonated to Kira and is acting leader of the South Cave.

KIRA—The first of the human women to be kidnapped, Kira had a large metallic translator attached to her ear by the aliens.

She is quiet and serious, with somber eyes. Her translator has been newly removed, and she has resonated to Aehako despite believing herself to be infertile.

KEMLI (Kemm-lee)—An elder female, mother to Salukh, Pashov, Zennek, and Farli. The tribe's expert on plants.

BORRAN (Bore-awn)—Kemli's much younger mate and an elder.

FARLI (Far-lee)—A preteen female sa-khui. Her brothers are Salukh, Pashov, and Zennek.

ASHA (Ah-shuh)—A mated female sa-khui. She is mated to Hemalo but has not been seen in his furs for some time. Their kit died shortly after birth.

HEMALO (Hee-mah-lo)—A tanner and a quiet sort. He is mated (unhappily) to Asha.

THE UNMATED HUMAN FEMALES

CLAIRE—A quiet, slender blonde with a pixie cut. She finds her new world extremely frightening.

JOSIE—One of the original kidnapped women, she broke her leg in the ship crash. Short and adorable, Josie is an excessive talker, a gossip, and a bit of a dreamer. Likes to sing.

TIFFANY—A "farm girl" back on Earth, she suffered greatly while waiting for Georgie to return. She has been traumatized by her alien abduction. She is a perfectionist and a hard worker.

THE UNMATED HUNTERS

BEK (Behk)—A hunter generally thought of as short-tempered and unpleasant. Brother to Maylak.

HAEDEN (Hi-den)—A grim and unsmiling hunter with "dead" eyes, Haeden formerly resonated but his female died of khui-sickness before they could mate. His current khui is new. He is very private.

HARREC (Hair-ek)—A hunter who has no family and finds his place in the tribe by constantly joking and teasing. A bit accident-prone.

HASSEN (Hass-en)—A passionate and brave hunter, Hassen is impulsive and tends to act before he thinks.

SALUKH (Sah-luke)—The brawny son of Kemli and Borran; brother to Farli, Pashov, and Zennek. Very strong and intense.

TAUSHEN (Tow—rhymes with "cow"—shen)—A teenage hunter, newly into adulthood. Eager to prove himself.

ELDERS

ELDER DRAYAN—A smiling elder who uses a cane to help him walk.

ELDER DRENOL—A grumpy, antisocial elder.

ELDER VADREN (Vaw-dren)—An elder.

ELDER VAZA (Vaw-zhuh)—A lonely widower and hunter. He tries to be as helpful as possible. He is very interested in the new females.

THE DEAD

DOMINIQUE—A redheaded human female. Her mind was broken when she was abused by the aliens on the ship. When she arrived on Not-Hoth, she ran out into the snow and deliberately froze.

HARLOW—One of the women kept in the stasis tubes. She has red hair and freckles, and is mechanically minded and excellent at problem-solving. Currently missing and believed dead.

KRISSY—A human female, dead in the crash.

PEG—A human female, dead in the crash.

ABOUT THE AUTHOR

RUBY DIXON is an author of all things science fiction romance. She is a Sagittarius and a Reylo shipper, and loves farming sims (but not actual housework). She lives in the South with her husband and a couple of geriatric cats, and can't think of anything else to put in her biography. Truly, she is boring.

CONNECT ONLINE

RubyDixon.com
🅕 RubyDixonBooks
🅘 Author.Ruby.Dixon

Ready to find
your next great read?

Let us help.

Visit prh.com/nextread